# Beauty And The Beast
## And Tales Of Home

*by*
Bayard Taylor

# Beauty And The Beast
## And Tales Of Home
### by Bayard Taylor

Copyright © 2023

All Rights reserved.

No part of this publication may be reproduced, stored in a retrieval system, or transmitted in any form or by any means, electronic, mechanical, photocopying or Otherwise, without the written permission of the publisher.
The author/editor asserts the moral right to be identified as the author/editor of this work.

ISBN: 978-93-61152-21-4

Published by

# DOUBLE 9 BOOKS
2/13-B, Ansari Road
Daryaganj, New Delhi – 110002
info@double9books.com
www.double9books.com
Tel. 011-40042856

This book is under public domain

# ABOUT THE AUTHOR

Bayard Taylor was an American poet, literary critic, translator, travel author, and diplomat. As a poet, he was extremely popular, with an audience of almost 4,000 attending a poetry reading once, setting a record that remained for 85 years. His travelogues were well-received in both the United States and Britain. He held diplomatic appointments in both Russia and Prussia. Taylor was born January 11, 1825, in Kennett Square, Chester County, Pennsylvania. He was the fourth son of Quaker couple Joseph and Rebecca Taylor, and the first to reach maturity. His mother was of half Swiss descent. His father was an affluent farmer. Charles Frederick Taylor, Bayard's younger brother, was a Union Army colonel killed in action during the Battle of Gettysburg in 1863. Bayard obtained his early education at an academy in West Chester, Pennsylvania, and later in nearby Unionville. At seventeen, he was apprenticed to a printer in West Chester. Rufus Wilmot Griswold, a renowned critic and editor, pushed him to produce poems. The resulting anthology, Ximena, or the Battle of the Sierra Morena and Other Poems, was published in 1844 and dedicated to Griswold.

# CONTENTS

**A STORY OF OLD RUSSIA**

I ........................................................................................... 7

II .......................................................................................... 8

III ....................................................................................... 12

IV ....................................................................................... 18

V ........................................................................................ 22

VI ....................................................................................... 26

VII ...................................................................................... 29

VIII ..................................................................................... 33

IX ....................................................................................... 38

X ........................................................................................ 40

XI ....................................................................................... 45

XII ...................................................................................... 48

**TALES OF HOME**

THE STRANGE FRIEND .................................................... 52

JACOB FLINT'S JOURNEY ................................................ 70

CAN A LIFE HIDE ITSELF? ............................................... 89

TWIN-LOVE ..................................................................... 106

THE EXPERIENCES OF THE A. C. ................................... 120

# FRIEND ELI'S DAUGHTER

I .................................................................................... 148
II ................................................................................... 152
III .................................................................................. 157
IV .................................................................................. 161
V ................................................................................... 165

# MISS BARTRAM'S TROUBLE

I .................................................................................... 173
II ................................................................................... 180
III .................................................................................. 183
MRS. STRONGITHARM'S REPORT ........................................ 188

# A STORY OF OLD RUSSIA

## I

We are about to relate a story of mingled fact and fancy. The facts are borrowed from the Russian author, Petjerski; the fancy is our own. Our task will chiefly be to soften the outlines of incidents almost too sharp and rugged for literary use, to supply them with the necessary coloring and sentiment, and to give a coherent and proportioned shape to the irregular fragments of an old chronicle. We know something, from other sources, of the customs described, something of the character of the people from personal observation, and may therefore the more freely take such liberties as we choose with the rude, vigorous sketches of the Russian original. One who happens to have read the work of Villebois can easily comprehend the existence of a state of society, on the banks of the Volga, a hundred years ago, which is now impossible, and will soon become incredible. What is strangest in our narrative has been declared to be true.

## II

We are in Kinesma, a small town on the Volga, between Kostroma and Nijni-Novgorod. The time is about the middle of the last century, and the month October.

There was trouble one day, in the palace of Prince Alexis, of Kinesma. This edifice, with its massive white walls, and its pyramidal roofs of green copper, stood upon a gentle mound to the eastward of the town, overlooking it, a broad stretch of the Volga, and the opposite shore. On a similar hill, to the westward, stood the church, glittering with its dozen bulging, golden domes. These two establishments divided the sovereignty of Kinesma between them.

Prince Alexis owned the bodies of the inhabitants, (with the exception of a few merchants and tradesmen,) and the Archimandrite Sergius owned their souls. But the shadow of the former stretched also over other villages, far beyond the ring of the wooded horizon. The number of his serfs was ten thousand, and his rule over them was even less disputed than theirs over their domestic animals.

The inhabitants of the place had noticed with dismay that the slumber-flag had not been hoisted on the castle, although it was half an hour after the usual time. So rare a circumstance betokened sudden wrath or disaster, on the part of Prince Alexis. Long experience had prepared the people for anything that might happen, and they were consequently not astonished at the singular event which presently transpired.

The fact is, that in the first place, the dinner had been prolonged full ten minutes beyond its accustomed limit, owing to a discussion between the Prince, his wife, the Princess Martha, and their son Prince Boris. The last was to leave for St. Petersburg in a fortnight, and wished to have his departure preceded by a festival at the castle. The Princess Martha was always ready to second the desires of her only child. Between the two they had pressed some twenty or thirty thousand rubles out of the old Prince, for the winter diversions of the young one. The festival, to be sure, would have been a slight expenditure for a noble of such immense wealth as Prince Alexis; but he never liked his wife, and he took a stubborn pleasure in thwarting her wishes. It was no satisfaction that Boris resembled her in character. That weak successor to the sovereignty of Kinesma preferred a game of cards to a bear hunt, and could never drink more than a quart of vodki without becoming dizzy and sick.

"Ugh!" Prince Alexis would cry, with a shudder of disgust, "the whelp barks after the dam!"

A state dinner he might give; but a festival, with dances, dramatic representations, burning tar-barrels, and cannon,—no! He knitted his heavy brows and drank deeply, and his fiery gray eyes shot such incessant glances from side to side that Boris and the Princess Martha could not exchange a single wink of silent advice. The pet bear, Mishka, plied with strong wines, which Prince Alexis poured out for him into a golden basin, became at last comically drunk, and in endeavoring to execute a dance, lost his balance, and fell at full length on his back.

The Prince burst into a yelling, shrieking fit of laughter. Instantly the yellow-haired serfs in waiting, the Calmucks at the hall-door, and the half-witted dwarf who crawled around the table in his tow shirt, began laughing in chorus, as violently as they could. The Princess Martha and Prince Boris laughed also; and while the old man's eyes were dimmed with streaming tears of mirth, quickly exchanged nods. The sound extended all over the castle, and was heard outside of the walls.

"Father!" said Boris, "let us have the festival, and Mishka shall perform again. Prince Paul of Kostroma would strangle, if he could see him."

"Good, by St. Vladimir!" exclaimed Prince Alexis. "Thou shalt have it, my Borka! 1 Where's Simon Petrovitch? May the Devil scorch that vagabond, if he doesn't do better than the last time! Sasha!"

A broad-shouldered serf stepped forward and stood with bowed head.

"Lock up Simon Petrovitch in the southwestern tower. Send the tailor and the girls to him, to learn their parts. Search every one of them before they go in, and if any one dares to carry vodki to the beast, twenty-five lashes on the back!"

Sasha bowed again and departed. Simon Petrovitch was the court-poet of Kinesma. He had a mechanical knack of preparing allegorical diversions which suited the conventional taste of society at that time; but he had also a failing,—he was rarely sober enough to write. Prince Alexis, therefore, was in the habit of locking him up and placing a guard over him, until the inspiration had done its work. The most comely young serfs of both sexes were selected to perform the parts, and the court-tailor arranged for them the appropriate dresses. It depended very much upon accident—that is to say, the mood of Prince Alexis—whether Simon Petrovitch was rewarded with stripes or rubles.

The matter thus settled, the Prince rose from the table and walked out upon an overhanging balcony, where an immense reclining arm-chair of stuffed leather was ready for his siesta. He preferred this indulgence in the open air; and although the weather was rapidly growing cold, a pelisse of sables enabled him to slumber sweetly in the face of the north wind. An attendant stood with the pelisse outspread; another held the halyards to which was attached the great red slumber-flag, ready to run it up and announce to all Kinesma that the noises of the town must cease; a few seconds more, and all things would have been fixed in their regular daily courses. The Prince, in fact, was just straightening his shoulders to receive the sables; his eyelids were dropping, and his eyes, sinking mechanically with them, fell upon the river-road, at the foot of the hill. Along this road walked a man, wearing the long cloth caftan of a merchant.

Prince Alexis started, and all slumber vanished out of his eyes. He leaned forward for a moment, with a quick, eager expression; then a loud roar, like that of an enraged wild beast, burst from his mouth. He gave a stamp that shook the balcony.

"Dog!" he cried to the trembling attendant, "my cap! my whip!"

The sables fell upon the floor, the cap and whip appeared in a twinkling, and the red slumber-flag was folded up again for the first time in several years, as the Prince stormed out of the castle. The traveller below had heard the cry,—for it might have been heard half a mile. He seemed to have a presentiment of evil, for he had already set off towards the town at full speed.

To explain the occurrence, we must mention one of the Prince's many peculiar habits. This was, to invite strangers or merchants of the neighborhood to dine with him, and, after regaling them bountifully, to take his pay in subjecting them to all sorts of outrageous tricks, with the help of his band of willing domestics. Now this particular merchant had been invited, and had attended; but, being a very wide-awake, shrewd person, he saw what was coming, and dexterously slipped away from the banquet without being perceived. The Prince vowed vengeance, on discovering the escape, and he was not a man to forget his word.

Impelled by such opposite passions, both parties ran with astonishing speed. The merchant was the taller, but his long caftan, hastily ungirdled, swung behind him and dragged in the air.

The short, booted legs of the Prince beat quicker time, and he grasped his short, heavy, leathern whip more tightly as he saw the space diminishing. They dashed into the town of Kinesma a hundred yards apart. The merchant entered the main street, or bazaar, looking rapidly to right and left, as he ran, in the hope of espying some place of refuge. The terrible voice behind him cried,—

"Stop, scoundrel! I have a crow to pick with you!"

And the tradesmen in their shops looked on and laughed, as well they might, being unconcerned spectators of the fun. The fugitive, therefore, kept straight on, notwithstanding a pond of water glittered across the farther end of the street.

Although Prince Alexis had gained considerably in the race, such violent exercise, after a heavy dinner, deprived him of breath. He again cried,—

"Stop!"

"But the merchant answered,—

"No, Highness! You may come to me, but I will not go to you."

"Oh, the villian!" growled the Prince, in a hoarse whisper, for he had no more voice.

The pond cut of all further pursuit. Hastily kicking off his loose boots, the merchant plunged into the water, rather than encounter the princely whip, which already began to crack and snap in fierce anticipation. Prince Alexis kicked off his boots and followed; the pond gradually deepened, and in a minute the tall merchant stood up to his chin in the icy water, and his short pursuer likewise but out of striking distance. The latter coaxed and entreated, but the victim kept his ground.

"You lie, Highness!" he said, boldly. "If you want me, come to me."

"Ah-h-h!" roared the Prince, with chattering teeth, "what a stubborn rascal you are! Come here, and I give you my word that I will not hurt you. Nay,"—seeing that the man did not move,—"you shall dine with me as often as you please. You shall be my friend; by St. Vladimir, I like you!"

"Make the sign of the cross, and swear it by all the Saints," said the merchant, composedly.

With a grim smile on his face, the Prince stepped back and shiveringly obeyed. Both then waded out, sat down upon the ground and pulled on their boots; and presently the people of Kinesma beheld the dripping pair walking side by side up the street, conversing in the most cordial manner. The merchant dried his clothes FROM WITHIN, at the castle table; a fresh keg of old Cognac was opened; and although the slumber-flag was not unfurled that afternoon, it flew from the staff and hushed the town nearly all the next day.

# III

The festival granted on behalf of Prince Boris was one of the grandest ever given at the castle. In character it was a singular cross between the old Muscovite revel and the French entertainments which were then introduced by the Empress Elizabeth.

All the nobility, for fifty versts around, including Prince Paul and the chief families of Kostroma, were invited. Simon Petrovitch had been so carefully guarded that his work was actually completed and the parts distributed; his superintendence of the performance, however, was still a matter of doubt, as it was necessary to release him from the tower, and after several days of forced abstinence he always manifested a raging appetite. Prince Alexis, in spite of this doubt, had been assured by Boris that the dramatic part of the entertainment would not be a failure. When he questioned Sasha, the poet's strong-shouldered guard, the latter winked familiarly and answered with a proverb,—

"I sit on the shore and wait for the wind,"—which was as much as to say that Sasha had little fear of the result.

The tables were spread in the great hall, where places for one hundred chosen guests were arranged on the floor, while the three or four hundred of minor importance were provided for in the galleries above. By noon the whole party were assembled. The halls and passages of the castle were already permeated with rich and unctuous smells, and a delicate nose might have picked out and arranged, by their finer or coarser vapors, the dishes preparing for the upper and lower tables. One of the parasites of Prince Alexis, a dilapidated nobleman, officiated as Grand Marshal,—an office which more than compensated for the savage charity he received, for it was performed in continual fear and trembling. The Prince had felt the stick of the Great Peter upon his own back, and was ready enough to imitate any custom of the famous monarch.

An orchestra, composed principally of horns and brass instruments, occupied a separate gallery at one end of the dining-hall. The guests were assembled in the adjoining apartments, according to their rank; and when the first loud blast of the instruments announced the beginning of the banquet, two very differently attired and freighted processions of servants made their appearance at the same time. Those intended for the princely table numbered two hundred,—two for each guest. They were the handsomest young men among the ten thousand serfs, clothed in loose white trousers and shirts of pink or lilac silk; their soft golden hair, parted in the middle, fell upon their shoulders, and a band of gold-thread about the brow prevented it from sweeping the dishes they carried. They entered the reception-room, bearing huge trays of sculptured silver, upon which were anchovies, the finest Finnish caviar, sliced oranges, cheese, and crystal flagons of Cognac, rum, and kummel. There were fewer servants for the remaining guests, who were gathered in a separate chamber, and regaled with the common black caviar, onions, bread, and vodki. At the second blast of trumpets, the two companies set themselves in motion and entered the dining-hall at opposite ends. Our business, however, is only with the principal personages, so we will allow the common crowd quietly to mount to the galleries and satisfy their senses with the coarser viands, while their imagination is stimulated by the sight of the splendor and luxury below.

Prince Alexis entered first, with a pompous, mincing gait, leading the Princess Martha by the tips of her fingers. He wore a caftan of green velvet laced with gold, a huge vest of crimson brocade, and breeches of yellow satin. A wig, resembling clouds boiling in the confluence of opposing winds, surged from his low, broad forehead, and flowed upon his shoulders. As his small, fiery eyes swept the hall, every servant trembled: he was as severe at the commencement as he was reckless at the close of a banquet. The Princess Martha wore a robe of pink satin embroidered with flowers made of small pearls, and a train and head-dress of crimson velvet.

Her emeralds were the finest outside of Moscow, and she wore them all. Her pale, weak, frightened face was quenched in the dazzle of the green fires which shot from her forehead, ears, and bosom, as she moved.

Prince Paul of Kostroma and the Princess Nadejda followed; but on reaching the table, the gentlemen took their seats at the head, while the ladies marched down to the foot. Their seats were determined by their relative rank, and woe to him who was so ignorant or so absent-minded as to make a mistake! The servants had been carefully trained in advance by the Grand Marshal; and whoever took a place above his rank or importance found, when he came to sit down, that his chair had miraculously disappeared, or, not noticing the fact, seated himself absurdly and violently upon the floor. The Prince at the head of the table, and the Princess at the foot, with their nearest guests of equal rank, ate from dishes of massive gold; the others from silver. As soon as the last of the company had entered the hall, a crowd of jugglers, tumblers, dwarfs, and Calmucks followed, crowding themselves into the corners under the galleries, where they awaited the conclusion of the banquet to display their tricks, and scolded and pummelled each other in the mean time.

On one side of Prince Alexis the bear Mishka took his station. By order of Prince Boris he had been kept from wine for several days, and his small eyes were keener and hungrier than usual. As he rose now and then, impatiently, and sat upon his hind legs, he formed a curious contrast to the Prince's other supporter, the idiot, who sat also in his tow-shirt, with a large pewter basin in his hand. It was difficult to say whether the beast was most man or the man most beast. They eyed each other and watched the motions of their lord with equal jealousy; and the dismal whine of the bear found an echo in the drawling, slavering laugh of the idiot. The Prince glanced form one to the other; they put him in a capital humor, which was not lessened as he perceived an expression of envy pass over the face of Prince Paul.

The dinner commenced with a botvinia—something between a soup and a salad—of wonderful composition. It contained cucumbers, cherries, salt fish, melons, bread, salt, pepper, and wine. While it was being served, four huge fishermen, dressed to represent mermen of the Volga, naked to the waist, with hair crowned with reeds, legs finned with silver tissue from the knees downward, and preposterous scaly tails, which dragged helplessly upon the floor, entered the hall, bearing a broad, shallow tank of silver. In the tank flapped and swam four superb sterlets, their ridgy backs rising out of the water like those of alligators. Great applause welcomed this new and classical adaptation of the old custom of showing the LIVING fish, before cooking them, to the guests at the table. The invention was due to Simon Petrovitch, and was (if the truth must be confessed) the result of certain carefully measured supplies of brandy which Prince Boris himself had carried to the imprisoned poet.

After the sterlets had melted away to their backbones, and the roasted geese had shrunk into drumsticks and breastplates, and here and there a guest's ears began to redden with more rapid blood, Prince Alexis judged that the time for diversion had arrived. He first filled up the idiot's basin with fragments of all the dishes within his reach,—fish, stewed fruits, goose fat, bread, boiled cabbage, and beer,—the idiot grinning with delight all the while, and singing, "Ne uyesjai golubchik moi," (Don't go away, my little pigeon), between the handfuls which he crammed into his mouth. The guests roared with laughter, especially when a juggler or Calmuck stole out from under the gallery, and pretended to have designs upon the basin. Mishka, the bear, had also been well fed, and greedily drank ripe old Malaga from the golden dish. But, alas! he would not dance. Sitting up on his hind legs, with his fore paws hanging before him, he cast a drunken, languishing eye upon the company, lolled out his tongue, and whined with an almost human voice. The domestics, secretly incited by the Grand Marshal, exhausted their ingenuity in coaxing him, but in vain. Finally, one of them took a goblet of wine in one hand, and, embracing Mishka with the other, began to waltz. The bear stretched out his paw and clumsily followed the movements, whirling round and round after the enticing goblet. The orchestra struck up, and the spectacle, though not exactly what Prince Alexis wished, was comical enough to divert the company immensely.

But the close of the performance was not upon the programme. The impatient bear, getting no nearer his goblet, hugged the man violently with the other paw, striking his claws through the thin shirt. The dance-measure was lost; the legs of the two tangled, and they fell to the floor, the bear undermost. With a growl of rage and disappointment, he brought his teeth together through the man's arm, and it might have fared badly with the latter, had not the goblet been refilled by some one and held to the animal's nose.

Then, releasing his hold, he sat up again, drank another bottle, and staggered out of the hall.

Now the health of Prince Alexis was drunk,—by the guests on the floor of the hall in Champagne, by those in the galleries in kislischi and hydromel. The orchestra played; a choir of serfs sang an ode by Simon Petrovitch, in which the departure of Prince Boris was mentioned; the tumblers began to posture; the jugglers came forth and played their tricks; and the cannon on the ramparts announced to all Kinesma, and far up and down the Volga, that the company were rising from the table.

Half an hour later, the great red slumber-flag floated over the castle. All slept,—except the serf with the wounded arm, the nervous Grand Marshal, and Simon Petrovich with his band of dramatists, guarded by the indefatigable Sasha. All others slept,—and the curious crowd outside, listening to the music, stole silently away; down in Kinesma, the mothers ceased to scold their children, and the merchants whispered to each other in the bazaar; the captains of vessels floating on the Volga directed their men by gestures; the mechanics laid aside hammer and axe, and lighted their pipes. Great silence fell upon the land, and continued unbroken so long as Prince Alexis and his guests slept the sleep of the just and the tipsy.

By night, however, they were all awake and busily preparing for the diversions of the evening. The ball-room was illuminated by thousands of wax-lights, so connected with inflammable threads, that the wicks could all be kindled in a moment. A pyramid of tar-barrels had been erected on each side of the castle-gate, and every hill or mound on the opposite bank of the Volga was similarly crowned. When, to a stately march,—the musicians blowing their loudest,—Prince Alexis and Princess Martha led the way to the ball-room, the signal was given: candles and tar-barrels burst into flame, and not only within the castle, but over the landscape for five or six versts, around everything was bright and clear in the fiery day. Then the noises of Kinesma were not only permitted, but encouraged. Mead and qvass flowed in the very streets, and the castle trumpets could not be heard for the sound of troikas and balalaikas.

After the Polonaise, and a few stately minuets, (copied from the court of Elizabeth), the company were ushered into the theatre. The hour of Simon Petrovitch had struck: with the inspiration smuggled to him by Prince Boris, he had arranged a performance which he felt to be his masterpiece. Anxiety as to its reception kept him sober. The overture had ceased, the spectators were all in their seats, and now the curtain rose. The background was a growth of enormous, sickly toad-stools, supposed to be clouds. On the stage stood a girl of eighteen, (the handsomest in Kinesma), in hoops and satin petticoat, powdered hair, patches, and high-heeled shoes. She held a fan in one hand, and a bunch of marigolds in the other. After a deep and graceful curtsy to the company, she came forward and said,—

"I am the goddess Venus. I have come to Olympus to ask some questions of Jupiter."

Thunder was heard, and a car rolled upon the stage. Jupiter sat therein, in a blue coat, yellow vest, ruffled shirt and three-cornered hat. One hand held a bunch of thunderbolts, which he occasionally lifted and shook; the other, a gold-headed cane.

"Here am, I Jupiter," said he; "what does Venus desire?"

A poetical dialogue then followed, to the effect that the favorite of the goddess, Prince Alexis of Kinesma, was about sending his son, Prince Boris, into the gay world, wherein himself had already displayed all the gifts of all the divinities of Olympus. He claimed from her, Venus, like favors for his son: was it possible to grant them? Jupiter dropped his head and meditated. He could not answer the question at once: Apollo, the Graces, and the Muses must be consulted: there were few precedents where the son had succeeded in rivalling the father,—yet the father's pious wishes could not be overlooked. Venus said,—

"What I asked for Prince Alexis was for HIS sake: what I ask for the son is for the father's sake."

Jupiter shook his thunderbolt and called "Apollo!"

Instantly the stage was covered with explosive and coruscating fires,— red, blue, and golden,—and amid smoke, and glare, and fizzing noises, and strong chemical smells, Apollo dropped down from above. He was accustomed to heat and smoke, being the cook's assistant, and was sweated down to a weight capable of being supported by the invisible wires. He wore a yellow caftan, and wide blue silk trousers. His yellow hair was twisted around and glued fast to gilded sticks, which stood out from his head in a circle, and represented rays of light. He first bowed to Prince Alexis, then to the guests, then to Jupiter, then to Venus. The matter was explained to him.

He promised to do what he could towards favoring the world with a second generation of the beauty, grace, intellect, and nobility of character which had already won his regard. He thought, however, that their gifts were unnecessary, since the model was already in existence, and nothing more could be done than to IMITATE it.

(Here there was another meaning bow towards Prince Alexis,—a bow in which Jupiter and Venus joined. This was the great point of the evening, in the opinion of Simon Petrovitch. He peeped through a hole in one of the clouds, and, seeing the delight of Prince Alexis and the congratulations of his friends, immediately took a large glass of Cognac).

The Graces were then summoned, and after them the Muses—all in hoops, powder, and paint. Their songs had the same burden,—intense admiration of the father, and good-will for the son, underlaid with a delicate doubt. The close was a chorus of all the deities and semi-deities in praise of the old Prince, with the accompaniment of fireworks. Apollo rose through the air like a frog, with his blue legs and yellow arms wide apart; Jupiter's chariot rolled off; Venus bowed herself back against a mouldy cloud; and the Muses came forward in a bunch, with a wreath of laurel, which they placed upon the venerated head.

Sasha was dispatched to bring the poet, that he might receive his well-earned praise and reward. But alas for Simon Petrovitch? His legs had already doubled under him. He was awarded fifty rubles and a new caftan, which he was not in a condition to accept until several days afterward.

The supper which followed resembled the dinner, except that there were fewer dishes and more bottles. When the closing course of sweatmeats had either been consumed or transferred to the pockets of the guests, the Princess Martha retired with the ladies. The guests of lower rank followed; and there remained only some fifteen or twenty, who were thereupon conducted by Prince Alexis to a smaller chamber, where he pulled off his coat, lit his pipe, and called for brandy. The others followed his example, and their revelry wore out the night.

Such was the festival which preceded the departure of Prince Boris for St. Petersburg.

# IV

Before following the young Prince and his fortunes, in the capital, we must relate two incidents which somewhat disturbed the ordered course of life in the castle of Kinesma, during the first month or two after his departure.

It must be stated, as one favorable trait in the character of Prince Alexis, that, however brutally he treated his serfs, he allowed no other man to oppress them. All they had and were—their services, bodies, lives—belonged to him; hence injustice towards them was disrespect towards their lord. Under the fear which his barbarity inspired lurked a brute-like attachment, kept alive by the recognition of this quality.

One day it was reported to him that Gregor, a merchant in the bazaar at Kinesma, had cheated the wife of one of his serfs in the purchase of a piece of cloth. Mounting his horse, he rode at once to Gregor's booth, called for the cloth, and sent the entire piece to the woman, in the merchant's name, as a confessed act of reparation.

"Now, Gregor, my child," said he, as he turned his horse's head, "have a care in future, and play me no more dishonest tricks. Do you hear? I shall come and take your business in hand myself, if the like happens again."

Not ten days passed before the like—or something fully as bad—did happen. Gregor must have been a new comer in Kinesma, or he would not have tried the experiment. In an hour from the time it was announced, Prince Alexis appeared in the bazaar with a short whip under his arm.

He dismounted at the booth with an ironical smile on his face, which chilled the very marrow in the merchant's bones.

"Ah, Gregor, my child," he shouted, "you have already forgotten my commands. Holy St. Nicholas, what a bad memory the boy has! Why, he can't be trusted to do business: I must attend to the shop myself. Out of the way! march!"

He swung his terrible whip; and Gregor, with his two assistants, darted under the counter, and made their escape. The Prince then entered the booth, took up a yard-stick, and cried out in a voice which could be heard from one end of the town to the other,—"Ladies and gentlemen, have the kindness to come and examine our stock of goods! We have silks and satins, and all kinds of ladies' wear; also velvet, cloth, cotton, and linen for the gentlemen. Will your Lordships deign to choose? Here are stockings and handkerchiefs of the finest. We understand how to measure, your Lordships, and we sell cheap. We give no change, and take no small money. Whoever has no cash may have credit. Every thing sold below cost, on account of closing up the establishment. Ladies and gentlemen, give us a call?"

Everybody in Kinesma flocked to the booth, and for three hours Prince Alexis measured and sold, either for scant cash or long credit, until the last article had been disposed of and the shelves were empty. There was great rejoicing in the community over the bargains made that day. When all was over, Gregor was summoned, and the cash received paid into his hands.

"It won't take you long to count it," said the Prince; "but here is a list of debts to be collected, which will furnish you with pleasant occupation, and enable you to exercise your memory. Would your Worship condescend to take dinner to-day with your humble assistant? He would esteem it a favor to be permitted to wait upon you with whatever his poor house can supply."

Gregor gave a glance at the whip under the Prince's arm, and begged to be excused. But the latter would take no denial, and carried out the comedy to the end by giving the merchant the place of honor at his table, and dismissing him with the present of a fine pup of his favorite breed. Perhaps the animal acted as a mnemonic symbol, for Gregor was never afterwards accused of forgetfulness.

If this trick put the Prince in a good humor, some thing presently occurred which carried him to the opposite extreme. While taking his customary siesta one afternoon, a wild young fellow—one of his noble poor relations, who "sponged" at the castle—happened to pass along a corridor outside of the very hall where his Highness was snoring. Two ladies in waiting looked down from an upper window. The young fellow perceived them, and made signs to attract their attention. Having succeeded in this, he attempted, by all sorts of antics and grimaces, to make them laugh or speak; but he failed, for the slumber-flag waved over them, and its fear was upon them. Then, in a freak of incredible rashness, he sang, in a loud voice, the first line of a popular ditty, and took to his heels.

No one had ever before dared to insult the sacred quiet. The Prince was on his feet in a moment, and rushed into the corridor, (dropping his mantle of sables by the way,) shouting.—

"Bring me the wretch who sang!"

The domestics scattered before him, for his face was terrible to look upon. Some of them had heard the voice, indeed, but not one of them had seen the culprit, who al ready lay upon a heap of hay in one of the stables, and appeared to be sunk in innocent sleep.

"Who was it? who was it?" yelled the Prince, foaming at the mouth with rage, as he rushed from chamber to chamber.

At last he halted at the top of the great flight of steps leading into the court-yard, and repeated his demand in a voice of thunder.

The servants, trembling, kept at a safe distance, and some of them ventured to state that the offender could not be discovered. The Prince turned and entered one of the state apartments, whence came the sound of porcelain smashed on the floor, and mirrors shivered on the walls. Whenever they heard that sound, the immates of the castle knew that a hurricane was let loose.

They deliberated hurriedly and anxiously. What was to be done? In his fits of blind animal rage, there was nothing of which the Prince was not capable, and the fit could be allayed only by finding a victim. No one, however, was willing to be a Curtius for the others, and meanwhile the storm was increasing from minute to minute. Some of the more active and shrewd of the household pitched upon the leader of the band, a simple-minded, good-natured serf, named Waska. They entreated him to take upon himself the crime of having sung, offering to have his punishment mitigated in every possible way. He was proof against their tears, but not against the money which they finally offered, in order to avert the storm. The agreement was made, although Waska both scratched his head and shook it, as he reflected upon the probable result.

The Prince, after his work of destruction, again appeared upon the steps, and with hoarse voice and flashing eyes, began to announce that every soul in the castle should receive a hundred lashes, when a noise was heard in the court, and amid cries of "Here he is!" "We've got him, Highness!" the poor Waska, bound hand and foot, was brought forward. They placed him at the bottom of the steps. The Prince descended until the two stood face to face. The others looked on from courtyard, door, and window. A pause ensued, during which no one dared to breathe.

At last Prince Alexis spoke, in a loud and terrible voice—

"It was you who sang it?"

"Yes, your Highness, it was I," Waska replied, in a scarcely audible tone, dropping his head and mechanically drawing his shoulders together, as if shrinking from the coming blow.

It was full three minutes before the Prince again spoke. He still held the whip in his hand, his eyes fixed and the muscles of his face rigid. All at once the spell seemed to dissolve: his hand fell, and he said in his ordinary voice—

"You sing remarkably well. Go, now: you shall have ten rubles and an embroidered caftan for your singing."

But any one would have made a great mistake who dared to awaken Prince Alexis a second time in the same manner.

# V

Prince Boris, in St. Petersburg, adopted the usual habits of his class. He dressed elegantly; he drove a dashing troika; he played, and lost more frequently than he won; he took no special pains to shun any form of fashionable dissipation. His money went fast, it is true; but twenty-five thousand rubles was a large sum in those days, and Boris did not inherit his father's expensive constitution. He was presented to the Empress; but his thin face, and mild, melancholy eyes did not make much impression upon that ponderous woman. He frequented the salons of the nobility, but saw no face so beautiful as that of Parashka, the serf-maiden who personated Venus for Simon Petrovitch. The fact is, he had a dim, undeveloped instinct of culture, and a crude, half-conscious worship of beauty,—both of which qualities found just enough nourishment in the life of the capital to tantalize and never satisfy his nature. He was excited by his new experience, but hardly happier.

Although but three-and-twenty, he would never know the rich, vital glow with which youth rushes to clasp all forms of sensation.

He had seen, almost daily, in his father's castle, excess in its most excessive development. It had grown to be repulsive, and he knew not how to fill the void in his life. With a single spark of genius, and a little more culture, he might have become a passable author or artist; but he was doomed to be one of those deaf and dumb natures that see the movements of the lips of others, yet have no conception of sound. No wonder his savage old father looked upon him with contempt, for even his vices were without strength or character.

The dark winter days passed by, one by one, and the first week of Lent had already arrived to subdue the glittering festivities of the court, when the only genuine adventure of the season happened to the young Prince. For adventures, in the conventional sense of the word, he was not distinguished; whatever came to him must come by its own force, or the force of destiny.

One raw, gloomy evening, as dusk was setting in, he saw a female figure in a droschky, which was about turning from the great Morskoi into the Gorokhovaya (Pea) Street. He noticed, listlessly, that the lady was dressed in black, closely veiled, and appeared to be urging the istvostchik (driver) to make better speed. The latter cut his horse sharply: it sprang forward, just at the turning, and the droschky, striking a lamp-post was instantly overturned. The lady, hurled with great force upon the solidly frozen snow, lay motionless, which the driver observing, he righted the sled and drove off at full speed, without looking behind him. It was not inhumanity, but fear of the knout that hurried him away.

Prince Boris looked up and down the Morskoi, but perceived no one near at hand. He then knelt upon the snow, lifted the lady's head to his knee, and threw back her veil. A face so lovely, in spite of its deadly pallor, he had never before seen. Never had he even imagined so perfect an oval, such a sweet, fair forehead, such delicately pencilled brows, so fine and straight a nose, such wonderful beauty of mouth and chin. It was fortunate that she was not very severely stunned, for Prince Boris was not only ignorant of the usual modes of restoration in such cases, but he totally forgot their necessity, in his rapt contemplation of the lady's face. Presently she opened her eyes, and they dwelt, expressionless, but bewildering in their darkness and depth, upon his own, while her consciousness of things slowly returned.

She strove to rise, and Boris gently lifted and supported her. She would have withdrawn from his helping arm, but was still too weak from the shock. He, also, was confused and (strange to say) embarrassed; but he had self-possession enough to shout, "Davei!" (Here!) at random. The call was answered from the Admiralty Square; a sled dashed up the Gorokhovaya and halted beside him. Taking the single seat, he lifted her gently upon his lap and held her very tenderly in his arms.

"Where?" asked the istvostchik.

Boris was about to answer "Anywhere!" but the lady whispered in a voice of silver sweetness, the name of a remote street, near the Smolnoi Church.

As the Prince wrapped the ends of his sable pelisse about her, he noticed that her furs were of the common foxskin worn by the middle classes. They, with her heavy boots and the threadbare cloth of her garments, by no means justified his first suspicion,—that she was a grande dame, engaged in some romantic "adventure." She was not more than nineteen or twenty years of age, and he felt—without knowing what it was—the atmosphere of sweet, womanly purity and innocence which surrounded her. The shyness of a lost boyhood surprised him.

By the time they had reached the Litenie, she had fully recovered her consciousness and a portion of her strength. She drew away from him as much as the narrow sled would allow.

"You have been very kind, sir, and I thank you," she said; "but I am now able to go home without your further assistance."

"By no means, lady!" said the Prince. "The streets are rough, and here are no lamps. If a second accident were to happen, you would be helpless. Will you not allow me to protect you?"

She looked him in the face. In the dusky light, she saw not the peevish, weary features of the worldling, but only the imploring softness of his eyes, the full and perfect honesty of his present emotion. She made no further objection; perhaps she was glad that she could trust the elegant stranger.

Boris, never before at a loss for words, even in the presence of the Empress, was astonished to find how awkward were his attempts at conversation. She was presently the more self-possessed of the two, and nothing was ever so sweet to his ears as the few commonplace remarks she uttered. In spite of the darkness and the chilly air, the sled seemed to fly like lightning. Before he supposed they had made half the way, she gave a sign to the istvostchik, and they drew up before a plain house of squared logs.

The two lower windows were lighted, and the dark figure of an old man, with a skull-cap upon his head, was framed in one of them. It vanished as the sled stopped; the door was thrown open and the man came forth hurriedly, followed by a Russian nurse with a lantern.

"Helena, my child, art thou come at last? What has befallen thee?"

He would evidently have said more, but the sight of Prince Boris caused him to pause, while a quick shade of suspicion and alarm passed over his face. The Prince stepped forward, instantly relieved of his unaccustomed timidity, and rapidly described the accident. The old nurse Katinka, had meanwhile assisted the lovely Helena into the house.

The old man turned to follow, shivering in the night-air. Suddenly recollecting himself, he begged the Prince to enter and take some refreshments, but with the air and tone of a man who hopes that his invitation will not be accepted. If such was really his hope, he was disappointed; for Boris instantly commanded the istvostchik to wait for him, and entered the humble dwelling.

The apartment into which he was ushered was spacious, and plainly, yet not shabbily furnished. A violoncello and clavichord, with several portfolios of music, and scattered sheets of ruled paper, proclaimed the profession or the taste of the occupant. Having excused himself a moment to look after his daughter's condition, the old man, on his return, found Boris turning over the leaves of a musical work.

"You see my profession," he said. "I teach music?"

"Do you not compose?" asked the Prince.

"That was once my ambition. I was a pupil of Sebastian Bach. But—circumstances—necessity—brought me here. Other lives changed the direction of mine. It was right!"

"You mean your daughter's?" the Prince gently suggested.

"Hers and her mother's. Our story was well known in St. Petersburg twenty years ago, but I suppose no one recollects it now. My wife was the daughter of a Baron von Plauen, and loved music and myself better than her home and a titled bridegroom. She escaped, we united our lives, suffered and were happy together,—and she died. That is all."

Further conversation was interrupted by the entrance of Helena, with steaming glasses of tea. She was even lovelier than before. Her close-fitting dress revealed the symmetry of her form, and the quiet, unstudied grace of her movements. Although her garments were of well-worn material, the lace which covered her bosom was genuine point d'Alencon, of an old and rare pattern. Boris felt that her air and manner were thoroughly noble; he rose and saluted her with the profoundest respect.

In spite of the singular delight which her presence occasioned him, he was careful not to prolong his visit beyond the limits of strict etiquette. His name, Boris Alexeivitch, only revealed to his guests the name of his father, without his rank; and when he stated that he was employed in one of the Departments, (which was true in a measure, for he was a staff officer,) they could only look upon him as being, at best, a member of some family whose recent elevation to the nobility did not release them from the necessity of Government service. Of course he employed the usual pretext of wishing to study music, and either by that or some other stratagem managed to leave matters in such a shape that a second visit could not occasion surprise.

As the sled glided homewards over the crackling snow, he was obliged to confess the existence of a new and powerful excitement. Was it the chance of an adventure, such as certain of his comrades were continually seeking? He thought not; no, decidedly not. Was it—could it be—love? He really could not tell; he had not the slightset idea what love was like.

# VI

It was something at least, that the plastic and not un-virtuous nature of the young man was directed towards a definite object. The elements out of which he was made, although somewhat diluted, were active enough to make him uncomfortable, so long as they remained in a confused state. He had very little power of introversion, but he was sensible that his temperament was changing,—that he grew more cheerful and contented with life,—that a chasm somewhere was filling up,—just in proportion as his acquaintance with the old music-master and his daughter became more familiar. His visits were made so brief, were so adroitly timed and accounted for by circumstances, that by the close of Lent he could feel justified in making the Easter call of a friend, and claim its attendant privileges, without fear of being repulsed.

That Easter call was an era in his life. At the risk of his wealth and rank being suspected, he dressed himself in new and rich garments, and hurried away towards the Smolnoi. The old nurse, Katinka, in her scarlet gown, opened the door for him, and was the first to say, "Christ is arisen!" What could he do but give her the usual kiss? Formerly he had kissed hundreds of serfs, men and women, on the sacred anniversary, with a passive good-will. But Katinka's kiss seemed bitter, and he secretly rubbed his mouth after it. The music-master came next: grisly though he might be, he was the St. Peter who stood at the gate of heaven. Then entered Helena, in white, like an angel. He took her hand, pronounced the Easter greeting, and scarcely waited for the answer, "Truly he has arisen!" before his lips found the way to hers. For a second they warmly trembled and glowed together; and in another second some new and sweet and subtle relation seemed to be established between their natures.

That night Prince Boris wrote a long letter to his "chere maman," in piquantly misspelt French, giving her the gossip of the court, and such family news as she usually craved. The purport of the letter, however, was only disclosed in the final paragraph, and then in so negative a way that it is doubtful whether the Princess Martha fully understood it.

"Poing de mariajes pour moix!" he wrote,—but we will drop the original,—"I don't think of such a thing yet. Pashkoff dropped a hint, the other day, but I kept my eyes shut. Perhaps you remember her?—fat, thick lips, and crooked teeth. Natalie D—— said to me, 'Have you ever been in love, Prince?" HAVE I, MAMAN? I did not know what answer to make. What is love? How does one feel, when one has it? They laugh at it here, and of course I should not wish to do what is laughable. Give me a hint: forewarned is forearmed, you know,'"—etc., etc.

Perhaps the Princess Martha DID suspect something; perhaps some word in her son's letter touched a secret spot far back in her memory, and renewed a dim, if not very intelligible, pain. She answered his question at length, in the style of the popular French romances of that day. She had much to say of dew and roses, turtledoves and the arrows of Cupid.

"Ask thyself," she wrote, "whether felicity comes with her presence, and distraction with her absence,—whether her eyes make the morning brighter for thee, and her tears fall upon thy heart like molten lava,—whether heaven would be black and dismal without her company, and the flames of hell turn into roses under her feet."

It was very evident that the good Princess Martha had never felt—nay, did not comprehend—a passion such as she described.

Prince Boris, however, whose veneration for his mother was unbounded, took her words literally, and applied the questions to himself. Although he found it difficult, in good faith and sincerity, to answer all of them affirmatively (he was puzzled, for instance, to know the sensation of molten lava falling upon the heart), yet the general conclusion was inevitable: Helena was necessary to his happiness.

Instead of returning to Kinesma for the summer, as had been arranged, he determined to remain in St. Petersburg, under the pretence of devoting himself to military studies. This change of plan occasioned more disappointment to the Princess Martha than vexation to Prince Alexis. The latter only growled at the prospect of being called upon to advance a further supply of rubles, slightly comforting himself with the muttered reflection,—

"Perhaps the brat will make a man of himself, after all."

It was not many weeks, in fact, before the expected petition came to hand. The Princess Martha had also foreseen it, and instructed her son how to attack his father's weak side. The latter was furiously jealous of certain other noblemen of nearly equal wealth, who were with him at the court of Peter the Great, as their sons now were at that of Elizabeth. Boris compared the splendor of these young noblemen with his own moderate estate, fabled a few "adventures" and drinking-bouts, and announced his determination of doing honor to the name which Prince Alexis of Kinesma had left behind him in the capital.

There was cursing at the castle when the letter arrived. Many serfs felt the sting of the short whip, the slumber-flag was hoisted five minutes later than usual, and the consumption of Cognac was alarming; but no mirror was smashed, and when Prince Alexis read the letter to his poor relations, he even chuckled over some portions of it. Boris had boldly demanded twenty thousand rubles, in the desperate hope of receiving half that amount,—and he had calculated correctly.

Before midsummer he was Helena's accepted lover. Not, however, until then, when her father had given his consent to their marriage in the autumn, did he disclose his true rank. The old man's face lighted up with a glow of selfish satisfaction; but Helena quietly took her lover's hand, and said,—

"Whatever you are, Boris, I will be faithful to you."

# VII

Leaving Boris to discover the exact form and substance of the passion of love, we will return for a time to the castle of Kinesma.

Whether the Princess Martha conjectured what had transpired in St. Petersburg, or was partially informed of it by her son, cannot now be ascertained. She was sufficiently weak, timid, and nervous, to be troubled with the knowledge of the stratagem in which she had assisted in order to procure money, and that the ever-present consciousness thereof would betray itself to the sharp eyes of her husband. Certain it is, that the demeanor of the latter towards her and his household began to change about the end of the summer. He seemed to have a haunting suspicion, that, in some way he had been, or was about to be, overreached. He grew peevish, suspicious, and more violent than ever in his excesses.

When Mishka, the dissipated bear already described, bit off one of the ears of Basil, a hunter belonging to the castle, and Basil drew his knife and plunged it into Mishka's heart, Prince Alexis punished the hunter by cutting off his other ear, and sending him away to a distant estate. A serf, detected in eating a few of the pickled cherries intended for the Prince's botvinia, was placed in a cask, and pickled cherries packed around him up to the chin. There he was kept until almost flayed by the acid. It was ordered that these two delinquents should never afterwards be called by any other names than "Crop-Ear" and "Cherry."

But the Prince's severest joke, which, strange to say, in no wise lessened his popularity among the serfs, occurred a month or two later. One of his leading passions was the chase, — especially the chase in his own forests, with from one to two hundred men, and no one to dispute his Lordship. On such occasions, a huge barrel of wine, mounted upon a sled, always accompanied the crowd, and the quantity which the hunters received depended upon the satisfaction of Prince Alexis with the game they collected.

Winter had set in early and suddenly, and one day, as the Prince and his retainers emerged from the forest with their forenoon's spoil, and found themselves on the bank of the Volga, the water was already covered with a thin sheet of ice. Fires were kindled, a score or two of hares and a brace of deer were skinned, and the flesh placed on sticks to broil; skins of mead foamed and hissed into the wooden bowls, and the cask of unbroached wine towered in the midst. Prince Alexis had a good appetite; the meal was after his heart; and by the time he had eaten a hare and half a flank of venison, followed by several bowls of fiery wine, he was in the humor for sport. He ordered a hole cut in the upper side of the barrel, as it lay; then, getting astride of it, like a grisly Bacchus, he dipped out the liquor with a ladle, and plied his thirsty serfs until they became as recklessly savage as he.

They were scattered over a slope gently falling from the dark, dense fir-forest towards the Volga, where it terminated in a rocky palisade, ten to fifteen feet in height. The fires blazed and crackled merrily in the frosty air; the yells and songs of the carousers were echoed back from the opposite shore of the river. The chill atmosphere, the lowering sky, and the approaching night could not touch the blood of that wild crowd. Their faces glowed and their eyes sparkled; they were ready for any deviltry which their lord might suggest.

Some began to amuse themselves by flinging the clean-picked bones of deer and hare along the glassy ice of the Volga. Prince Alexis, perceiving this diverson, cried out in ecstasy, —

"Oh, by St. Nicholas the Miracle-Worker, I'll give you better sport than that, ye knaves! Here's the very place for a reisak, — do you hear me children? — a reisak! Could there be better ice? and then the rocks to jump from! Come, children, come! Waska, Ivan, Daniel, you dogs, over with you!"

Now the reisak was a gymnastic performance peculiar to old Russia, and therefore needs to be described. It could become popular only among a people of strong physical qualities, and in a country where swift rivers freeze rapidly from sudden cold. Hence we are of the opinion that it will not be introduced into our own winter diversions. A spot is selected where the water is deep and the current tolerably strong; the ice must be about half an inch in thickness. The performer leaps head foremost from a rock or platform, bursts through the ice, is carried under by the current, comes up some distance below, and bursts through again. Both skill and strength are required to do the feat successfully.

Waska, Ivan, Daniel, and a number of others, sprang to the brink of the rocks and looked over. The wall was not quite perpendicular, some large fragments having fallen from above and lodged along the base. It would therefore require a bold leap to clear the rocks and strike the smooth ice. They hesitated, — and no wonder.

Prince Alexis howled with rage and disappointment.

"The Devil take you, for a pack of whimpering hounds!" he cried. "Holy Saints! they are afraid to make a reisak!"

Ivan crossed himself and sprang. He cleared the rocks, but, instead of bursting through the ice with his head, fell at full length upon his back.

"O knave!" yelled the Prince,—"not to know where his head is! Thinks it's his back! Give him fifteen stripes."

Which was instantly done.

The second attempt was partially successful. One of the hunters broke through the ice, head foremost, going down, but he failed to come up again; so the feat was only half performed.

The Prince became more furiously excited.

"This is the way I'm treated!" he cried. "He forgets all about finishing the reisak, and goes to chasing sterlet! May the carps eat him up for an ungrateful vagabond! Here, you beggars!" (addressing the poor relations,) "take your turn, and let me see whether you are men."

Only one of the frightened parasites had the courage to obey. On reaching the brink, he shut his eyes in mortal fear, and made a leap at random. The next moment he lay on the edge of the ice with one leg broken against a fragment of rock.

This capped the climax of the Prince's wrath. He fell into a state bordering on despair, tore his hair, gnashed his teeth, and wept bitterly.

"They will be the death of me!" was his lament. "Not a man among them! It wasn't so in the old times. Such beautiful reisaks as I have seen! But the people are becoming women,—hares,—chickens,—skunks! Villains, will you force me to kill you? You have dishonored and disgraced me; I am ashamed to look my neighbors in the face. Was ever a man so treated?"

The serfs hung down their heads, feeling somehow responsible for their master's misery. Some of them wept, out of a stupid sympathy with his tears.

All at once he sprang down from the cask, crying in a gay, triumphant tone,—

"I have it! Bring me Crop-Ear. He's the fellow for a reisak,—he can make three, one after another."

One of the boldest ventured to suggest that Crop-Ear had been sent away in disgrace to another of the Prince's estates.

"Bring him here, I say? Take horses, and don't draw rein going or coming. I will not stir from this spot until Crop-Ear comes."

With these words, he mounted the barrel, and recommenced ladling out the wine. Huge fires were made, for the night was falling, and the cold had become intense. Fresh game was skewered and set to broil, and the tragic interlude of the revel was soon forgotten.

Towards midnight the sound of hoofs was heard, and the messengers arrived with Crop-Ear. But, although the latter had lost his ears, he was not inclined to split his head. The ice, meanwhile, had become so strong that a cannon-ball would have made no impression upon it. Crop-Ear simply threw down a stone heavier than himself, and, as it bounced and slid along the solid floor, said to Prince Alexis, —

"Am I to go back, Highness, or stay here?"

"Here, my son. Thou'rt a man. Come hither to me."

Taking the serf's head in his hands, he kissed him on both cheeks. Then he rode homeward through the dark, iron woods, seated astride on the barrel, and steadying himself with his arms around Crop-Ear's and Waska's necks.

# VIII

The health of the Princess Martha, always delicate, now began to fail rapidly. She was less and less able to endure her husband's savage humors, and lived almost exclusively in her own apartments. She never mentioned the name of Boris in his presence, for it was sure to throw him into a paroxysm of fury. Floating rumors in regard to the young Prince had reached him from the capital, and nothing would convince him that his wife was not cognizant of her son's doings. The poor Princess clung to her boy as to all that was left her of life, and tried to prop her failing strength with the hope of his speedy return. She was now too helpless to thwart his wishes in any way; but she dreaded, more than death, the terrible SOMETHING which would surely take place between father and son if her conjectures should prove to be true.

One day, in the early part of November, she received a letter from Boris, announcing his marriage. She had barely strength and presence of mind enough to conceal the paper in her bosom before sinking in a swoon. By some means or other the young Prince had succeeded in overcoming all the obstacles to such a step: probably the favor of the Empress was courted, in order to obtain her consent. The money he had received, he wrote, would be sufficient to maintain them for a few months, though not in a style befitting their rank. He was proud and happy; the Princess Helena would be the reigning beauty of the court, when he should present her, but he desired the sanction of his parents to the marriage, before taking his place in society. He would write immediately to his father, and hoped, that, if the news brought a storm, Mishka might be on hand to divert its force, as on a former occasion.

Under the weight of this imminent secret, the Princess Martha could neither eat nor sleep. Her body wasted to a shadow; at every noise in the castle, she started and listened in terror, fearing that the news had arrived.

Prince Boris, no doubt, found his courage fail him when he set about writing the promised letter; for a fortnight elapsed before it made its appearance. Prince Alexis received it on his return from the chase. He read it hastily through, uttered a prolonged roar like that of a wounded bull, and rushed into the castle. The sound of breaking furniture, of crashing porcelain and shivered glass, came from the state apartments: the domestics fell on their knees and prayed; the Princess, who heard the noise and knew what it portended, became almost insensible from fright.

One of the upper servants entered a chamber as the Prince was in the act of demolishing a splendid malachite table, which had escaped all his previous attacks. He was immediately greeted with a cry of,—

"Send the Princess to me!"

"Her Highness is not able to leave her chamber," the man replied.

How it happened he could never afterwards describe but he found himself lying in a corner of the room. When he arose, there seemed to be a singular cavity in his mouth: his upper front teeth were wanting.

We will not narrate what took place in the chamber of the Princess.

The nerves of the unfortunate woman had been so wrought upon by her fears, that her husband's brutal rage, familiar to her from long experience, now possessed a new and alarming significance. His threats were terrible to hear; she fell into convulsions, and before morning her tormented life was at an end.

There was now something else to think of, and the smashing of porcelain and cracking of whips came to an end. The Archimandrite was summoned, and preparations, both religious and secular, were made for a funeral worthy the rank of the deceased. Thousands flocked to Kinesma; and when the immense procession moved away from the castle, although very few of the persons had ever known or cared in the least, for the Princess Martha, all, without exception, shed profuse tears. Yes, there was one exception,— one bare, dry rock, rising alone out of the universal deluge,—Prince Alexis himself, who walked behind the coffin, his eyes fixed and his features rigid as stone. They remarked that his face was haggard, and that the fiery tinge on his cheeks and nose had faded into livid purple. The only sign of emotion which he gave was a convulsive shudder, which from time to time passed over his whole body.

Three archimandrites (abbots) and one hundred priests headed the solemn funeral procession from the castle to the church on the opposite hill. There the mass for the dead was chanted, the responses being sung by a choir of silvery boyish voices. All the appointments were of the costliest character. Not only all those within the church, but the thousands outside, spared not their tears, but wept until the fountains were exhausted. Notice was given, at the close of the services, that "baked meats" would be furnished to the multitude, and that all beggars who came to Kinesma would be charitably fed for the space of six weeks. Thus, by her death, the amiable Princess Martha was enabled to dispense more charity than had been permitted to her life.

At the funeral banquet which followed, Prince Alexis placed the Abbot Sergius at his right hand, and conversed with him in the most edifying manner upon the necessity of leading a pure and godly life. His remarks upon the duty of a Christian, upon brotherly love, humility, and self-sacrifice, brought tears into the eyes of the listening priests. He expressed his conviction that the departed Princess, by the piety of her life, had attained unto salvation,—and added, that his own life had now no further value unless he should devote it to religious exercises.

"Can you not give me a place in your monastery?" he asked, turning to the Abbot. "I will endow it with a gift of forty thousand rubles, for the privilege of occupying a monk's cell."

"Pray, do not decide too hastily, Highness," the Abbot replied. "You have yet a son."

"What!" yelled Prince Alexis, with flashing eyes, every trace of humility and renunciation vanishing like smoke,—"what! Borka? The infamous wretch who has ruined me, killed his mother, and brought disgrace upon our name? Do you know that he has married a wench of no family and without a farthing,—who would be honored, if I should allow her to feed my hogs? Live for HIM? live for HIM? Ah-R-R-R!"

This outbreak terminated in a sound between a snarl and a bellow. The priests turned pale, but the Abbot devoutly remarked—

"Encompassed by sorrows, Prince, you should humbly submit to the will of the Lord."

"Submit to Borka?" the Prince scornfully laughed. "I know what I'll do. There's time enough yet for a wife and another child,—ay,—a dozen children! I can have my pick in the province; and if I couldn't I'd sooner take Masha, the goose-girl, than leave Borka the hope of stepping into my shoes. Beggars they shall be,—beggars!"

What further he might have said was interrupted by the priests rising to chant the Blajennon uspennie (blessed be the dead),—after which, the trisna, a drink composed of mead, wine, and rum, was emptied to the health of the departed soul. Every one stood during this ceremony, except Prince Alexis, who fell suddenly prostrate before the consecrated pictures, and sobbed so passionately that the tears of the guests flowed for the third time. There he lay until night; for whenever any one dared to touch him, he struck out furiously with fists and feet. Finally he fell asleep on the floor, and the servants then bore him to his sleeping apartment.

For several days afterward his grief continued to be so violent that the occupants of the castle were obliged to keep out of his way. The whip was never out of his hand, and he used it very recklessly, not always selecting the right person. The parasitic poor relations found their situation so uncomfortable, that they decided, one and all, to detach themselves from the tree upon which they fed and fattened, even at the risk of withering on a barren soil. Night and morning the serfs prayed upon their knees, with many tears and groans, that the Saints might send consolation, in any form, to their desperate lord.

The Saints graciously heard and answered the prayer. Word came that a huge bear had been seen in the forest stretching towards Juriewetz. The sorrowing Prince pricked up his ears, threw down his whip, and ordered a chase. Sasha, the broad-shouldered, the cunning, the ready, the untiring companion of his master, secretly ordered a cask of vodki to follow the crowd of hunters and serfs. There was a steel-bright sky, a low, yellow sun, and a brisk easterly wind from the heights of the Ural. As the crisp snow began to crunch under the Prince's sled, his followers saw the old expression come back to his face. With song and halloo and blast of horns, they swept away into the forest.

Saint John the Hunter must have been on guard over Russia that day.

The great bear was tracked, and after a long and exciting chase, fell by the hand of Prince Alexis himself. Halt was made in an open space in the forest, logs were piled together and kindled on the snow, and just at the right moment (which no one knew better than Sasha) the cask of vodki rolled into its place. When the serfs saw the Prince mount astride of it, with his ladle in his hand, they burst into shouts of extravagant joy. "Slava Bogu!" (Glory be to God!) came fervently from the bearded lips of those hard, rough, obedient children. They tumbled headlong over each other, in their efforts to drink first from the ladle, to clasp the knees or kiss the hands of the restored Prince. And the dawn was glimmering against the eastern stars, as they took the way to the castle, making the ghostly fir-woods ring with shout and choric song.

Nevertheless, Prince Alexis was no longer the same man; his giant strength and furious appetite were broken. He was ever ready, as formerly, for the chase and the drinking-bout; but his jovial mood no longer grew into a crisis which only utter physical exhaustion or the stupidity of drunkenness could overcome. Frequently, while astride the cask, his shouts of laughter would suddenly cease, the ladle would drop from his hand, and he would sit motionless, staring into vacancy for five minutes at a time. Then the serfs, too, became silent, and stood still, awaiting a change. The gloomy mood passed away as suddenly. He would start, look about him, and say, in a melancholy voice,—

"Have I frightened you, my children? It seems to me that I am getting old. Ah, yes, we must all die, one day. But we need not think about it, until the time comes. The Devil take me for putting it into my head! Why, how now? can't you sing, children?"

Then he would strike up some ditty which they all knew: a hundred voices joined in the strain, and the hills once more rang with revelry.

Since the day when the Princess Martha was buried, the Prince had not again spoken of marriage. No one, of course, dared to mention the name of Boris in his presence.

# IX

The young Prince had, in reality, become the happy husband of Helena. His love for her had grown to be a shaping and organizing influence, without which his nature would have fallen into its former confusion. If a thought of a less honorable relation had ever entered his mind, it was presently banished by the respect which a nearer intimacy inspired; and thus Helena, magnetically drawing to the surface only his best qualities, loved, unconsciously to herself, her own work in him. Ere long, she saw that she might balance the advantages he had conferred upon her in their marriage by the support and encouragement which she was able to impart to him; and this knowledge, removing all painful sense of obligation, made her both happy and secure in her new position.

The Princess Martha, under some presentiment of her approaching death, had intrusted one of the ladies in attendance upon her with the secret of her son's marriage, in addition to a tender maternal message, and such presents of money and jewelry as she was able to procure without her husband's knowledge. These presents reached Boris very opportunely; for, although Helena developed a wonderful skill in regulating his expenses, the spring was approaching, and even the limited circle of society in which they had moved during the gay season had made heavy demands upon his purse. He became restless and abstracted, until his wife, who by this time clearly comprehended the nature of his trouble, had secretly decided how it must be met.

The slender hoard of the old music-master, with a few thousand rubles from Prince Boris, sufficed for his modest maintenance. Being now free from the charge of his daughter, he determined to visit Germany, and, if circumstances were propitious, to secure a refuge for his old age in his favorite Leipsic. Summer was at hand, and the court had already removed to Oranienbaum. In a few weeks the capital would be deserted.

"Shall we go to Germany with your father?" asked Boris, as he sat at a window with Helena, enjoying the long twilight.

"No, my Boris," she answered; "we will go to Kinesma."

"But—Helena,—golubchik, mon ange,—are you in earnest?"

"Yes, my Boris. The last letter from your—our cousin Nadejda convinces me that the step must be taken. Prince Alexis has grown much older since your mother's death; he is lonely and unhappy. He may not welcome us, but he will surely suffer us to come to him; and we must then begin the work of reconciliation. Reflect, my Boris, that you have keenly wounded him in the tenderest part,—his pride,—and you must therefore cast away your own pride, and humbly and respectfully, as becomes a son, solicit his pardon."

"Yes," said he, hesitatingly, "you are right. But I know his violence and recklessness, as you do not. For myself, alone, I am willing to meet him; yet I fear for your sake. Would you not tremble to encounter a maddened and brutal mujik?—then how much more to meet Alexis Pavlovitch of Kinesma!"

"I do not and shall not tremble," she replied. "It is not your marriage that has estranged your father, but your marriage with ME. Having been, unconsciously, the cause of the trouble, I shall deliberately, and as a sacred duty, attempt to remove it. Let us go to Kinesma, as humble, penitent children, and cast ourselves upon your father's mercy. At the worst, he can but reject us; and you will have given me the consolation of knowing that I have tried, as your wife, to annul the sacrifice you have made for my sake."

"Be it so, then!" cried Boris, with a mingled feeling of relief and anxiety.

He was not unwilling that the attempt should be made, especially since it was his wife's desire; but he knew his father too well to anticipate immediate success. All threatening POSSIBILITIES suggested themselves to his mind; all forms of insult and outrage which he had seen perpetrated at Kinesma filled his memory. The suspense became at last worse than any probable reality. He wrote to his father, announcing a speedy visit from himself and his wife; and two days afterwards the pair left St. Petersburg in a large travelling kibitka.

# X

When Prince Alexis received his son's letter, an expression of fierce, cruel delight crept over his face, and there remained, horribly illuminating its haggard features. The orders given for swimming horses in the Volga—one of his summer diversions—were immediately countermanded; he paced around the parapet of the castle-wall until near midnight, followed by Sasha with a stone jug of vodki. The latter had the useful habit, notwithstanding his stupid face, of picking up the fragments of soliloquy which the Prince dropped, and answering them as if talking to himself. Thus he improved upon and perfected many a hint of cruelty, and was too discreet ever to dispute his master's claim to the invention.

Sasha, we may be sure, was busy with his devil's work that night. The next morning the stewards and agents of Prince Alexis, in castle, village, and field, were summoned to his presence.

"Hark ye!" said he; "Borka and his trumpery wife send me word that they will be here to-morrow. See to it that every man, woman, and child, for ten versts out on the Moskovskoi road, knows of their coming. Let it be known that whoever uncovers his head before them shall uncover his back for a hundred lashes. Whomsoever they greet may bark like a dog, meeouw like a cat, or bray like an ass, as much as he chooses; but if he speaks a decent word, his tongue shall be silenced with stripes. Whoever shall insult them has my pardon in advance. Oh, let them come!—ay, let them come! Come they may: but how they go away again"——

The Prince Alexis suddenly stopped, shook his head, and walked up and down the hall, muttering to himself. His eyes were bloodshot, and sparkled with a strange light. What the stewards had heard was plain enough; but that something more terrible than insult was yet held in reserve they did not doubt. It was safe, therefore, not only to fulfil, but to exceed, the letter of their instructions. Before night the whole population were acquainted with their duties; and an unusual mood of expectancy, not unmixed with brutish glee, fell upon Kinesma.

By the middle of the next forenoon, Boris and his wife, seated in the open kibitka, drawn by post-horses, reached the boundaries of the estate, a few versts from the village. They were both silent and slightly pale at first, but now began to exchange mechanical remarks, to divert each other's thoughts from the coming reception.

"Here are the fields of Kinesma at last!" exclaimed Prince Boris. "We shall see the church and castle from the top of that hill in the distance. And there is Peter, my playmate, herding the cattle!

"Peter! Good-day, brotherkin!"

Peter looked, saw the carriage close upon him, and, after a moment of hesitation, let his arms drop stiffly by his sides, and began howling like a mastiff by moonlight. Helena laughed heartily at this singular response to the greeting; but Boris, after the first astonishment was over, looked terrified.

"That was done by order," said he, with a bitter smile. "The old bear stretches his claws out. Dare you try his hug?"

"I do not fear," she answered, her face was calm.

Every serf they passed obeyed the order of Prince Alexis according to his own idea of disrespect. One turned his back; another made contemptuous grimaces and noises; another sang a vulgar song; another spat upon the ground or held his nostrils. Nowhere was a cap raised, or the stealthy welcome of a friendly glance given.

The Princess Helena met these insults with a calm, proud indifference. Boris felt them more keenly; for the fields and hills were prospectively his property, and so also were the brutish peasants. It was a form of chastisement which he had never before experienced, and knew not how to resist. The affront of an entire community was an offence against which he felt himself to be helpless.

As they approached the town, the demonstrations of insolence were redoubled. About two hundred boys, between the ages of ten and fourteen, awaited them on the hill below the church, forming themselves into files on either side of the road. These imps had been instructed to stick out their tongues in derision, and howl, as the carriage passed between them. At the entrance of the long main street of Kinesma, they were obliged to pass under a mock triumphal arch, hung with dead dogs and drowned cats; and from this point the reception assumed an outrageous character. Howls, hootings, and hisses were heard on all sides; bouquets of nettles and vile weeds were flung to them; even wreaths of spoiled fish dropped from the windows. The women were the most eager and uproarious in this carnival of insult: they beat their saucepans, threw pails of dirty water upon the horses, pelted the coachman with rotten cabbages, and filled the air with screeching and foul words.

It was impossible to pass through this ordeal with indifference. Boris, finding that his kindly greetings were thrown away,—that even his old acquaintances in the bazaar howled like the rest,—sat with head bowed and despair in his heart. The beautiful eyes of Helena were heavy with tears; but she no longer trembled, for she knew the crisis was yet to come.

As the kibitka slowly climbed the hill on its way to the castle-gate, Prince Alexis, who had heard and enjoyed the noises in the village from a balcony on the western tower, made his appearance on the head of the steps which led from the court-yard to the state apartments. The dreaded whip was in his hand; his eyes seemed about to start from their sockets, in their wild, eager, hungry gaze; the veins stood out like cords on his forehead; and his lips, twitching involuntarily, revealed the glare of his set teeth. A frightened hush filled the castle. Some of the domestics were on their knees; others watching, pale and breathless, from the windows: for all felt that a greater storm than they had ever experienced was about to burst. Sasha and the castle-steward had taken the wise precaution to summon a physician and a priest, provided with the utensils for extreme unction. Both of these persons had been smuggled in through a rear entrance, and were kept concealed until their services should be required.

The noise of wheels was heard outside the gate, which stood invitingly open. Prince Alexis clutched his whip with iron fingers, and unconsciously took the attitude of a wild beast about to spring from its ambush. Now the hard clatter of hoofs and the rumbling, of wheels echoed from the archway, and the kibitka rolled into the courtyard. It stopped near the foot of the grand staircase. Boris, who sat upon the farther side, rose to alight, in order to hand down his wife; but no sooner had he made a movement than Prince Alexis, with lifted whip and face flashing fire, rushed down the steps. Helena rose, threw back her veil, let her mantle (which Boris had grasped, in his anxiety to restrain her action,) fall behind her, and stepped upon the pavement.

Prince Alexis had already reached the last step, and but a few feet separated them. He stopped as if struck by lightning,—his body still retaining, in every limb, the impress of motion. The whip was in his uplifted fist; one foot was on the pavement of the court, and the other upon the edge of the last step; his head was bent forward, his mouth open, and his eyes fastened upon the Princess Helena's face.

She, too, stood motionless, a form of simple and perfect grace, and met his gaze with soft, imploring, yet courageous and trustful eyes. The women who watched the scene from the galleries above always declared that an invisible saint stood beside her in that moment, and surrounded her with a dazzling glory. The few moments during which the suspense of a hundred hearts hung upon those encountering eyes seemed an eternity.

Prince Alexis did not move, but he began to tremble from head to foot. His fingers relaxed, and the whip fell ringing upon the pavement. The wild fire of his eyes changed from wrath into an ecstasy as intense, and a piercing cry of mingled wonder, admiration and delight burst from his throat. At that cry Boris rushed forward and knelt at his feet. Helena, clasping her fairest hands, sank beside her husband, with upturned face, as if seeking the old man's eyes, and perfect the miracle she had wrought.

The sight of that sweet face, so near his own, tamed the last lurking ferocity of the beast. His tears burst forth in a shower; he lifted and embraced the Princess, kissing her brow, her cheeks, her chin, and her hands, calling her his darling daughter, his little white dove, his lambkin.

"And, father, my Boris, too!" said she.

The pure liquid voice sent thrills of exquisite delight through his whole frame. He embraced and blessed Boris, and then, throwing an arm around each, held them to his breast, and wept passionately upon their heads. By this time the whole castle overflowed with weeping. Tears fell from every window and gallery; they hissed upon the hot saucepans of the cooks; they moistened the oats in the manger; they took the starch out of the ladies' ruffles, and weakened the wine in the goblets of the guests. Insult was changed into tenderness in a moment. Those who had barked or stuck out their tongues at Boris rushed up to kiss his boots; a thousand terms of endearment were showered upon him.

Still clasping his children to his breast, Prince Alexis mounted the steps with them. At the top he turned, cleared his throat, husky from sobbing, and shouted—

"A feast! a feast for all Kinesma! Let there be rivers of vodki, wine and hydromel! Proclaim it everywhere that my dear son Boris and my dear daughter Helena have arrived, and whoever fails to welcome them to Kinesma shall be punished with a hundred stripes! Off, ye scoundrels, ye vagabonds, and spread the news!"

It was not an hour before the whole sweep of the circling hills resounded with the clang of bells, the blare of horns, and the songs and shouts of the rejoicing multitude. The triumphal arch of unsavory animals was whirled into the Volga; all signs of the recent reception vanished like magic; festive fir-boughs adorned the houses, and the gardens and window-pots were stripped of their choicest flowers to make wreaths of welcome. The two hundred boys, not old enough to comprehend this sudden bouleversement of sentiment, did not immediately desist from sticking out their tongues: whereupon they were dismissed with a box on the ear. By the middle of the afternoon all Kinesma was eating, drinking, and singing; and every song was sung, and every glass emptied in honor of the dear, good Prince Boris, and the dear, beautiful Princess Helena. By night all Kinesma was drunk.

# XI

In the castle a superb banquet was improvised. Music, guests, and rare dishes were brought together with wonderful speed, and the choicest wines of the cellar were drawn upon. Prince Boris, bewildered by this sudden and incredible change in his fortunes, sat at his father's right hand, while the Princess filled, but with much more beauty and dignity, the ancient place of the Princess Martha. The golden dishes were set before her, and the famous family emeralds—in accordance with the command of Prince Alexis—gleamed among her dark hair and flashed around her milk-white throat. Her beauty was of a kind so rare in Russia that it silenced all question and bore down all rivalry. Every one acknowledged that so lovely a creature had never before been seen. "Faith, the boy has eyes!" the old Prince constantly repeated, as he turned away from a new stare of admiration, down the table.

The guests noticed a change in the character of the entertainment. The idiot, in his tow shirt, had been crammed to repletion in the kitchen, and was now asleep in the stable. Razboi, the new bear,—the successor of the slaughtered Mishka,—was chained up out of hearing. The jugglers, tumblers, and Calmucks still occupied their old place under the gallery, but their performances were of a highly decorous character. At the least-sign of a relapse into certain old tricks, more grotesque than refined, the brows of Prince Alexis would grow dark, and a sharp glance at Sasha was sufficient to correct the indiscretion. Every one found this natural enough; for they were equally impressed with the elegance and purity of the young wife. After the healths had been drunk and the slumber-flag was raised over the castle, Boris led her into the splendid apartments of his mother,—now her own,—and knelt at her feet.

"Have I done my part, my Boris?" she asked.

"You are an angel!" he cried. "It was a miracle! My life was not worth a copek, and I feared for yours. If it will only last!—if it will only last!"

"It WILL," said she. "You have taken me from poverty, and given me rank, wealth, and a proud place in the world: let it be my work to keep the peace which God has permitted me to establish between you and your father!"

The change in the old Prince, in fact, was more radical than any one who knew his former ways of life would have considered possible. He stormed and swore occasionally, flourished his whip to some purpose, and rode home from the chase, not outside of a brandy cask, as once, but with too much of its contents inside of him: but these mild excesses were comparative virtues. His accesses of blind rage seemed to be at an end. A powerful, unaccustomed feeling of content subdued his strong nature, and left its impress on his voice and features. He joked and sang with his "children," but not with the wild recklessness of the days of reisaks and indiscriminate floggings. Both his exactions and his favors diminished in quantity. Week after week passed by, and there was no sign of any return to his savage courses.

Nothing annoyed him so much as a reference to his former way of life, in the presence of the Princess Helena. If her gentle, questioning eyes happened to rest on him at such times, something very like a blush rose into his face, and the babbler was silenced with a terribly significant look. It was enough for her to say, when he threatened an act of cruelty and injustice, "Father, is that right?" He confusedly retracted his orders, rather than bear the sorrow of her face.

The promise of another event added to his happiness: Helena would soon become a mother. As the time drew near he stationed guards at the distance of a verst around the castle, that no clattering vehicles should pass, no dogs bark loudly, nor any other disturbance occur which might agitate the Princess. The choicest sweetmeats and wines, flowers from Moscow and fruits from Astrakhan, were procured for her; and it was a wonder that the midwife performed her duty, for she had the fear of death before her eyes. When the important day at last arrived the slumber-flag was instantly hoisted, and no mouse dared to squeak in Kinesma until the cannon announced the advent of a new soul.

That night Prince Alexis lay down in the corridor, outside of Helena's door: he glared fiercely at the nurse as she entered with the birth-posset for the young mother. No one else was allowed to pass, that night, nor the next. Four days afterwards, Sasha, having a message to the Princess, and supposing the old man to be asleep, attempted to step noiselessly over his body. In a twinkle the Prince's teeth fastened themselves in the serf's leg, and held him with the tenacity of a bull-dog. Sasha did not dare to cry out: he stood, writhing with pain, until the strong jaws grew weary of their hold, and then crawled away to dress the bleeding wound. After that, no one tried to break the Prince's guard.

The christening was on a magnificent scale. Prince Paul of Kostroma was godfather, and gave the babe the name of Alexis. As the Prince had paid his respects to Helena just before the ceremony, it may be presumed that the name was not of his own inspiration. The father and mother were not allowed to be present, but they learned that the grandfather had comported himself throughout with great dignity and propriety. The Archimandrite Sergius obtained from the Metropolitan at Moscow a very minute fragment of the true cross, which was encased in a hollow bead of crystal, and hung around the infant's neck by a fine gold chain, as a precious amulet.

Prince Alexis was never tired of gazing at his grandson and namesake.

"He has more of his mother than of Boris," he would say. "So much the better! Strong dark eyes, like the Great Peter,—and what a goodly leg for a babe! Ha! he makes a tight little fist already,—fit to handle a whip,—or" (seeing the expression of Helena's face)—"or a sword. He'll be a proper Prince of Kinesma, my daughter, and we owe it to you."

Helena smiled, and gave him a grateful glance in return. She had had her secret fears as to the complete conversion of Prince Alexis; but now she saw in this babe a new spell whereby he might be bound. Slight as was her knowledge of men, she yet guessed the tyranny of long-continued habits; and only her faith, powerful in proportion as it was ignorant, gave her confidence in the result of the difficult work she had undertaken.

# XII

Alas! the proud predictions of Prince Alexis, and the protection of the sacred amulet, were alike unavailing. The babe sickened, wasted away, and died in less than two months after its birth. There was great and genuine sorrow among the serfs of Kinesma. Each had received a shining ruble of silver at the christening; and, moreover, they were now beginning to appreciate the milder regime of their lord, which this blow might suddenly terminate. Sorrow, in such natures as his, exasperates instead of chastening: they knew him well enough to recognize the danger.

At first the old man's grief appeared to be of a stubborn, harmless nature. As soon as the funeral ceremonies were over he betook himself to his bed, and there lay for two days and nights, without eating a morsel of food. The poor Princess Helena, almost prostrated by the blow, mourned alone, or with Boris, in her own apartments. Her influence, no longer kept alive by her constant presence, as formerly, began to decline. When the old Prince aroused somewhat from his stupor, it was not meat that he demanded, but drink; and he drank to angry excess. Day after day the habit resumed its ancient sway, and the whip and the wild-beast yell returned with it. The serfs even began to tremble as they never had done, so long as his vices were simply those of a strong man; for now a fiendish element seemed to be slowly creeping in. He became horribly profane: they shuddered when he cursed the venerable Metropolitan of Moscow, declaring that the old sinner had deliberately killed his grandson, by sending to him, instead of the true cross of the Saviour, a piece of the tree to which the impenitent thief was nailed.

Boris would have spared his wife the knowledge of this miserable relapse, in her present sorrow, but the information soon reached her in other ways. She saw the necessity of regaining, by a powerful effort, what she had lost. She therefore took her accustomed place at the table, and resumed her inspection of household matters. Prince Alexis, as if determined to cast off the yoke which her beauty and gentleness had laid upon him, avoided looking at her face or speaking to her, as much as possible: when he did so, his manner was cold and unfriendly. During her few days of sad retirement he had brought back the bear Razboi and the idiot to his table, and vodki was habitually poured out to him and his favorite serfs in such a measure that the nights became hideous with drunken tumult.

The Princess Helena felt that her beauty no longer possessed the potency of its first surprise. It must now be a contest of nature with nature, spiritual with animal power. The struggle would be perilous, she foresaw, but she did not shrink; she rather sought the earliest occasion to provoke it.

That occasion came. Some slight disappointment brought on one of the old paroxysms of rage, and the ox-like bellow of Prince Alexis rang through the castle. Boris was absent, but Helena delayed not a moment to venture into his father's presence. She found him in a hall over-looking the court-yard, with his terrible whip in his hand, giving orders for the brutal punishment of some scores of serfs. The sight of her, coming thus unexpectedly upon him, did not seem to produce the least effect.

"Father!" she cried, in an earnest, piteous tone, "what is it you do?"

"Away, witch!" he yelled. "I am the master in Kinesma, not thou! Away, or—"

The fierceness with which he swung and cracked the whip was more threatening than any words. Perhaps she grew a shade paler, perhaps her hands were tightly clasped in order that they might not tremble; but she did not flinch from the encounter. She moved a step nearer, fixed her gaze upon his flashing eyes, and said, in a low, firm voice—

"It is true, father, you are master here. It is easy to rule over those poor, submissive slaves. But you are not master over yourself; you are lashed and trampled upon by evil passions, and as much a slave as any of these. Be not weak, my father, but strong!"

An expression of bewilderment came into his face. No such words had ever before been addressed to him, and he knew not how to reply to them. The Princess Helena followed up the effect—she was not sure that it was an advantage—by an appeal to the simple, childish nature which she believed to exist under his ferocious exterior. For a minute it seemed as if she were about to re-establish her ascendancy: then the stubborn resistance of the beast returned.

Among the portraits in the hall was one of the deceased Princess Martha. Pointing to this, Helena cried—

"See, my father! here are the features of your sainted wife! Think that she looks down from her place among the blessed, sees you, listens to your words, prays that your hard heart may be softened! Remember her last farewell to you on earth, her hope of meeting you—"

A cry of savage wrath checked her. Stretching one huge, bony hand, as if to close her lips, trembling with rage and pain, livid and convulsed in every feature of his face, Prince Alexis reversed the whip in his right hand, and weighed its thick, heavy butt for one crashing, fatal blow. Life and death were evenly balanced. For an instant the Princess became deadly pale, and a sickening fear shot through her heart. She could not understand the effect of her words: her mind was paralyzed, and what followed came without her conscious volition.

Not retreating a step, not removing her eyes from the terrible picture before her, she suddenly opened her lips and sang. Her voice of exquisite purity, power, and sweetness, filled the old hall and overflowed it, throbbing in scarcely weakened vibrations through court-yard and castle. The melody was a prayer—the cry of a tortured heart for pardon and repose; and she sang it with almost supernatural expression. Every sound in the castle was hushed: the serfs outside knelt and uncovered their heads.

The Princess could never afterwards describe, or more than dimly recall, the exaltation of that moment. She sang in an inspired trance: from the utterance of the first note the horror of the imminent fate sank out of sight. Her eyes were fixed upon the convulsed face, but she beheld it not: all the concentrated forces of her life flowed into the music. She remembered, however, that Prince Alexis looked alternately from her face to the portrait of his wife; that he at last shuddered and grew pale; and that, when with the closing note her own strength suddenly dissolved, he groaned and fell upon the floor.

She sat down beside him, and took his head upon her lap. For a long time he was silent, only shivering as if in fever.

"Father!" she finally whispered, "let me take you away!"

He sat up on the floor and looked around; but as his eyes encountered the portrait, he gave a loud howl and covered his face with his hands.

"She turns her head!" he cried. "Take her away,—she follows me with her eyes! Paint her head black, and cover it up!"

With some difficulty he was borne to his bed, but he would not rest until assured that his orders had been obeyed, and the painting covered for the time with a coat of lamp-black. A low, prolonged attack of fever followed, during which the presence of Helena was indispensable to his comfort. She ventured to leave the room only while he slept. He was like a child in her hands; and when she commended his patience or his good resolutions, his face beamed with joy and gratitude. He determined (in good faith, this time) to enter a monastery and devote the rest of his life to pious works.

But, even after his recovery, he was still too weak and dependent on his children's attentions to carry out this resolution. He banished from the castle all those of his poor relations who were unable to drink vodki in moderation; he kept careful watch over his serfs, and those who became intoxicated (unless they concealed the fact in the stables and outhouses) were severely punished: all excess disappeared, and a reign of peace and gentleness descended upon Kinesma.

In another year another Alexis was born, and lived, and soon grew strong enough to give his grandfather the greatest satisfaction he had ever known in his life, by tugging at his gray locks, and digging the small fingers into his tamed and merry eyes. Many years after Prince Alexis was dead the serfs used to relate how they had seen him, in the bright summer afternoons, asleep in his armchair on the balcony, with the rosy babe asleep on his bosom, and the slumber-flag waving over both.

Legends of the Prince's hunts, reisaks, and brutal revels are still current along the Volga; but they are now linked to fairer and more gracious stories; and the free Russian farmers (no longer serfs) are never tired of relating incidents of the beauty, the courage, the benevolence, and the saintly piety of the Good Lady of Kinesma.

# TALES OF HOME

# THE STRANGE FRIEND

It would have required an intimate familiarity with the habitual demeanor of the people of Londongrove to detect in them an access of interest (we dare not say excitement), of whatever kind. Expression with them was pitched to so low a key that its changes might be compared to the slight variations in the drabs and grays in which they were clothed. Yet that there was a moderate, decorously subdued curiosity present in the minds of many of them on one of the First-days of the Ninth-month, in the year 1815, was as clearly apparent to a resident of the neighborhood as are the indications of a fire or a riot to the member of a city mob.

The agitations of the war which had so recently come to an end had hardly touched this quiet and peaceful community. They had stoutly "borne their testimony," and faced the question where it could not be evaded; and although the dashing Philadelphia militia had been stationed at Camp Bloomfield, within four miles of them, the previous year, these good people simply ignored the fact. If their sons ever listened to the trumpets at a distance, or stole nearer to have a peep at the uniforms, no report of what they had seen or heard was likely to be made at home. Peace brought to them a relief, like the awakening from an uncomfortable dream: their lives at once reverted to the calm which they had breathed for thirty years preceding the national disturbance. In their ways they had not materially changed for a hundred years. The surplus produce of their farms more than sufficed for the very few needs which those farms did not supply, and they seldom touched the world outside of their sect except in matters of business. They were satisfied with themselves and with their lot; they lived to a ripe and beautiful age, rarely "borrowed trouble," and were patient to endure that which came in the fixed course of things. If the spirit of curiosity, the yearning for an active, joyous grasp of life, sometimes pierced through this placid temper, and stirred the blood of the adolescent members, they were persuaded by grave voices, of almost prophetic authority, to turn their hearts towards "the Stillness and the Quietness."

It was the pleasant custom of the community to arrive at the meeting-house some fifteen or twenty minutes before the usual time of meeting, and exchange quiet and kindly greetings before taking their places on the plain benches inside. As most of the families had lived during the week on the solitude of their farms, they liked to see their neighbors' faces, and resolve, as it were, their sense of isolation into the common atmosphere, before yielding to the assumed abstraction of their worship. In this preliminary meeting, also, the sexes were divided, but rather from habit than any prescribed rule. They were already in the vestibule of the sanctuary; their voices were subdued and their manner touched with a kind of reverence.

If the Londongrove Friends gathered together a few minutes earlier on that September First-day; if the younger members looked more frequently towards one of the gates leading into the meeting-house yard than towards the other; and if Abraham Bradbury was the centre of a larger circle of neighbors than Simon Pennock (although both sat side by side on the highest seat of the gallery),—the cause of these slight deviations from the ordinary behavior of the gathering was generally known. Abraham's son had died the previous Sixth-month, leaving a widow incapable of taking charge of his farm on the Street Road, which was therefore offered for rent. It was not always easy to obtain a satisfactory tenant in those days, and Abraham was not more relieved than surprised on receiving an application from an unexpected quarter. A strange Friend, of stately appearance, called upon him, bearing a letter from William Warner, in Adams County, together with a certificate from a Monthly Meeting on Long Island. After inspecting the farm and making close inquiries in regard to the people of the neighborhood, he accepted the terms of rent, and had now, with his family, been three or four days in possession.

In this circumstance, it is true, there was nothing strange, and the interest of the people sprang from some other particulars which had transpired. The new-comer, Henry Donnelly by name, had offered, in place of the usual security, to pay the rent annually in advance; his speech and manner were not, in all respects, those of Friends, and he acknowledged that he was of Irish birth; and moreover, some who had passed the wagons bearing his household goods had been struck by the peculiar patterns of the furniture piled upon them. Abraham Bradbury had of course been present at the arrival, and the Friends upon the adjoining farms had kindly given their assistance, although it was a busy time of the year. While, therefore, no one suspected that the farmer could possibly accept a tenant of doubtful character, a general sentiment of curious expectancy went forth to meet the Donnelly family.

Even the venerable Simon Pennock, who lived in the opposite part of the township, was not wholly free from the prevalent feeling. "Abraham," he said, approaching his colleague, "I suppose thee has satisfied thyself that the strange Friend is of good repute."

Abraham was assuredly satisfied of one thing—that the three hundred silver dollars in his antiquated secretary at home were good and lawful coin. We will not say that this fact disposed him to charity, but will only testify that he answered thus:

"I don't think we have any right to question the certificate from Islip, Simon; and William Warner's word (whom thee knows by hearsay) is that of a good and honest man. Henry himself will stand ready to satisfy thee, if it is needful."

Here he turned to greet a tall, fresh-faced youth, who had quietly joined the group at the men's end of the meeting-house. He was nineteen, blue-eyed, and rosy, and a little embarrassed by the grave, scrutinizing, yet not unfriendly eyes fixed upon him.

"Simon, this is Henry's oldest son, De Courcy," said Abraham.

Simon took the youth's hand, saying, "Where did thee get thy outlandish name?"

The young man colored, hesitated, and then said, in a low, firm voice, "It was my grandfather's name."

One of the heavy carriages of the place and period, new and shiny, in spite of its sober colors, rolled into the yard. Abraham Bradbury and De Courcy Donnelly set forth side by side, to meet it.

Out of it descended a tall, broad-shouldered figure—a man in the prime of life, whose ripe, aggressive vitality gave his rigid Quaker garb the air of a military undress. His blue eyes seemed to laugh above the measured accents of his plain speech, and the close crop of his hair could not hide its tendency to curl. A bearing expressive of energy and the habit of command was not unusual in the sect, strengthening, but not changing, its habitual mask; yet in Henry Donnelly this bearing suggested—one could scarcely explain why—a different experience. Dress and speech, in him, expressed condescension rather than fraternal equality.

He carefully assisted his wife to alight, and De Courcy led the horse to the hitching-shed. Susan Donnelly was a still blooming woman of forty; her dress, of the plainest color, was yet of the richest texture; and her round, gentle, almost timid face looked forth like a girl's from the shadow of her scoop bonnet. While she was greeting Abraham Bradbury, the two daughters, Sylvia and Alice, who had been standing shyly by themselves on the edge of the group of women, came forward. The latter was a model of the demure Quaker maiden; but Abraham experienced as much surprise as was possible to his nature on observing Sylvia's costume. A light-blue dress, a dark-blue cloak, a hat with ribbons, and hair in curls—what Friend of good standing ever allowed his daughter thus to array herself in the fashion of the world?

Henry read the question in Abraham's face, and preferred not to answer it at that moment. Saying, "Thee must make me acquainted with the rest of our brethren," he led the way back to the men's end. When he had been presented to the older members, it was time for them to assemble in meeting.

The people were again quietly startled when Henry Donnelly deliberately mounted to the third and highest bench facing them, and sat down beside Abraham and Simon. These two retained, possibly with some little inward exertion, the composure of their faces, and the strange Friend became like unto them. His hands were clasped firmly in his lap; his full, decided lips were set together, and his eyes gazed into vacancy from under the broad brim. De Courcy had removed his hat on entering the house, but, meeting his father's eyes, replaced it suddenly, with a slight blush.

When Simon Pennock and Ruth Treadwell had spoken the thoughts which had come to them in the stillness, the strange Friend arose. Slowly, with frequent pauses, as if waiting for the guidance of the Spirit, and with that inward voice which falls so naturally into the measure of a chant, he urged upon his hearers the necessity of seeking the Light and walking therein. He did not always employ the customary phrases, but neither did he seem to speak the lower language of logic and reason; while his tones were so full and mellow that they gave, with every slowly modulated sentence, a fresh satisfaction to the ear. Even his broad a's and the strong roll of his r's verified the rumor of his foreign birth, did not detract from the authority of his words. The doubts which had preceded him somehow melted away in his presence, and he came forth, after the meeting had been dissolved by the shaking of hands, an accepted tenant of the high seat.

That evening, the family were alone in their new home. The plain rush-bottomed chairs and sober carpet, in contrast with the dark, solid mahogany table, and the silver branched candle-stick which stood upon it, hinted of former wealth and present loss; and something of the same contrast was reflected in the habits of the inmates. While the father, seated in a stately arm-chair, read aloud to his wife and children, Sylvia's eyes rested on a guitar-case in the corner, and her fingers absently adjusted themselves to the imaginary frets. De Courcy twisted his neck as if the straight collar of his coat were a bad fit, and Henry, the youngest boy, nodded drowsily from time to time.

"There, my lads and lasses!" said Henry Donnelly, as he closed the book, "now we're plain farmers at last,—and the plainer the better, since it must be. There's only one thing wanting—"

He paused; and Sylvia, looking up with a bright, arch determination, answered: "It's too late now, father,—they have seen me as one of the world's people, as I meant they should. When it is once settled as something not to be helped, it will give us no trouble."

"Faith, Sylvia!" exclaimed De Courcy, "I almost wish I had kept you company."

"Don't be impatient, my boy," said the mother, gently. "Think of the vexations we have had, and what a rest this life will be!"

"Think, also," the father added, "that I have the heaviest work to do, and that thou'lt reap the most of what may come of it. Don't carry the old life to a land where it's out of place. We must be what we seem to be, every one of us!"

"So we will!" said Sylvia, rising from her seat,—"I, as well as the rest. It was what I said in the beginning, you—no, THEE knows, father. Somebody must be interpreter when the time comes; somebody must remember while the rest of you are forgetting. Oh, I shall be talked about, and set upon, and called hard names; it won't be so easy. Stay where you are, De Courcy; that coat will fit sooner than you think."

Her brother lifted his shoulders and made a grimace. "I've an unlucky name, it seems," said he. "The old fellow—I mean Friend Simon—pronounced it outlandish. Couldn't I change it to Ezra or Adonijah?"

"Boy, boy—"

"Don't be alarmed, father. It will soon be as Sylvia says; thee's right, and mother is right. I'll let Sylvia keep my memory, and start fresh from here. We must into the field to-morrow, Hal and I. There's no need of a collar at the plough-tail."

They went to rest, and on the morrow not only the boys, but their father were in the field. Shrewd, quick, and strong, they made available what they knew of farming operations, and disguised much of their ignorance, while they learned. Henry Donnelly's first public appearance had made a strong public impression in his favor, which the voice of the older Friends soon stamped as a settled opinion. His sons did their share, by the amiable, yielding temper they exhibited, in accommodating themselves to the manners and ways of the people. The graces which came from a better education, possibly, more refined associations, gave them an attraction, which was none the less felt because it was not understood, to the simple-minded young men who worked with the hired hands in their fathers' fields. If the Donnelly family had not been accustomed, in former days, to sit at the same table with laborers in shirt-sleeves, and be addressed by the latter in fraternal phrase, no little awkwardnesses or hesitations betrayed the fact. They were anxious to make their naturalization complete, and it soon became so.

The "strange Friend" was now known in Londongrove by the familiar name of "Henry." He was a constant attendant at meeting, not only on First-days, but also on Fourth-days, and whenever he spoke his words were listened to with the reverence due to one who was truly led towards the Light. This respect kept at bay the curiosity that might still have lingered in some minds concerning his antecedent life. It was known that he answered Simon Pennock, who had ventured to approach him with a direct question, in these words:

"Thee knows, Friend Simon, that sometimes a seal is put upon our mouths for a wise purpose. I have learned not to value the outer life except in so far as it is made the manifestation of the inner life, and I only date my own from the time when I was brought to a knowledge of the truth. It is not pleasant to me to look upon what went before; but a season may come when it shall be lawful for me to declare all things—nay, when it shall be put upon me as a duty.

"Thee must suffer me to wait the call."

After this there was nothing more to be said. The family was on terms of quiet intimacy with the neighbors; and even Sylvia, in spite of her defiant eyes and worldly ways, became popular among the young men and maidens. She touched her beloved guitar with a skill which seemed marvellous to the latter; and when it was known that her refusal to enter the sect arose from her fondness for the prohibited instrument, she found many apologists among them. She was not set upon, and called hard names, as she had anticipated. It is true that her father, when appealed to by the elders, shook his head and said, "It is a cross to us!"—but he had been known to remain in the room while she sang "Full high in Kilbride," and the keen light which arose in his eyes was neither that of sorrow nor anger.

At the end of their first year of residence the farm presented evidences of much more orderly and intelligent management than at first, although the adjoining neighbors were of the opinion that the Donnellys had hardly made their living out of it. Friend Henry, nevertheless, was ready with the advance rent, and his bills were promptly paid. He was close at a bargain, which was considered rather a merit than otherwise,—and almost painfully exact in observing the strict letter of it, when made.

As time passed by, and the family became a permanent part and parcel of the remote community, wearing its peaceful color and breathing its untroubled atmosphere, nothing occurred to disturb the esteem and respect which its members enjoyed. From time to time the postmaster at the corner delivered to Henry Donnelly a letter from New York, always addressed in the same hand. The first which arrived had an "Esq." added to the name, but this "compliment" (as the Friends termed it) soon ceased. Perhaps the official may have vaguely wondered whether there was any connection between the occasional absence of Friend Henry—not at Yearly-Meeting time—and these letters. If he had been a visitor at the farm-house he might have noticed variations in the moods of its inmates, which must have arisen from some other cause than the price of stock or the condition of the crops. Outside of the family circle, however, they were serenely reticent.

In five or six years, when De Courcy had grown to be a hale, handsome man of twenty-four, and as capable of conducting a farm as any to the township born, certain aberrations from the strict line of discipline began to be rumored. He rode a gallant horse, dressed a little more elegantly than his membership prescribed, and his unusually high, straight collar took a knack of falling over. Moreover, he was frequently seen to ride up the Street Road, in the direction of Fagg's Manor, towards those valleys where the brick Presbyterian church displaces the whitewashed Quaker meeting-house.

Had Henry Donnelly not occupied so high a seat, and exercised such an acknowledged authority in the sect, he might sooner have received counsel, or proffers of sympathy, as the case might be; but he heard nothing until the rumors of De Courcy's excursions took a more definite form.

But one day, Abraham Bradbury, after discussing some Monthly-Meeting matters, suddenly asked: "Is this true that I hear, Henry,—that thy son De Courcy keeps company with one of the Alison girls?"

"Who says that?" Henry asked, in a sharp voice.

"Why, it's the common talk! Surely, thee's heard of it before?"

"No!"

Henry set his lips together in a manner which Abraham understood. Considering that he had fully performed his duty, he said no more.

That evening, Sylvia, who had been gently thrumming to herself at the window, began singing "Bonnie Peggie Alison." Her father looked at De Courcy, who caught his glance, then lowered his eyes, and turned to leave the room.

"Stop, De Courcy," said the former; "I've heard a piece of news about thee to-day, which I want thee to make clear."

"Shall I go, father?" asked Sylvia.

"No; thee may stay to give De Courcy his memory. I think he is beginning to need it. I've learned which way he rides on Seventh-day evenings."

"Father, I am old enough to choose my way," said De Courcy.

"But no such ways NOW, boy! Has thee clean forgotten? This was among the things upon which we agreed, and you all promised to keep watch and guard over yourselves. I had my misgivings then, but for five years I've trusted you, and now, when the time of probation is so nearly over—"

He hesitated, and De Courcy, plucking up courage, spoke again. With a strong effort the young man threw off the yoke of a self-taught restraint, and asserted his true nature. "Has O'Neil written?" he asked.

"Not yet."

"Then, father," he continued, "I prefer the certainty of my present life to the uncertainty of the old. I will not dissolve my connection with the Friends by a shock which might give thee trouble; but I will slowly work away from them. Notice will be taken of my ways; there will be family visitations, warnings, and the usual routine of discipline, so that when I marry Margaret Alison, nobody will be surprised at my being read out of meeting. I shall soon be twenty-five, father, and this thing has gone on about as long as I can bear it. I must decide to be either a man or a milksop."

The color rose to Henry Donnelly's cheeks, and his eyes flashed, but he showed no signs of anger. He moved to De Courcy's side and laid his hand upon his shoulder.

"Patience, my boy!" he said. "It's the old blood, and I might have known it would proclaim itself. Suppose I were to shut my eyes to thy ridings, and thy merry-makings, and thy worldly company. So far I might go; but the girl is no mate for thee. If O'Neil is alive, we are sure to hear from him soon; and in three years, at the utmost, if the Lord favors us, the end will come. How far has it gone with thy courting? Surely, surely, not too far to withdraw, at least under the plea of my prohibition?"

De Courcy blushed, but firmly met his father's eyes. "I have spoken to her," he replied, "and it is not the custom of our family to break plighted faith."

"Thou art our cross, not Sylvia. Go thy ways now. I will endeavor to seek for guidance."

"Sylvia," said the father, when De Courcy had left the room, "what is to be the end of this?"

"Unless we hear from O'Neil, father, I am afraid it cannot be prevented. De Courcy has been changing for a year past; I am only surprised that you did not sooner notice it. What I said in jest has become serious truth; he has already half forgotten. We might have expected, in the beginning, that one of two things would happen: either he would become a plodding Quaker farmer or take to his present courses. Which would be worse, when this life is over,—if that time ever comes?"

Sylvia sighed, and there was a weariness in her voice which did not escape her father's ear. He walked up and down the room with a troubled air. She sat down, took the guitar upon her lap, and began to sing the verse, commencing, "Erin, my country, though sad and forsaken," when—perhaps opportunely—Susan Donnelly entered the room.

"Eh, lass!" said Henry, slipping his arm around his wife's waist, "art thou tired yet? Have I been trying thy patience, as I have that of the children? Have there been longings kept from me, little rebellions crushed, battles fought that I supposed were over?"

"Not by me, Henry," was her cheerful answer. "I have never have been happier than in these quiet ways with thee. I've been thinking, what if something has happened, and the letters cease to come? And it has seemed to me—now that the boys are as good farmers as any, and Alice is such a tidy housekeeper—that we could manage very well without help. Only for thy sake, Henry: I fear it would be a terrible disappointment to thee. Or is thee as accustomed to the high seat as I to my place on the women's side?"

"No!" he answered emphatically. "The talk with De Courcy has set my quiet Quaker blood in motion. The boy is more than half right; I am sure Sylvia thinks so too. What could I expect? He has no birthright, and didn't begin his task, as I did, after the bravery of youth was over. It took six generations to establish the serenity and content of our brethren here, and the dress we wear don't give us the nature. De Courcy is tired of the masquerade, and Sylvia is tired of seeing it. Thou, my little Susan, who wert so timid at first, puttest us all to shame now!"

"I think I was meant for it,—Alice, and Henry, and I," said she.

No outward change in Henry Donnelly's demeanor betrayed this or any other disturbance at home. There were repeated consultations between the father and son, but they led to no satisfactory conclusion. De Courcy was sincerely attached to the pretty Presbyterian maiden, and found livelier society in her brothers and cousins than among the grave, awkward Quaker youths of Londongrove.

With the occasional freedom from restraint there awoke in him a desire for independence—a thirst for the suppressed license of youth. His new acquaintances were accustomed to a rigid domestic regime, but of a different character, and they met on a common ground of rebellion. Their aberrations, it is true, were not of a very formidable character, and need not have been guarded but for the severe conventionalities of both sects. An occasional fox-chase, horse-race, or a "stag party" at some outlying tavern, formed the sum of their dissipation; they sang, danced reels, and sometimes ran into little excesses through the stimulating sense of the trespass they were committing.

By and by reports of certain of these performances were brought to the notice of the Londongrove Friends, and, with the consent of Henry Donnelly himself, De Courcy received a visit of warning and remonstrance. He had foreseen the probability of such a visit and was prepared. He denied none of the charges brought against him, and accepted the grave counsel offered, simply stating that his nature was not yet purified and chastened; he was aware he was not walking in the Light; he believed it to be a troubled season through which he must needs pass. His frankness, as he was shrewd enough to guess, was a source of perplexity to the elders; it prevented them from excommunicating him without further probation, while it left him free to indulge in further recreations.

Some months passed away, and the absence from which Henry Donnelly always returned with a good supply of ready money did not take place. The knowledge of farming which his sons had acquired now came into play. It was necessary to exercise both skill and thrift in order to keep up the liberal footing upon which the family had lived; for each member of it was too proud to allow the community to suspect the change in their circumstances. De Courcy, retained more than ever at home, and bound to steady labor, was man enough to subdue his impatient spirit for the time; but he secretly determined that with the first change for the better he would follow the fate he had chosen for himself.

Late in the fall came the opportunity for which he had longed. One evening he brought home a letter, in the well-known handwriting. His father opened and read it in silence.

"Well, father?" he said.

"A former letter was lost, it seems. This should have come in the spring; it is only the missing sum."

"Does O'Neil fix any time?"

"No; but he hopes to make a better report next year."

"Then, father," said De Courcy, "it is useless for me to wait longer; I am satisfied as it is. I should not have given up Margaret in any case; but now, since thee can live with Henry's help, I shall claim her."

"MUST it be, De Courcy?"

"It must."

But it was not to be. A day or two afterwards the young man, on his mettled horse, set off up the Street Road, feeling at last that the fortune and the freedom of his life were approaching. He had become, in habits and in feelings, one of the people, and the relinquishment of the hope in which his father still indulged brought him a firmer courage, a more settled content. His sweetheart's family was in good circumstances; but, had she been poor, he felt confident of his power to make and secure for her a farmer's home. To the past—whatever it might have been—he said farewell, and went carolling some cheerful ditty, to look upon the face of his future.

That night a country wagon slowly drove up to Henry Donnelly's door. The three men who accompanied it hesitated before they knocked, and, when the door was opened, looked at each other with pale, sad faces, before either spoke. No cries followed the few words that were said, but silently, swiftly, a room was made ready, while the men lifted from the straw and carried up stairs an unconscious figure, the arms of which hung down with a horrible significance as they moved. He was not dead, for the heart beat feebly and slowly; but all efforts to restore his consciousness were in vain. There was concussion of the brain the physician said. He had been thrown from his horse, probably alighting upon his head, as there were neither fractures nor external wounds. All that night and next day the tenderest, the most unwearied care was exerted to call back the flickering gleam of life. The shock had been too great; his deadly torpor deepened into death.

In their time of trial and sorrow the family received the fullest sympathy, the kindliest help, from the whole neighborhood. They had never before so fully appreciated the fraternal character of the society whereof they were members. The plain, plodding people living on the adjoining farms became virtually their relatives and fellow-mourners. All the external offices demanded by the sad occasion were performed for them, and other eyes than their own shed tears of honest grief over De Courcy's coffin. All came to the funeral, and even Simon Pennock, in the plain yet touching words which he spoke beside the grave, forgot the young man's wandering from the Light, in the recollection of his frank, generous, truthful nature.

If the Donnellys had sometimes found the practical equality of life in Londongrove a little repellent they were now gratefully moved by the delicate and refined ways in which the sympathy of the people sought to express itself. The better qualities of human nature always develop a temporary good-breeding. Wherever any of the family went, they saw the reflection of their own sorrow; and a new spirit informed to their eyes the quiet pastoral landscapes.

In their life at home there was little change. Abraham Bradbury had insisted on sending his favorite grandson, Joel, a youth of twenty-two, to take De Courcy's place for a few months. He was a shy quiet creature, with large brown eyes like a fawn's, and young Henry Donnelly and he became friends at once. It was believed that he would inherit the farm at his grandfather's death; but he was as subservient to Friend Donnelly's wishes in regard to the farming operations as if the latter held the fee of the property. His coming did not fill the terrible gap which De Courcy's death had made, but seemed to make it less constantly and painfully evident.

Susan Donnelly soon remarked a change, which she could neither clearly define nor explain to herself, both in her husband and in their daughter Sylvia. The former, although in public he preserved the same grave, stately face,—its lines, perhaps, a little more deeply marked,—seemed to be devoured by an internal unrest. His dreams were of the old times: words and names long unused came from his lips as he slept by her side. Although he bore his grief with more strength than she had hoped, he grew nervous and excitable,—sometimes unreasonably petulant, sometimes gay to a pitch which impressed her with pain. When the spring came around, and the mysterious correspondence again failed, as in the previous year, his uneasiness increased. He took his place on the high seat on First-days, as usual, but spoke no more.

Sylvia, on the other hand, seemed to have wholly lost her proud, impatient character. She went to meeting much more frequently than formerly, busied herself more actively about household matters, and ceased to speak of the uncertain contingency which had been so constantly present in her thoughts. In fact, she and her father had changed places. She was now the one who preached patience, who held before them all the bright side of their lot, who brought Margaret Alison to the house and justified her dead brother's heart to his father's, and who repeated to the latter, in his restless moods, "De Courcy foresaw the truth, and we must all in the end decide as he did."

"Can THEE do it, Sylvia?" her father would ask.

"I believe I have done it already," she said. "If it seems difficult, pray consider how much later I begin my work. I have had all your memories in charge, and now I must not only forget for myself, but for you as well."

Indeed, as the spring and summer months came and went, Sylvia evidently grew stronger in her determination. The fret of her idle force was allayed, and her content increased as she saw and performed the possible duties of her life. Perhaps her father might have caught something of her spirit, but for his anxiety in regard to the suspended correspondence. He wearied himself in guesses, which all ended in the simple fact that, to escape embarrassment, the rent must again be saved from the earnings of the farm.

The harvests that year were bountiful; wheat, barley, and oats stood thick and heavy in the fields. No one showed more careful thrift or more cheerful industry than young Joel Bradbury, and the family felt that much of the fortune of their harvest was owing to him.

On the first day after the crops had been securely housed, all went to meeting, except Sylvia. In the walled graveyard the sod was already green over De Courcy's unmarked mound, but Alice had planted a little rose-tree at the head, and she and her mother always visited the spot before taking their seats on the women's side. The meeting-house was very full that day, as the busy season of the summer was over, and the horses of those who lived at a distance had no longer such need of rest.

It was a sultry forenoon, and the windows and doors of the building were open. The humming of insects was heard in the silence, and broken lights and shadows of the poplar-leaves were sprinkled upon the steps and sills. Outside there were glimpses of quiet groves and orchards, and blue fragments of sky,—no more semblance of life in the external landscape than there was in the silent meeting within. Some quarter of an hour before the shaking of hands took place, the hoofs of a horse were heard in the meeting-house yard—the noise of a smart trot on the turf, suddenly arrested.

The boys pricked up their ears at this unusual sound, and stole glances at each other when they imagined themselves unseen by the awful faces in the gallery. Presently those nearest the door saw a broader shadow fall over those flickering upon the stone. A red face appeared for a moment, and was then drawn back out of sight. The shadow advanced and receded, in a state of peculiar restlessness. Sometimes the end of a riding-whip was visible, sometimes the corner of a coarse gray coat. The boys who noticed these apparitions were burning with impatience, but they dared not leave their seats until Abraham Bradbury had reached his hand to Henry Donnelly.

Then they rushed out. The mysterious personage was still beside the door, leaning against the wall. He was a short, thick-set man of fifty, with red hair, round gray eyes, a broad pug nose, and projecting mouth. He wore a heavy gray coat, despite the heat, and a waistcoat with many brass buttons; also corduroy breeches and riding boots. When they appeared, he started forward with open mouth and eyes, and stared wildly in their faces. They gathered around the poplar-trunks, and waited with some uneasiness to see what would follow.

Slowly and gravely, with the half-broken ban of silence still hanging over them, the people issued from the house. The strange man stood, leaning forward, and seemed to devour each, in turn, with his eager eyes. After the young men came the fathers of families, and lastly the old men from the gallery seats. Last of these came Henry Donnelly. In the meantime, all had seen and wondered at the waiting figure; its attitude was too intense and self-forgetting to be misinterpreted. The greetings and remarks were suspended until the people had seen for whom the man waited, and why.

Henry Donnelly had no sooner set his foot upon the door-step than, with something between a shout and a howl, the stranger darted forward, seized his hand, and fell upon one knee, crying: "O my lord! my lord! Glory be to God that I've found ye at last!"

If these words burst like a bomb on the ears of the people, what was their consternation when Henry Donnelly exclaimed, "The Divel! Jack O'Neil, can that be you?"

"It's me, meself, my lord! When we heard the letters went wrong last year, I said 'I'll trust no such good news to their blasted mail-posts: I'll go meself and carry it to his lordship,—if it is t'other side o' the say. Him and my lady and all the children went, and sure I can go too. And as I was the one that went with you from Dunleigh Castle, I'll go back with you to that same, for it stands awaitin', and blessed be the day that sees you back in your ould place!"

"All clear, Jack? All mine again?"

"You may believe it, my lord! And money in the chest beside. But where's my lady, bless her sweet face! Among yon women, belike, and you'll help me to find her, for it's herself must have the news next, and then the young master—"

With that word Henry Donnelly awoke to a sense of time and place. He found himself within a ring of staring, wondering, scandalized eyes. He met them boldly, with a proud, though rather grim smile, took hold of O'Neil's arm and led him towards the women's end of the house, where the sight of Susan in her scoop bonnet so moved the servant's heart that he melted into tears. Both husband and wife were eager to get home and hear O'Neil's news in private; so they set out at once in their plain carriage, followed by the latter on horseback. As for the Friends, they went home in a state of bewilderment.

Alice Donnelly, with her brother Henry and Joel Bradbury, returned on foot. The two former remembered O'Neil, and, although they had not witnessed his first interview with their father, they knew enough of the family history to surmise his errand. Joel was silent and troubled.

"Alice, I hope it doesn't mean that we are going back, don't you?" said Henry.

"Yes," she answered, and said no more.

They took a foot-path across the fields, and reached the farm-house at the same time with the first party. As they opened the door Sylvia descended the staircase dressed in a rich shimmering brocade, with a necklace of amethysts around her throat. To their eyes, so long accustomed to the absence of positive color, she was completely dazzling. There was a new color on her cheeks, and her eyes seemed larger and brighter. She made a stately courtesy, and held open the parlor door.

"Welcome, Lord Henry Dunleigh, of Dunleigh Castle!" she cried; "welcome, Lady Dunleigh!"

Her father kissed her on the forehead. "Now give us back our memories, Sylvia!" he said, exultingly.

Susan Donnelly sank into a chair, overcome by the mixed emotions of the moment.

"Come in, my faithful Jack! Unpack thy portmanteau of news, for I see thou art bursting to show it; let us have every thing from the beginning. Wife, it's a little too much for thee, coming so unexpectedly. Set out the wine, Alice!"

The decanter was placed upon the table. O'Neil filled a tumbler to the brim, lifted it high, made two or three hoarse efforts to speak, and then walked away to the window, where he drank in silence. This little incident touched the family more than the announcement of their good fortune. Henry Donnelly's feverish exultation subsided: he sat down with a grave, thoughtful face, while his wife wept quietly beside him. Sylvia stood waiting with an abstracted air; Alice removed her mother's bonnet and shawl; and Henry and Joel, seated together at the farther end of the room, looked on in silent anticipation.

O'Neil's story was long, and frequently interrupted. He had been Lord Dunleigh's steward in better days, as his father had been to the old lord, and was bound to the family by the closest ties of interest and affection. When the estates became so encumbered that either an immediate change or a catastrophe was inevitable, he had been taken into his master's confidence concerning the plan which had first been proposed in jest, and afterwards adopted in earnest.

The family must leave Dunleigh Castle for a period of probably eight or ten years, and seek some part of the world where their expenses could be reduced to the lowest possible figure. In Germany or Italy there would be the annoyance of a foreign race and language, of meeting of tourists belonging to the circle in which they had moved, a dangerous idleness for their sons, and embarrassing restrictions for their daughters. On the other hand, the suggestion to emigrate to America and become Quakers during their exile offered more advantages the more they considered it. It was original in character; it offered them economy, seclusion, entire liberty of action inside the limits of the sect, the best moral atmosphere for their children, and an occupation which would not deteriorate what was best in their blood and breeding.

How Lord Dunleigh obtained admission into the sect as plain Henry Donnelly is a matter of conjecture with the Londongrove Friends. The deception which had been practised upon them—although it was perhaps less complete than they imagined—left a soreness of feeling behind it. The matter was hushed up after the departure of the family, and one might now live for years in the neighborhood without hearing the story. How the shrewd plan was carried out by Lord Dunleigh and his family, we have already learned. O'Neil, left on the estate, in the north of Ireland, did his part with equal fidelity. He not only filled up the gaps made by his master's early profuseness, but found means to move the sympathies of a cousin of the latter—a rich, eccentric old bachelor, who had long been estranged by a family quarrel. To this cousin he finally confided the character of the exile, and at a lucky time; for the cousin's will was altered in Lord Dunleigh's favor, and he died before his mood of reconciliation passed away. Now, the estate was not only unencumbered, but there was a handsome surplus in the hands of the Dublin bankers. The family might return whenever they chose, and there would be a festival to welcome them, O'Neil said, such as Dunleigh Castle had never known since its foundations were laid.

"Let us go at once!" said Sylvia, when he had concluded his tale. "No more masquerading,—I never knew until to-day how much I have hated it! I will not say that your plan was not a sensible one, father; but I wish it might have been carried out with more honor to ourselves. Since De Courcy's death I have begun to appreciate our neighbors: I was resigned to become one of these people had our luck gone the other way. Will they give us any credit for goodness and truth, I wonder? Yes, in mother's case, and Alice's; and I believe both of them would give up Dunleigh Castle for this little farm."

"Then," her father exclaimed, "it IS time that we should return, and without delay. But thee wrongs us somewhat, Sylvia: it has not all been masquerading. We have become the servants, rather than the masters, of our own parts, and shall live a painful and divided life until we get back in our old place. I fear me it will always be divided for thee, wife, and Alice and Henry. If I am subdued by the element which I only meant to assume, how much more deeply must it have wrought in your natures! Yes, Sylvia is right, we must get away at once. To-morrow we must leave Londongrove forever!"

He had scarcely spoken, when a new surprise fell upon the family. Joel Bradbury arose and walked forward, as if thrust by an emotion so powerful that it transformed his whole being. He seemed to forget every thing but Alice Donnelly's presence. His soft brown eyes were fixed on her face with an expression of unutterable tenderness and longing. He caught her by the hands. "Alice, O, Alice!" burst from his lips; "you are not going to leave me?"

The flush in the girl's sweet face faded into a deadly paleness. A moan came from her lips; her head dropped, and she would have fallen, swooning, from the chair had not Joel knelt at her feet and caught her upon his breast.

For a moment there was silence in the room.

Presently, Sylvia, all her haughtiness gone, knelt beside the young man, and took her sister from his arms. "Joel, my poor, dear friend," she said, "I am sorry that the last, worst mischief we have done must fall upon you."

Joel covered his face with his hands, and convulsively uttered the words, "MUST she go?"

Then Henry Donnelly—or, rather, Lord Dunleigh, as we must now call him—took the young man's hand. He was profoundly moved; his strong voice trembled, and his words came slowly. "I will not appeal to thy heart, Joel," he said, "for it would not hear me now.

"But thou hast heard all our story, and knowest that we must leave these parts, never to return. We belong to another station and another mode of life than yours, and it must come to us as a good fortune that our time of probation is at an end. Bethink thee, could we leave our darling Alice behind us, parted as if by the grave? Nay, could we rob her of the life to which she is born—of her share in our lives? On the other hand, could we take thee with us into relations where thee would always be a stranger, and in which a nature like thine has no place? This is a case where duty speaks clearly, though so hard, so very hard, to follow."

He spoke tenderly, but inflexibly, and Joel felt that his fate was pronounced. When Alice had somewhat revived, and was taken to another room, he stumbled blindly out of the house, made his way to the barn, and there flung himself upon the harvest-sheaves which, three days before, he had bound with such a timid, delicious hope working in his arm.

The day which brought such great fortune had thus a sad and troubled termination. It was proposed that the family should start for Philadelphia on the morrow, leaving O'Neil to pack up and remove such furniture as they wished to retain; but Susan, Lady Dunleigh, could not forsake the neighborhood without a parting visit to the good friends who had mourned with her over her firstborn; and Sylvia was with her in this wish. So two more days elapsed, and then the Dunleighs passed down the Street Road, and the plain farm-house was gone from their eyes forever. Two grieved over the loss of their happy home; one was almost broken-hearted; and the remaining two felt that the trouble of the present clouded all their happiness in the return to rank and fortune.

They went, and they never came again. An account of the great festival at Dunleigh Castle reached Londongrove two years later, through an Irish laborer, who brought to Joel Bradbury a letter of recommendation signed "Dunleigh." Joel kept the man upon his farm, and the two preserved the memory of the family long after the neighborhood had ceased to speak of it. Joel never married; he still lives in the house where the great sorrow of his life befell.

His head is gray, and his face deeply wrinkled; but when he lifts the shy lids of his soft brown eyes, I fancy I can see in their tremulous depths the lingering memory of his love for Alice Dunleigh.

# JACOB FLINT'S JOURNEY

If there ever was a man crushed out of all courage, all self-reliance, all comfort in life, it was Jacob Flint. Why this should have been, neither he nor any one else could have explained; but so it was. On the day that he first went to school, his shy, frightened face marked him as fair game for the rougher and stronger boys, and they subjected him to all those exquisite refinements of torture which boys seem to get by the direct inspiration of the Devil. There was no form of their bullying meanness or the cowardice of their brutal strength which he did not experience. He was born under a fading or falling star,—the inheritor of some anxious or unhappy mood of his parents, which gave its fast color to the threads out of which his innocent being was woven.

Even the good people of the neighborhood, never accustomed to look below the externals of appearance and manner, saw in his shrinking face and awkward motions only the signs of a cringing, abject soul.

"You'll be no more of a man than Jake Flint!" was the reproach which many a farmer addressed to his dilatory boy; and thus the parents, one and all, came to repeat the sins of the children.

If, therefore, at school and "before folks," Jacob's position was always uncomfortable and depressing, it was little more cheering at home. His parents, as all the neighbors believed, had been unhappily married, and, though the mother died in his early childhood, his father remained a moody, unsocial man, who rarely left his farm except on the 1st of April every year, when he went to the county town for the purpose of paying the interest upon a mortgage. The farm lay in a hollow between two hills, separated from the road by a thick wood, and the chimneys of the lonely old house looked in vain for a neighbor-smoke when they began to grow warm of a morning.

Beyond the barn and under the northern hill there was a log tenant-house, in which dwelt a negro couple, who, in the course of years had become fixtures on the place and almost partners in it. Harry, the man, was the medium by which Samuel Flint kept up his necessary intercourse with the world beyond the valley; he took the horses to the blacksmith, the grain to the mill, the turkeys to market, and through his hands passed all the incomings and outgoings of the farm, except the annual interest on the mortgage. Sally, his wife, took care of the household, which, indeed, was a light and comfortable task, since the table was well supplied for her own sake, and there was no sharp eye to criticise her sweeping, dusting, and bed-making. The place had a forlorn, tumble-down aspect, quite in keeping with its lonely situation; but perhaps this very circumstance flattered the mood of its silent, melancholy owner and his unhappy son.

In all the neighborhood there was but one person with whom Jacob felt completely at ease—but one who never joined in the general habit of making his name the butt of ridicule or contempt. This was Mrs. Ann Pardon, the hearty, active wife of Farmer Robert Pardon, who lived nearly a mile farther down the brook. Jacob had won her good-will by some neighborly services, something so trifling, indeed, that the thought of a favor conferred never entered his mind. Ann Pardon saw that it did not; she detected a streak of most unconscious goodness under his uncouth, embarrassed ways, and she determined to cultivate it. No little tact was required, however, to coax the wild, forlorn creature into so much confidence as she desired to establish; but tact is a native quality of the heart no less than a social acquirement, and so she did the very thing necessary without thinking much about it.

Robert Pardon discovered by and by that Jacob was a steady, faithful hand in the harvest-field at husking-time, or whenever any extra labor was required, and Jacob's father made no objection to his earning a penny in this way; and so he fell into the habit of spending his Saturday evenings at the Pardon farm-house, at first to talk over matters of work, and finally because it had become a welcome relief from his dreary life at home.

Now it happened that on a Saturday in the beginning of haying-time, the village tailor sent home by Harry a new suit of light summer clothes, for which Jacob had been measured a month before. After supper he tried them on, the day's work being over, and Sally's admiration was so loud and emphatic that he felt himself growing red even to the small of his back.

"Now, don't go for to take 'em off, Mr. Jake," said she. "I spec' you're gwine down to Pardon's, and so you jist keep 'em on to show 'em all how nice you KIN look."

The same thought had already entered Jacob's mind. Poor fellow! It was the highest form of pleasure of which he had ever allowed himself to conceive. If he had been called upon to pass through the village on first assuming the new clothes, every stitch would have pricked him as if the needle remained in it; but a quiet walk down the brookside, by the pleasant path through the thickets and over the fragrant meadows, with a consciousness of his own neatness and freshness at every step, and with kind Ann Pardon's commendation at the close, and the flattering curiosity of the children,—the only ones who never made fun of him,—all that was a delightful prospect. He could never, NEVER forget himself, as he had seen other young fellows do; but to remember himself agreeably was certainly the next best thing.

Jacob was already a well-grown man of twenty-three, and would have made a good enough appearance but for the stoop in his shoulders, and the drooping, uneasy way in which he carried his head. Many a time when he was alone in the fields or woods he had straightened himself, and looked courageously at the buts of the oak-trees or in the very eyes of the indifferent oxen; but, when a human face drew near, some spring in his neck seemed to snap, some buckle around his shoulders to be drawn three holes tighter, and he found himself in the old posture. The ever-present thought of this weakness was the only drop of bitterness in his cup, as he followed the lonely path through the thickets.

Some spirit in the sweet, delicious freshness of the air, some voice in the mellow babble of the stream, leaping in and out of sight between the alders, some smile of light, lingering on the rising corn-fields beyond the meadow and the melting purple of a distant hill, reached to the seclusion of his heart. He was soothed and cheered; his head lifted itself in the presentiment of a future less lonely than the past, and the everlasting trouble vanished from his eyes.

Suddenly, at a turn of the path, two mowers from the meadow, with their scythes upon their shoulders, came upon him. He had not heard their feet on the deep turf. His chest relaxed, and his head began to sink; then, with the most desperate effort in his life, he lifted it again, and, darting a rapid side glance at the men, hastened by. They could not understand the mixed defiance and supplication of his face; to them he only looked "queer."

"Been committin' a murder, have you?" asked one of them, grinning.

"Startin' off on his journey, I guess," said the other.

The next instant they were gone, and Jacob, with set teeth and clinched hands, smothered something that would have been a howl if he had given it voice. Sharp lines of pain were marked on his face, and, for the first time, the idea of resistance took fierce and bitter possession of his heart. But the mood was too unusual to last; presently he shook his head, and walked on towards Pardon's farm-house.

Ann wore a smart gingham dress, and her first exclamation was: "Why, Jake! how nice you look. And so you know all about it, too?"

"About what?"

"I see you don't," said she. "I was too fast; but it makes no difference. I know you are willing to lend me a helping hand."

"Oh, to be sure," Jacob answered.

"And not mind a little company?"

Jacob's face suddenly clouded; but he said, though with an effort: "No—not much—if I can be of any help."

"It's rather a joke, after all," Ann Pardon continued, speaking rapidly; "they meant a surprise, a few of the young people; but sister Becky found a way to send me word, or I might have been caught like Meribah Johnson last week, in the middle of my work; eight or ten, she said, but more may drop in: and it's moonlight and warm, so they'll be mostly under the trees; and Robert won't be home till late, and I DO want help in carrying chairs, and getting up some ice, and handing around; and, though I know you don't care for merry makings, you CAN help me out, you see—"

Here she paused. Jacob looked perplexed, but said nothing.

"Becky will help what she can, and while I'm in the kitchen she'll have an eye to things outside," she said.

Jacob's head was down again, and, moreover, turned on one side, but his ear betrayed the mounting blood. Finally he answered, in a quick, husky voice: "Well, I'll do what I can. What's first?"

Thereupon he began to carry some benches from the veranda to a grassy bank beside the sycamore-tree. Ann Pardon wisely said no more of the coming surprise-party, but kept him so employed that, as the visitors arrived by twos and threes, the merriment was in full play almost before he was aware of it. Moreover, the night was a protecting presence: the moonlight poured splendidly upon the open turf beyond the sycamore, but every lilac-bush or trellis of woodbine made a nook of shade, wherein he could pause a moment and take courage for his duties. Becky Morton, Ann Pardon's youngest sister, frightened him a little every time she came to consult about the arrangement of seats or the distribution of refreshments; but it was a delightful, fascinating fear, such as he had never felt before in his life. He knew Becky, but he had never seen her in white and pink, with floating tresses, until now. In fact, he had hardly looked at her fairly, but now, as she glided into the moonlight and he paused in the shadow, his eyes took note of her exceeding beauty. Some sweet, confusing influence, he knew not what, passed into his blood.

The young men had brought a fiddler from the village, and it was not long before most of the company were treading the measures of reels or cotillons on the grass. How merry and happy they all were! How freely and unembarrassedly they moved and talked! By and by all became involved in the dance, and Jacob, left alone and unnoticed, drew nearer and nearer to the gay and beautiful life from which he was expelled.

With a long-drawn scream of the fiddle the dance came to an end, and the dancers, laughing, chattering, panting, and fanning themselves, broke into groups and scattered over the enclosure before the house. Jacob was surrounded before he could escape. Becky, with two lively girls in her wake, came up to him and said: "Oh Mr. Flint, why don't you dance?"

If he had stopped to consider, he would no doubt have replied very differently. But a hundred questions, stirred by what he had seen, were clamoring for light, and they threw the desperate impulse to his lips.

"If I COULD dance, would you dance with me?"

The two lively girls heard the words, and looked at Becky with roguish faces.

"Oh yes, take him for your next partner!" cried one.

"I will," said Becky, "after he comes back from his journey."

Then all three laughed. Jacob leaned against the tree, his eyes fixed on the ground.

"Is it a bargain?" asked one of the girls.

"No," said he, and walked rapidly away.

He went to the house, and, finding that Robert had arrived, took his hat, and left by the rear door. There was a grassy alley between the orchard and garden, from which it was divided by a high hawthorn hedge. He had scarcely taken three paces on his way to the meadow, when the sound of the voice he had last heard, on the other side of the hedge, arrested his feet.

"Becky, I think you rather hurt Jake Flint," said the girl.

"Hardly," answered Becky; "he's used to that."

"Not if he likes you; and you might go further and fare worse."

"Well, I MUST say!" Becky exclaimed, with a laugh; "you'd like to see me stuck in that hollow, out of your way!"

"It's a good farm, I've heard," said the other.

"Yes, and covered with as much as it'll bear!"

Here the girls were called away to the dance. Jacob slowly walked up the dewy meadow, the sounds of fiddling, singing, and laughter growing fainter behind him.

"My journey!" he repeated to himself,—"my journey! why shouldn't I start on it now? Start off, and never come back?"

It was a very little thing, after all, which annoyed him, but the mention of it always touched a sore nerve of his nature. A dozen years before, when a boy at school, he had made a temporary friendship with another boy of his age, and had one day said to the latter, in the warmth of his first generous confidence: "When I am a little older, I shall make a great journey, and come back rich, and buy Whitney's place!"

Now, Whitney's place, with its stately old brick mansion, its avenue of silver firs, and its two hundred acres of clean, warm-lying land, was the finest, the most aristocratic property in all the neighborhood, and the boy-friend could not resist the temptation of repeating Jacob's grand design, for the endless amusement of the school. The betrayal hurt Jacob more keenly than the ridicule. It left a wound that never ceased to rankle; yet, with the inconceivable perversity of unthinking natures, precisely this joke (as the people supposed it to be) had been perpetuated, until "Jake Flint's Journey" was a synonyme for any absurd or extravagant expectation. Perhaps no one imagined how much pain he was keeping alive; for almost any other man than Jacob would have joined in the laugh against himself and thus good-naturedly buried the joke in time. "He's used to that," the people said, like Becky Morton, and they really supposed there was nothing unkind in the remark!

After Jacob had passed the thickets and entered the lonely hollow in which his father's house lay, his pace became slower and slower.

He looked at the shabby old building, just touched by the moonlight behind the swaying shadows of the weeping-willow, stopped, looked again, and finally seated himself on a stump beside the path.

"If I knew what to do!" he said to himself, rocking backwards and forwards, with his hands clasped over his knees,—"if I knew what to do!"

The spiritual tension of the evening reached its climax: he could bear no more. With a strong bodily shudder his tears burst forth, and the passion of his weeping filled him from head to foot. How long he wept he knew not; it seemed as if the hot fountains would never run dry. Suddenly and startlingly a hand fell upon his shoulder.

"Boy, what does this mean?"

It was his father who stood before him.

Jacob looked up like some shy animal brought to bay, his eyes full of a feeling mixed of fierceness and terror; but he said nothing.

His father seated himself on one of the roots of the old stump, laid one hand upon Jacob's knee, and said with an unusual gentleness of manner, "I'd like to know what it is that troubles you so much."

After a pause, Jacob suddenly burst forth with: "Is there any reason why I should tell you? Do you care any more for me than the rest of 'em?"

"I didn't know as you wanted me to care for you particularly," said the father, almost deprecatingly. "I always thought you had friends of your own age."

"Friends? Devils!" exclaimed Jacob. "Oh, what have I done—what is there so dreadful about me that I should always be laughed at, and despised, and trampled upon? You are a great deal older than I am, father: what do you see in me? Tell me what it is, and how to get over it!"

The eyes of the two men met. Jacob saw his father's face grow pale in the moonlight, while he pressed his hand involuntarily upon his heart, as if struggling with some physical pain. At last he spoke, but his words were strange and incoherent.

"I couldn't sleep," he said; "I got up again and came out o' doors. The white ox had broken down the fence at the corner, and would soon have been in the cornfield. I thought it was that, maybe, but still your—your mother would come into my head. I was coming down the edge of the wood when I saw you, and I don't know why it was that you seemed so different, all at once—"

Here he paused, and was silent for a minute. Then he said, in a grave, commanding tone: "Just let me know the whole story. I have that much right yet."

Jacob related the history of the evening, somewhat awkwardly and confusedly, it is true; but his father's brief, pointed questions kept him to the narrative, and forced him to explain the full significance of the expressions he repeated. At the mention of "Whitney's place," a singular expression of malice touched the old man's face.

"Do you love Becky Morton?" he asked bluntly, when all had been told.

"I don't know," Jacob stammered; "I think not; because when I seem to like her most, I feel afraid of her."

"It's lucky that you're not sure of it!" exclaimed the old man with energy; "because you should never have her."

"No," said Jacob, with a mournful acquiescence, "I can never have her, or any other one."

"But you shall—and will I when I help you. It's true I've not seemed to care much about you, and I suppose you're free to think as you like; but this I say: I'll not stand by and see you spit upon! 'Covered with as much as it'll bear!' THAT'S a piece o' luck anyhow. If we're poor, your wife must take your poverty with you, or she don't come into MY doors. But first of all you must make your journey!"

"My journey!" repeated Jacob.

"Weren't you thinking of it this night, before you took your seat on that stump? A little more, and you'd have gone clean off, I reckon."

Jacob was silent, and hung his head.

"Never mind! I've no right to think hard of it. In a week we'll have finished our haying, and then it's a fortnight to wheat; but, for that matter, Harry and I can manage the wheat by ourselves. You may take a month, two months, if any thing comes of it. Under a month I don't mean that you shall come back. I'll give you twenty dollars for a start; if you want more you must earn it on the road, any way you please. And, mark you, Jacob! since you ARE poor, don't let anybody suppose you are rich. For my part, I shall not expect you to buy Whitney's place; all I ask is that you'll tell me, fair and square, just what things and what people you've got acquainted with. Get to bed now—the matter's settled; I will have it so."

They rose and walked across the meadow to the house. Jacob had quite forgotten the events of the evening in the new prospect suddenly opened to him, which filled him with a wonderful confusion of fear and desire. His father said nothing more. They entered the lonely house together at midnight, and went to their beds; but Jacob slept very little.

Six days afterwards he left home, on a sparkling June morning, with a small bundle tied in a yellow silk handkerchief under his arm. His father had furnished him with the promised money, but had positively refused to tell him what road he should take, or what plan of action he should adopt. The only stipulation was that his absence from home should not be less than a month.

After he had passed the wood and reached the highway which followed the course of the brook, he paused to consider which course to take. Southward the road led past Pardon's, and he longed to see his only friends once more before encountering untried hazards; but the village was beyond, and he had no courage to walk through its one long street with a bundle, denoting a journey, under his arm. Northward he would have to pass the mill and blacksmith's shop at the cross-roads. Then he remembered that he might easily wade the stream at a point where it was shallow, and keep in the shelter of the woods on the opposite hill until he struck the road farther on, and in that direction two or three miles would take him into a neighborhood where he was not known.

Once in the woods, an exquisite sense of freedom came upon him. There was nothing mocking in the soft, graceful stir of the expanded foliage, in the twittering of the unfrightened birds, or the scampering of the squirrels, over the rustling carpet of dead leaves. He lay down upon the moss under a spreading beech-tree and tried to think; but the thoughts would not come. He could not even clearly recall the keen troubles and mortifications he had endured: all things were so peaceful and beautiful that a portion of their peace and beauty fell upon men and invested them with a more kindly character.

Towards noon Jacob found himself beyond the limited geography of his life. The first man he encountered was a stranger, who greeted him with a hearty and respectful "How do you do, sir?"

"Perhaps," thought Jacob, "I am not so very different from other people, if I only thought so myself."

At noon, he stopped at a farm-house by the roadside to get a drink of water. A pleasant woman, who came from the door at that moment with a pitcher, allowed him to lower the bucket and haul it up dripping with precious coolness. She looked upon him with good-will, for he had allowed her to see his eyes, and something in their honest, appealing expression went to her heart.

"We're going to have dinner in five minutes," said she; "won't you stay and have something?"

Jacob stayed and brake bread with the plain, hospitable family. Their kindly attention to him during the meal gave him the lacking nerve; for a moment he resolved to offer his services to the farmer, but he presently saw that they were not really needed, and, besides, the place was still too near home.

Towards night he reached an old country tavern, lording it over an incipient village of six houses. The landlord and hostler were inspecting a drooping-looking horse in front of the stables. Now, if there was any thing which Jacob understood, to the extent of his limited experience, it was horse nature. He drew near, listened to the views of the two men, examined the animal with his eyes, and was ready to answer, "Yes, I guess so," when the landlord said, "Perhaps, sir, you can tell what is the matter with him."

His prompt detection of the ailment, and prescription of a remedy which in an hour showed its good effects, installed him in the landlord's best graces. The latter said, "Well, it shall cost you nothing to-night," as he led the way to the supper-room. When Jacob went to bed he was surprised on reflecting that he had not only been talking for a full hour in the bar-room, but had been looking people in the face.

Resisting an offer of good wages if he would stay and help look after the stables, he set forward the next morning with a new and most delightful confidence in himself. The knowledge that now nobody knew him as "Jake Flint" quite removed his tortured self-consciousness. When he met a person who was glum and ungracious of speech, he saw, nevertheless, that he was not its special object. He was sometimes asked questions, to be sure, which a little embarrassed him, but he soon hit upon answers which were sufficiently true without betraying his purpose.

Wandering sometimes to the right and sometimes to the left, he slowly made his way into the land, until, on the afternoon of the fourth day after leaving home, he found himself in a rougher region—a rocky, hilly tract, with small and not very flourishing farms in the valleys. Here the season appeared to be more backward than in the open country; the hay harvest was not yet over.

Jacob's taste for scenery was not particularly cultivated, but something in the loneliness and quiet of the farms reminded him of his own home; and he looked at one house after another, deliberating with himself whether it would not be a good place to spend the remainder of his month of probation. He seemed to be very far from home—about forty miles, in fact,—and was beginning to feel a little tired of wandering.

Finally the road climbed a low pass of the hills, and dropped into a valley on the opposite side. There was but one house in view—a two-story building of logs and plaster, with a garden and orchard on the hillside in the rear. A large meadow stretched in front, and when the whole of it lay clear before him, as the road issued from a wood, his eye was caught by an unusual harvest picture.

Directly before him, a woman, whose face was concealed by a huge, flapping sun-bonnet, was seated upon a mowing machine, guiding a span of horses around the great tract of thick grass which was still uncut. A little distance off, a boy and girl were raking the drier swaths together, and a hay-cart, drawn by oxen and driven by a man, was just entering the meadow from the side next the barn.

Jacob hung his bundle upon a stake, threw his coat and waistcoat over the rail, and, resting his chin on his shirted arms, leaned on the fence, and watched the hay-makers. As the woman came down the nearer side she appeared to notice him, for her head was turned from time to time in his direction. When she had made the round, she stopped the horses at the corner, sprang lightly from her seat and called to the man, who, leaving his team, met her half-way. They were nearly a furlong distant, but Jacob was quite sure that she pointed to him, and that the man looked in the same direction. Presently she set off across the meadow, directly towards him.

When within a few paces of the fence, she stopped, threw back the flaps of her sun-bonnet, and said, "Good day to you!" Jacob was so amazed to see a bright, fresh, girlish face, that he stared at her with all his eyes, forgetting to drop his head. Indeed, he could not have done so, for his chin was propped upon the top rail of the fence.

"You are a stranger, I see," she added.

"Yes, in these parts," he replied.

"Looking for work?"

He hardly knew what answer to make, so he said, at a venture, "That's as it happens." Then he colored a little, for the words seemed foolish to his ears.

"Time's precious," said the girl, "so I'll tell you at once we want help. Our hay MUST be got in while the fine weather lasts."

"I'll help you!" Jacob exclaimed, taking his arms from the rail, and looking as willing as he felt.

"I'm so glad! But I must tell you, at first, that we're not rich, and the hands are asking a great deal now. How much do you expect?"

"Whatever you please?" said he, climbing the fence.

"No, that's not our way of doing business. What do you say to a dollar a day, and found?"

"All right!" and with the words he was already at her side, taking long strides over the elastic turf.

"I will go on with my mowing," said she, when they reached the horses, "and you can rake and load with my father. What name shall I call you by?"

"Everybody calls me Jake."

"'Jake!' Jacob is better. Well, Jacob, I hope you'll give us all the help you can."

With a nod and a light laugh she sprang upon the machine. There was a sweet throb in Jacob's heart, which, if he could have expressed it, would have been a triumphant shout of "I'm not afraid of her! I'm not afraid of her!"

The farmer was a kindly, depressed man, with whose quiet ways Jacob instantly felt himself at home. They worked steadily until sunset, when the girl, detaching her horses from the machine, mounted one of them and led the other to the barn. At the supper-table, the farmer's wife said: "Susan, you must be very tired."

"Not now, mother!" she cheerily answered. "I was, I think, but after I picked up Jacob I felt sure we should get our hay in."

"It was a good thing," said the farmer; "Jacob don't need to be told how to work."

Poor Jacob! He was so happy he could have cried. He sat and listened, and blushed a little, with a smile on his face which it was a pleasure to see. The honest people did not seem to regard him in the least as a stranger; they discussed their family interests and troubles and hopes before him, and in a little while it seemed as if he had known them always.

How faithfully he worked! How glad and tired he felt when night came, and the hay-mow was filled, and the great stacks grew beside the barn! But ah! the haying came to an end, and on the last evening, at supper, everybody was constrained and silent. Even Susan looked grave and thoughtful.

"Jacob," said the farmer, finally, "I wish we could keep you until wheat harvest; but you know we are poor, and can't afford it. Perhaps you could—"

He hesitated; but Jacob, catching at the chance and obeying his own unselfish impulse, cried: "Oh, yes, I can; I'll be satisfied with my board, till the wheat's ripe."

Susan looked at him quickly, with a bright, speaking face. "It's hardly fair to you," said the farmer.

"But I like to be here so much!" Jacob cried. "I like—all of you!"

"We DO seem to suit," said the farmer, "like as one family. And that reminds me, we've not heard your family name yet."

"Flint."

"Jacob FLINT!" exclaimed the farmer's wife, with sudden agitation.

Jacob was scared and troubled. They had heard of him, he thought, and who knew what ridiculous stories? Susan noticed an anxiety on his face which she could not understand, but she unknowingly came to his relief.

"Why, mother," she asked, "do you know Jacob's family?"

"No, I think not," said her mother, "only somebody of the name, long ago."

His offer, however, was gratefully accepted. The bright, hot summer days came and went, but no flower of July ever opened as rapidly and richly and warmly as his chilled, retarded nature. New thoughts and instincts came with every morning's sun, and new conclusions were reached with every evening's twilight. Yet as the wheat harvest drew towards the end, he felt that he must leave the place. The month of absence had gone by, he scarce knew how. He was free to return home, and, though he might offer to bridge over the gap between wheat and oats, as he had already done between hay and wheat, he imagined the family might hesitate to accept such an offer. Moreover, this life at Susan's side was fast growing to be a pain, unless he could assure himself that it would be so forever.

They were in the wheat-field, busy with the last sheaves; she raking and he binding. The farmer and younger children had gone to the barn with a load. Jacob was working silently and steadily, but when they had reached the end of a row, he stopped, wiped his wet brow, and suddenly said, "Susan, I suppose to-day finishes my work here."

"Yes," she answered very slowly.

"And yet I'm very sorry to go."

"I—WE don't want you to go, if we could help it."

Jacob appeared to struggle with himself. He attempted to speak. "If I could—" he brought out, and then paused. "Susan, would you be glad if I came back?"

His eyes implored her to read his meaning. No doubt she read it correctly, for her face flushed, her eyelids fell, and she barely murmured, "Yes, Jacob."

"Then I'll come!" he cried; "I'll come and help you with the oats. Don't talk of pay! Only tell me I'll be welcome! Susan, don't you believe I'll keep my word?"

"I do indeed," said she, looking him firmly in the face.

That was all that was said at the time; but the two understood each other tolerably well.

On the afternoon of the second day, Jacob saw again the lonely house of his father. His journey was made, yet, if any of the neighbors had seen him, they would never have believed that he had come back rich.

Samuel Flint turned away to hide a peculiar smile when he saw his son; but little was said until late that evening, after Harry and Sally had left. Then he required and received an exact account of Jacob's experience during his absence. After hearing the story to the end, he said, "And so you love this Susan Meadows?"

"I'd—I'd do any thing to be with her."

"Are you afraid of her?"

"No!" Jacob uttered the word so emphatically that it rang through the house.

"Ah, well!" said the old man, lifting his eyes, and speaking in the air, "all the harm may be mended yet. But there must be another test." Then he was silent for some time.

"I have it!" he finally exclaimed. "Jacob, you must go back for the oats harvest. You must ask Susan to be your wife, and ask her parents to let you have her. But,—pay attention to my words!—you must tell her that you are a poor, hired man on this place, and that she can be engaged as housekeeper. Don't speak of me as your father, but as the owner of the farm. Bring her here in that belief, and let me see how honest and willing she is. I can easily arrange matters with Harry and Sally while you are away; and I'll only ask you to keep up the appearance of the thing for a month or so."

"But, father,"—Jacob began.

"Not a word! Are you not willing to do that much for the sake of having her all your life, and this farm after me? Suppose it is covered with a mortgage, if she is all you say, you two can work it off. Not a word more! It is no lie, after all, that you will tell her."

"I am afraid," said Jacob, "that she could not leave her home now. She is too useful there, and the family is so poor."

"Tell them that both your wages, for the first year, shall go to them. It'll be my business to rake and scrape the money together somehow. Say, too, that the housekeeper's place can't be kept for her—must be filled at once. Push matters like a man, if you mean to be a complete one, and bring her here, if she carries no more with her than the clothes on her back!"

During the following days Jacob had time to familiarize his mind with this startling proposal. He knew his father's stubborn will too well to suppose that it could be changed; but the inevitable soon converted itself into the possible and desirable. The sweet face of Susan as she had stood before him in the wheat-field was continually present to his eyes, and ere long, he began to place her, in his thoughts, in the old rooms at home, in the garden, among the thickets by the brook, and in Ann Pardon's pleasant parlor. Enough; his father's plan became his own long before the time was out.

On his second journey everybody seemed to be an old acquaintance and an intimate friend. It was evening as he approached the Meadows farm, but the younger children recognized him in the dusk, and their cry of, "Oh, here's Jacob!" brought out the farmer and his wife and Susan, with the heartiest of welcomes. They had all missed him, they said—even the horses and oxen had looked for him, and they were wondering how they should get the oats harvested without him.

Jacob looked at Susan as the farmer said this, and her eyes seemed to answer, "I said nothing, but I knew you would come." Then, first, he felt sufficient courage for the task before him.

He rose the next morning, before any one was stirring, and waited until she should come down stairs. The sun had not risen when she appeared, with a milk-pail in each hand, walking unsuspectingly to the cow-yard. He waylaid her, took the pails in his hand and said in nervous haste, "Susan, will you be my wife?"

She stopped as if she had received a sudden blow; then a shy, sweet consent seemed to run through her heart. "O Jacob!" was all she could say.

"But you will, Susan?" he urged; and then (neither of them exactly knew how it happened) all at once his arms were around her, and they had kissed each other.

"Susan," he said, presently, "I am a poor man—only a farm hand, and must work for my living. You could look for a better husband."

"I could never find a better than you, Jacob."

"Would you work with me, too, at the same place?"

"You know I am not afraid of work," she answered, "and I could never want any other lot than yours."

Then he told her the story which his father had prompted. Her face grew bright and happy as she listened, and he saw how from her very heart she accepted the humble fortune. Only the thought of her parents threw a cloud over the new and astonishing vision. Jacob, however, grew bolder as he saw fulfilment of his hope so near. They took the pails and seated themselves beside neighbor cows, one raising objections or misgivings which the other manfully combated. Jacob's earnestness unconsciously ran into his hands, as he discovered when the impatient cow began to snort and kick.

The harvesting of the oats was not commenced that morning. The children were sent away, and there was a council of four persons held in the parlor. The result of mutual protestations and much weeping was, that the farmer and his wife agreed to receive Jacob as a son-in-law; the offer of the wages was four times refused by them, and then accepted; and the chance of their being able to live and labor together was finally decided to be too fortunate to let slip. When the shock and surprise was over all gradually became cheerful, and, as the matter was more calmly discussed, the first conjectured difficulties somehow resolved themselves into trifles.

It was the simplest and quietest wedding,—at home, on an August morning. Farmer Meadows then drove the bridal pair half-way on their journey, to the old country tavern, where a fresh conveyance had been engaged for them. The same evening they reached the farm-house in the valley, and Jacob's happy mood gave place to an anxious uncertainty as he remembered the period of deception upon which Susan was entering. He keenly watched his father's face when they arrived, and was a little relieved when he saw that his wife had made a good first impression.

"So, this is my new housekeeper," said the old man. "I hope you will suit me as well as your husband does."

"I'll do my best, sir," said she; "but you must have patience with me for a few days, until I know your ways and wishes."

"Mr. Flint," said Sally, "shall I get supper ready?" Susan looked up in astonishment at hearing the name.

"Yes," the old man remarked, "we both have the same name. The fact is, Jacob and I are a sort of relations."

Jacob, in spite of his new happiness, continued ill at ease, although he could not help seeing how his father brightened under Susan's genial influence, how satisfied he was with her quick, neat, exact ways and the cheerfulness with which she fulfilled her duties. At the end of a week, the old man counted out the wages agreed upon for both, and his delight culminated at the frank simplicity with which Susan took what she supposed she had fairly earned.

"Jacob," he whispered when she had left the room, "keep quiet one more week, and then I'll let her know."

He had scarcely spoken, when Susan burst into the room again, crying, "Jacob, they are coming, they have come!"

"Who?"

"Father and mother; and we didn't expect them, you know, for a week yet."

All three went to the door as the visitors made their appearance on the veranda. Two of the party stood as if thunderstruck, and two exclamations came together:

"Samuel Flint!"

"Lucy Wheeler!"

There was a moment's silence; then the farmer's wife, with a visible effort to compose herself, said, "Lucy Meadows, now."

The tears came into Samuel Flint's eyes. "Let us shake hands, Lucy," he said: "my son has married your daughter."

All but Jacob were freshly startled at these words. The two shook hands, and then Samuel, turning to Susan's father, said: "And this is your husband, Lucy. I am glad to make his acquaintance."

"Your father, Jacob!" Susan cried; "what does it all mean?"

Jacob's face grew red, and the old habit of hanging his head nearly came back upon him. He knew not what to say, and looked wistfully at his father.

"Come into the house and sit down," said the latter. "I think we shall all feel better when we have quietly and comfortably talked the matter over."

They went into the quaint, old-fashioned parlor, which had already been transformed by Susan's care, so that much of its shabbiness was hidden. When all were seated, and Samuel Flint perceived that none of the others knew what to say, he took a resolution which, for a man of his mood and habit of life, required some courage.

"Three of us here are old people," he began, "and the two young ones love each other. It was so long ago, Lucy, that it cannot be laid to my blame if I speak of it now. Your husband, I see, has an honest heart, and will not misunderstand either of us. The same thing often turns up in life; it is one of those secrets that everybody knows, and that everybody talks about except the persons concerned. When I was a young man, Lucy, I loved you truly, and I faithfully meant to make you my wife."

"I thought so too, for a while," said she, very calmly.

Farmer Meadows looked at his wife, and no face was ever more beautiful than his, with that expression of generous pity shining through it.

"You know how I acted," Samuel Flint continued, "but our children must also know that I broke off from you without giving any reason. A woman came between us and made all the mischief. I was considered rich then, and she wanted to secure my money for her daughter. I was an innocent and unsuspecting young man, who believed that everybody else was as good as myself; and the woman never rested until she had turned me from my first love, and fastened me for life to another. Little by little I discovered the truth; I kept the knowledge of the injury to myself; I quickly got rid of the money which had so cursed me, and brought my wife to this, the loneliest and dreariest place in the neighborhood, where I forced upon her a life of poverty. I thought it was a just revenge, but I was unjust. She really loved me: she was, if not quite without blame in the matter, ignorant of the worst that had been done (I learned all that too late), and she never complained, though the change in me slowly wore out her life. I know now that I was cruel; but at the same time I punished myself, and was innocently punishing my son. But to HIM there was one way to make amends. 'I will help him to a wife,' I said, 'who will gladly take poverty with him and for his sake.' I forced him, against his will, to say that he was a hired hand on this place, and that Susan must be content to be a hired housekeeper. Now that I know Susan, I see that this proof might have been left out; but I guess it has done no harm. The place is not so heavily mortgaged as people think, and it will be Jacob's after I am gone. And now forgive me, all of you,—Lucy first, for she has most cause; Jacob next; and Susan,—that will be easier; and you, Friend Meadows, if what I have said has been hard for you to hear."

The farmer stood up like a man, took Samuel's hand and his wife's, and said, in a broken voice: "Lucy, I ask you, too, to forgive him, and I ask you both to be good friends to each other."

Susan, dissolved in tears, kissed all of them in turn; but the happiest heart there was Jacob's.

It was now easy for him to confide to his wife the complete story of his troubles, and to find his growing self-reliance strengthened by her quick, intelligent sympathy. The Pardons were better friends than ever, and the fact, which at first created great astonishment in the neighborhood, that Jacob Flint had really gone upon a journey and brought home a handsome wife, began to change the attitude of the people towards him. The old place was no longer so lonely; the nearest neighbors began to drop in and insist on return visits. Now that Jacob kept his head up, and they got a fair view of his face, they discovered that he was not lacking, after all, in sense or social qualities.

In October, the Whitney place, which had been leased for several years, was advertised to be sold at public sale. The owner had gone to the city and become a successful merchant, had outlived his local attachments, and now took advantage of a rise in real estate to disburden himself of a property which he could not profitably control.

Everybody from far and wide attended the sale, and, when Jacob Flint and his father arrived, everybody said to the former: "Of course you've come to buy, Jacob." But each man laughed at his own smartness, and considered the remark original with himself.

Jacob was no longer annoyed. He laughed, too, and answered: "I'm afraid I can't do that; but I've kept half my word, which is more than most men do."

"Jake's no fool, after all," was whispered behind him.

The bidding commenced, at first very spirited, and then gradually slacking off, as the price mounted above the means of the neighboring farmers. The chief aspirant was a stranger, a well-dressed man with a lawyer's air, whom nobody knew. After the usual long pauses and passionate exhortations, the hammer fell, and the auctioneer, turning to the stranger, asked, "What name?"

"Jacob Flint!"

There was a general cry of surprise. All looked at Jacob, whose eyes and mouth showed that he was as dumbfounded as the rest.

The stranger walked coolly through the midst of the crowd to Samuel Flint, and said, "When shall I have the papers drawn up?"

"As soon as you can," the old man replied; then seizing Jacob by the arm, with the words, "Let's go home now!" he hurried him on.

The explanation soon leaked out. Samuel Flint had not thrown away his wealth, but had put it out of his own hands. It was given privately to trustees, to be held for his son, and returned when the latter should have married with his father's consent. There was more than enough to buy the Whitney place.

Jacob and Susan are happy in their stately home, and good as they are happy. If any person in the neighborhood ever makes use of the phrase "Jacob Flint's Journey," he intends thereby to symbolize the good fortune which sometimes follows honesty, reticence, and shrewdness.

# CAN A LIFE HIDE ITSELF?

I had been reading, as is my wont from time to time, one of the many volumes of "The New Pitaval," that singular record of human crime and human cunning, and also of the inevitable fatality which, in every case, leaves a gate open for detection. Were it not for the latter fact, indeed, one would turn with loathing from such endless chronicles of wickedness. Yet these may be safely contemplated, when one has discovered the incredible fatuity of crime, the certain weak mesh in a network of devilish texture; or is it rather the agency of a power outside of man, a subtle protecting principle, which allows the operation of the evil element only that the latter may finally betray itself? Whatever explanation we may choose, the fact is there, like a tonic medicine distilled from poisonous plants, to brace our faith in the ascendancy of Good in the government of the world.

Laying aside the book, I fell into a speculation concerning the mixture of the two elements in man's nature. The life of an individual is usually, it seemed to me, a series of RESULTS, the processes leading to which are not often visible, or observed when they are so. Each act is the precipitation of a number of mixed influences, more or less unconsciously felt; the qualities of good and evil are so blended therein that they defy the keenest moral analysis; and how shall we, then, pretend to judge of any one? Perhaps the surest indication of evil (I further reflected) is that it always tries to conceal itself, and the strongest incitement to good is that evil cannot be concealed. The crime, or the vice, or even the self-acknowledged weakness, becomes a part of the individual consciousness; it cannot be forgotten or outgrown. It follows a life through all experiences and to the uttermost ends of the earth, pressing towards the light with a terrible, demoniac power. There are noteless lives, of course—lives that accept obscurity, mechanically run their narrow round of circumstance, and are lost; but when a life endeavors to lose itself,—to hide some conscious guilt or failure,—can it succeed? Is it not thereby lifted above the level of common experience, compelling attention to itself by the very endeavor to escape it?

I turned these questions over in my mind, without approaching, or indeed expecting, any solution,—since I knew, from habit, the labyrinths into which they would certainly lead me,—when a visitor was announced.

It was one of the directors of our county almshouse, who came on an errand to which he attached no great importance. I owed the visit, apparently, to the circumstance that my home lay in his way, and he could at once relieve his conscience of a very trifling pressure and his pocket of a small package, by calling upon me. His story was told in a few words; the package was placed upon my table, and I was again left to my meditations.

Two or three days before, a man who had the appearance of a "tramp" had been observed by the people of a small village in the neighborhood. He stopped and looked at the houses in a vacant way, walked back and forth once or twice as if uncertain which of the cross-roads to take, and presently went on without begging or even speaking to any one. Towards sunset a farmer, on his way to the village store, found him sitting at the roadside, his head resting against a fence-post. The man's face was so worn and exhausted that the farmer kindly stopped and addressed him; but he gave no other reply than a shake of the head.

The farmer thereupon lifted him into his light country-wagon, the man offering no resistance, and drove to the tavern, where, his exhaustion being so evident, a glass of whiskey was administered to him. He afterwards spoke a few words in German, which no one understood. At the almshouse, to which he was transported the same evening, he refused to answer the customary questions, although he appeared to understand them. The physician was obliged to use a slight degree of force in administering nourishment and medicine, but neither was of any avail. The man died within twenty-four hours after being received. His pockets were empty, but two small leathern wallets were found under his pillow; and these formed the package which the director left in my charge. They were full of papers in a foreign language, he said, and he supposed I might be able to ascertain the stranger's name and home from them.

I took up the wallets, which were worn and greasy from long service, opened them, and saw that they were filled with scraps, fragments, and folded pieces of paper, nearly every one of which had been carried for a long time loose in the pocket. Some were written in pen and ink, and some in pencil, but all were equally brown, worn, and unsavory in appearance. In turning them over, however, my eye was caught by some slips in the Russian character, and three or four notes in French; the rest were German. I laid aside "Pitaval" at once, emptied all the leathern pockets carefully, and set about examining the pile of material.

I first ran rapidly through the papers to ascertain the dead man's name, but it was nowhere to be found. There were half a dozen letters, written on sheets folded and addressed in the fashion which prevailed before envelopes were invented; but the name was cut out of the address in every case. There was an official permit to embark on board a Bremen steamer, mutilated in the same way; there was a card photograph, from which the face had been scratched by a penknife. There were Latin sentences; accounts of expenses; a list of New York addresses, covering eight pages; and a number of notes, written either in Warsaw or Breslau. A more incongruous collection I never saw, and I am sure that had it not been for the train of thought I was pursuing when the director called upon me, I should have returned the papers to him without troubling my head with any attempt to unravel the man's story.

The evidence, however, that he had endeavored to hide his life, had been revealed by my first superficial examination; and here, I reflected, was a singular opportunity to test both his degree of success and my own power of constructing a coherent history out of the detached fragments. Unpromising as is the matter, said I, let me see whether he can conceal his secret from even such unpractised eyes as mine.

I went through the papers again, read each one rapidly, and arranged them in separate files, according to the character of their contents. Then I rearranged these latter in the order of time, so far as it was indicated; and afterwards commenced the work of picking out and threading together whatever facts might be noted. The first thing I ascertained, or rather conjectured, was that the man's life might be divided into three very distinct phases, the first ending in Breslau, the second in Poland, and the third and final one in America. Thereupon I once again rearranged the material, and attacked that which related to the first phase.

It consisted of the following papers: Three letters, in a female hand, commencing "My dear brother," and terminating with "Thy loving sister, Elise;" part of a diploma from a gymnasium, or high school, certifying that [here the name was cut out] had successfully passed his examination, and was competent to teach,—and here again, whether by accident or design, the paper was torn off; a note, apparently to a jeweller, ordering a certain gold ring to be delivered to "Otto," and signed "B. V. H.;" a receipt from the package-post for a box forwarded to Warsaw, to the address of Count Ladislas Kasincsky; and finally a washing-list, at the bottom of which was written, in pencil, in a trembling hand: "May God protect thee! But do not stay away so very long."

In the second collection, relating to Poland, I found the following: Six orders in Russian and three in French, requesting somebody to send by "Jean" sums of money, varying from two to eight hundred rubles. These orders were in the same hand, and all signed "Y." A charming letter in French, addressed "cher ami," and declining, in the most delicate and tender way, an offer of marriage made to the sister of the writer, of whose signature only "Amelie de" remained, the family name having been torn off. A few memoranda of expenses, one of which was curious: "Dinner with Jean, 58 rubles;" and immediately after it: "Doctor, 10 rubles." There were, moreover, a leaf torn out of a journal, and half of a note which had been torn down the middle, both implicating "Jean" in some way with the fortunes of the dead man.

The papers belonging to the American phase, so far as they were to be identified by dates, or by some internal evidence, were fewer, but even more enigmatical in character. The principal one was a list of addresses in New York, divided into sections, the street boundaries of which were given. There were no names, but some of the addresses were marked , and others?, and a few had been crossed out with a pencil. Then there were some leaves of a journal of diet and bodily symptoms, of a very singular character; three fragments of drafts of letters, in pencil, one of them commencing, "Dog and villain!" and a single note of "Began work, September 10th, 1865." This was about a year before his death.

The date of the diploma given by the gymnasium at Breslau was June 27, 1855, and the first date in Poland was May 3, 1861. Belonging to the time between these two periods there were only the order for the ring (1858), and a little memorandum in pencil, dated "Posen, Dec., 1859." The last date in Poland was March 18, 1863, and the permit to embark at Bremen was dated in October of that year. Here, at least, was a slight chronological framework. The physician who attended the county almshouse had estimated the man's age at thirty, which, supposing him to have been nineteen at the time of receiving the diploma, confirmed the dates to that extent.

I assumed, at the start, that the name which had been so carefully cut out of all the documents was the man's own. The "Elise" of the letters was therefore his sister. The first two letters related merely to "mother's health," and similar details, from which it was impossible to extract any thing, except that the sister was in some kind of service. The second letter closed with: "I have enough work to do, but I keep well. Forget thy disappointment so far as *I* am concerned, for I never expected any thing; I don't know why, but I never did."

Here was a disappointment, at least, to begin with. I made a note of it opposite the date, on my blank programme, and took up the next letter. It was written in November, 1861, and contained a passage which keenly excited my curiosity. It ran thus: "Do, pray, be more careful of thy money. It may be all as thou sayest, and inevitable, but I dare not mention the thing to mother, and five thalers is all I can spare out of my own wages. As for thy other request, I have granted it, as thou seest, but it makes me a little anxious. What is the joke? And how can it serve thee? That is what I do not understand, and I have plagued myself not a little to guess."

Among the Polish memoranda was this: "Sept. 1 to Dec. 1, 200 rubles," which I assumed to represent a salary. This would give him eight hundred a year, at least twelve times the amount which his sister—who must either have been cook or housekeeper, since she spoke of going to market for the family—could have received. His application to her for money, and the manner of her reference to it, indicated some imprudence or irregularity on his part. What the "other request" was, I could not guess; but as I was turning and twisting the worn leaf in some perplexity, I made a sudden discovery. One side of the bottom edge had been very slightly doubled over in folding, and as I smoothed it out, I noticed some diminutive letters in the crease. The paper had been worn nearly through, but I made out the words: "Write very soon, dear Otto!"

This was the name in the order for the gold ring, signed "B. V. H."—a link, indeed, but a fresh puzzle. Knowing the stubborn prejudices of caste in Germany, and above all in Eastern Prussia and Silesia, I should have been compelled to accept "Otto," whose sister was in service, as himself the servant of "B. V. H.," but for the tenderly respectful letter of "Amelie de— —," declining the marriage offer for her sister. I re-read this letter very carefully, to determine whether it was really intended for "Otto." It ran thus:

> "DEAR FRIEND,—I will not say that your letter was entirely unexpected, either to Helmine or myself. I should, perhaps, have less faith in the sincerity of your attachment if you had not already involuntarily betrayed it. When I say that although I detected the inclination of your heart some weeks ago, and that I also saw it was becoming evident to my sister, yet I refrained from mentioning the subject at all until she came to me last evening with your letter in her hand,—when I say this, you will understand that I have acted towards you with the respect and sympathy which I profoundly feel. Helmine fully shares this feeling, and her poor heart is too painfully moved to allow her to reply. Do I not say, in saying this, what her reply must be? But, though her heart cannot respond to your love, she hopes you will always believe her a friend to whom your proffered devotion was an honor, and will be—if you will subdue it to her deserts—a grateful thing to remember. We shall remain in Warsaw a fortnight longer, as I think yourself will agree that it is better we should not immediately return to the castle. Jean, who must carry a fresh order already, will bring you this, and

*we hope to have good news of Henri. I send back the papers, which were unnecessary; we never doubted you, and we shall of course keep your secret so long as you choose to wear it.*

"*AMELIE DE — —*"

The more light I seemed to obtain, the more inexplicable the circumstances became. The diploma and the note of salary were grounds for supposing that "Otto" occupied the position of tutor in a noble Polish family. There was the receipt for a box addressed to Count Ladislas Kasincsky, and I temporarily added his family name to the writer of the French letter, assuming her to be his wife. "Jean" appeared to be a servant, and "Henri" I set down as the son whom Otto was instructing in the castle or family seat in the country, while the parents were in warsaw. Plausible, so far; but the letter was not such a one as a countess would have written to her son's tutor, under similar circumstances. It was addressed to a social equal, apparently to a man younger than herself, and for whom — supposing him to have been a tutor, secretary, or something of the kind — she must have felt a special sympathy. Her mention of "the papers" and "your secret" must refer to circumstances which would explain the mystery. "So long as you choose to WEAR it," she had written: then it was certainly a secret connected with his personal history.

Further, it appeared that "Jean" was sent to him with "an order." What could this be, but one of the nine orders for money which lay before my eyes? I examined the dates of the latter, and lo! there was one written upon the same day as the lady's letter. The sums drawn by these orders amounted in all to four thousand two hundred rubles. But how should a tutor or secretary be in possession of his employer's money? Still, this might be accounted for; it would imply great trust on the part of the latter, but no more than one man frequently reposes in another. Yet, if it were so, one of the memoranda confronted me with a conflicting fact: "Dinner with Jean, 58 rubles." The unusual amount — nearly fifty dollars — indicated an act of the most reckless dissipation, and in company with a servant, if "Jean," as I could scarcely doubt, acted in that character. I finally decided to assume both these conjectures as true, and apply them to the remaining testimony.

I first took up the leaf which had been torn out of a small journal or pocket note-book, as was manifested by the red edge on three sides. It was scribbled over with brief notes in pencil, written at different times. Many of them were merely mnemonic signs; but the recurrence of the letters J and Y seemed to point to transactions with "Jean," and the drawer of the various sums of money. The letter Y reminded me that I had been too hasty in giving the name of Kasincsky to the noble family; indeed, the name upon the post-office receipt might have no connection with the matter I was trying to investigate.

Suddenly I noticed a "Ky" among the mnemonic signs, and the suspicion flashed across my mind that Count Kasincsky had signed the order with the last letter of his family name! To assume this, however, suggested a secret reason for doing so; and I began to think that I had already secrets enough on hand.

The leaf was much rubbed and worn, and it was not without considerable trouble that I deciphered the following (omitting the unintelligible signs):

"Oct. 30 (Nov. 12)—talk with Y; 20—Jean. Consider.

"Nov. 15—with J—H—hope.

"Dec. 1—Told the C. No knowledge of S—therefore safe. Uncertain of——C to Warsaw. Met J. as agreed. Further and further.

"Dec. 27—All for naught! All for naught!

"Jan. 19, '63—Sick. What is to be the end? Threats. No tidings of Y. Walked the streets all day. At night as usual.

"March 1—News. The C. and H. left yesterday. No more to hope. Let it come, then!"

These broken words warmed my imagination powerfully. Looking at them in the light of my conjecture, I was satisfied that "Otto" was involved in some crime, or dangerous secret, of which "Jean" was either the instigator or the accomplice. "Y.," or Count Kasincsky,—and I was more than ever inclined to connect the two,——also had his mystery, which might, or might not, be identical with the first. By comparing dates, I found that the entry made December 27 was three days later than the date of the letter of "Amelie de——"; and the exclamation "All for naught!" certainly referred to the disappointment it contained. I now guessed the "H." in the second entry to mean "Helmine." The two last suggested a removal to Warsaw from the country. Here was a little more ground to stand on; but how should I ever get at the secret?

I took up the torn half of a note, which, after the first inspection, I had laid aside as a hopeless puzzle. A closer examination revealed several things which failed to impress me at the outset. It was written in a strong and rather awkward masculine hand; several words were underscored, two misspelled, and I felt—I scarcely knew why—that it was written in a spirit of mingled contempt and defiance. Let me give the fragment just as it lay before me:

"ARON!

*It is quite time*
*be done. Who knows*
*is not his home by this*
CONCERN FOR THE
*that they are well off,*
*sian officers are*
*cide at once, my*
*risau, or I must*
*t* TEN DAYS DELAY
*money can be divi-*
*tier, and you may*
*ever you please.*
*untess goes, and she*
*will know who you*
*time, unless you carry*
*friend or not*
*decide,*
*ann Helm."*

Here, I felt sure, was the clue to much of the mystery. The first thing that struck me was the appearance of a new name. I looked at it again, ran through in my mind all possible German names, and found that it could only be "Johann,"—and in the same instant I recalled the frequent habit of the Prussian and Polish nobility of calling their German valets by French names. This, then, was "Jean!" The address was certainly "Baron," and why thrice underscored, unless in contemptuous satire? Light began to break upon the matter at last. "Otto" had been playing the part, perhaps assuming the name, of a nobleman, seduced to the deception by his passion for the Countess' sister, Helmine. This explained the reference to "the papers," and "the secret," and would account for the respectful and sympathetic tone of the Countess' letter. But behind this there was certainly another secret, in which "Y." (whoever he might be) was concerned, and which related to money. The close of the note, which I filled out to read, "Your friend or not, as you may decide," conveyed a threat, and, to judge from the halves of lines immediately preceding it, the threat referred to the money, as well as to the betrayal of an assumed character.

Here, just as the story began to appear in faint outline, my discoveries stopped for a while. I ascertained the breadth of the original note by a part of the middle-crease which remained, filled out the torn part with blank paper, completed the divided words in the same character of manuscript, and endeavored to guess the remainder, but no clairvoyant power of divination came to my aid. I turned over the letters again, remarking the neatness with which the addresses had been cut off, and wondering why the man had not destroyed the letters and other memoranda entirely, if he wished to hide a possible crime. The fact that they were not destroyed showed the hold which his past life had had upon him even to his dying hour. Weak and vain, as I had already suspected him to be,—wanting in all manly fibre, and of the very material which a keen, energetic villain would mould to his needs,—I felt that his love for his sister and for "Helmine," and other associations connected with his life in Germany and Poland, had made him cling to these worn records.

I know not what gave me the suspicion that he had not even found the heart to destroy the exscinded names; perhaps the care with which they had been removed; perhaps, in two instances, the circumstance of their taking words out of the body of the letters with them. But the suspicion came, and led to a re-examination of the leathern wallets. I could scarcely believe my eyes, when feeling something rustle faintly as I pressed the thin lining of an inner pocket, I drew forth three or four small pellets of paper, and unrolling them, found the lost addresses! I fitted them to the vacant places, and found that the first letters of the sister in Breslau had been forwarded to "Otto Lindenschmidt," while the letter to Poland was addressed "Otto von Herisau."

I warmed with this success, which exactly tallied with the previous discoveries, and returned again to the Polish memoranda The words "[Rus]sian officers" in "Jean's" note led me to notice that it had been written towards the close of the last insurrection in Poland—a circumstance which I immediately coupled with some things in the note and on the leaf of the journal. "No tidings of Y" might indicate that Count Kasincsky had been concerned in the rebellion, and had fled, or been taken prisoner. Had he left a large amount of funds in the hands of the supposed Otto von Herisau, which were drawn from time to time by orders, the form of which had been previously agreed upon? Then, when he had disappeared, might it not have been the remaining funds which Jean urged Otto to divide with him, while the latter, misled and entangled in deception rather than naturally dishonest, held back from such a step? I could hardly doubt so much, and it now required but a slight effort of the imagination to complete the torn note.

The next letter of the sister was addressed to Bremen. After having established so many particulars, I found it easily intelligible. "I have done what I can," she wrote. "I put it in this letter; it is all I have. But do not ask me for money again; mother is ailing most of the time, and I have not yet dared to tell her all. I shall suffer great anxiety until I hear that the vessel has sailed. My mistress is very good; she has given me an advance on my wages, or I could not have sent thee any thing. Mother thinks thou art still in Leipzig: why didst thou stay there so long? but no difference; thy money would have gone anyhow."

It was nevertheless singular that Otto should be without money, so soon after the appropriation of Count Kasincsky's funds. If the "20" in the first memorandum on the leaf meant "twenty thousand rubles," as I conjectured, and but four thousand two hundred were drawn by the Count previous to his flight or imprisonment, Otto's half of the remainder would amount to nearly eight thousand rubles; and it was, therefore, not easy to account for his delay in Leipzig, and his destitute condition.

Before examining the fragments relating to the American phase of his life,—which illustrated his previous history only by occasional revelations of his moods and feelings,—I made one more effort to guess the cause of his having assumed the name of "Von Herisau." The initials signed to the order for the ring ("B. V. H.") certainly stood for the same family name; and the possession of papers belonging to one of the family was an additional evidence that Otto had either been in the service of, or was related to, some Von Herisau. Perhaps a sentence in one of the sister's letters—"Forget thy disappointment so far as *I* am concerned, for I never expected any thing"— referred to something of the kind. On the whole, service seemed more likely than kinship; but in that case the papers must have been stolen.

I had endeavored, from the start, to keep my sympathies out of the investigation, lest they should lead me to misinterpret the broken evidence, and thus defeat my object. It must have been the Countess' letter, and the brief, almost stenographic, signs of anxiety and unhappiness on the leaf of the journal, that first beguiled me into a commiseration, which the simple devotion and self-sacrifice of the poor, toiling sister failed to neutralize. However, I detected the feeling at this stage of the examination, and turned to the American records, in order to get rid of it.

The principal paper was the list of addresses of which I have spoken. I looked over it in vain, to find some indication of its purpose; yet it had been carefully made out and much used. There was no name of a person upon it,—only numbers and streets, one hundred and thirty-eight in all. Finally, I took these, one by one, to ascertain if any of the houses were known to me, and found three, out of the whole number, to be the residences of persons whom I knew. One was a German gentleman, and the other two were Americans who had visited Germany. The riddle was read! During a former residence in New York, I had for a time been quite overrun by destitute Germans,—men, apparently, of some culture, who represented themselves as theological students, political refugees, or unfortunate clerks and secretaries,—soliciting assistance. I found that, when I gave to one, a dozen others came within the next fortnight; when I refused, the persecution ceased for about the same length of time. I became convinced, at last, that these persons were members of an organized society of beggars, and the result proved it; for when I made it an inviolable rule to give to no one who could not bring me an indorsement of his need by some person whom I knew, the annoyance ceased altogether.

The meaning of the list of addresses was now plain. My nascent commiseration for the man was not only checked, but I was in danger of changing my role from that of culprit's counsel to that of prosecuting attorney.

When I took up again the fragment of the first draught of a letter commencing, "Dog and villain!" and applied it to the words "Jean" or "Johann Helm," the few lines which could be deciphered became full of meaning. "Don't think," it began, "that I have forgotten you, or the trick you played me! If I was drunk or drugged the last night, I know how it happened, for all that. I left, but I shall go back. And if you make use of" (here some words were entirely obliterated).... "is true. He gave me the ring, and meant".... This was all I could make out. The other papers showed only scattered memoranda, of money, or appointments, or addresses, with the exception of the diary in pencil.

I read the letter attentively, and at first with very little idea of its meaning. Many of the words were abbreviated, and there were some arbitrary signs. It ran over a period of about four months, terminating six weeks before the man's death. He had been wandering about the country during this period, sleeping in woods and barns, and living principally upon milk. The condition of his pulse and other physical functions was scrupulously set down, with an occasional remark of "good" or "bad." The conclusion was at last forced upon me that he had been endeavoring to commit suicide by a slow course of starvation and exposure. Either as the cause or the result of this attempt, I read, in the final notes, signs of an aberration of mind. This also explained the singular demeanor of the man when found, and his refusal to take medicine or nourishment. He had selected a long way to accomplish his purpose, but had reached the end at last.

The confused material had now taken shape; the dead man, despite his will, had confessed to me his name and the chief events of his life. It now remained—looking at each event as the result of a long chain of causes—to deduce from them the elements of his individual character, and then fill up the inevitable gaps in the story from the probabilities of the operation of those elements. This was not so much a mere venture as the reader may suppose, because the two actions of the mind test each other. If they cannot, thus working towards a point and back again, actually discover what WAS, they may at least fix upon a very probable MIGHT HAVE BEEN.

A person accustomed to detective work would have obtained my little stock of facts with much less trouble, and would, almost instinctively, have filled the blanks as he went along. Being an apprentice in such matters, I had handled the materials awkwardly. I will not here retrace my own mental zigzags between character and act, but simply repeat the story as I finally settled and accepted it.

Otto Lindenschmidt was the child of poor parents in or near Breslau. His father died when he was young; his mother earned a scanty subsistence as a washerwoman; his sister went into service. Being a bright, handsome boy, he attracted the attention of a Baron von Herisau, an old, childless, eccentric gentleman, who took him first as page or attendant, intending to make him a superior valet de chambre. Gradually, however, the Baron fancied that he detected in the boy a capacity for better things; his condescending feeling of protection had grown into an attachment for the handsome, amiable, grateful young fellow, and he placed him in the gymnasium at Breslau, perhaps with the idea, now, of educating him to be an intelligent companion.

The boy and his humble relatives, dazzled by this opportunity, began secretly to consider the favor as almost equivalent to his adoption as a son. (The Baron had once been married, but his wife and only child had long been dead.) The old man, of course, came to look upon the growing intelligence of the youth as his own work: vanity and affection became inextricably blended in his heart, and when the cursus was over, he took him home as the companion of his lonely life. After two or three years, during which the young man was acquiring habits of idleness and indulgence, supposing his future secure, the Baron died,—perhaps too suddenly to make full provision for him, perhaps after having kept up the appearance of wealth on a life-annuity, but, in any case, leaving very little, if any, property to Otto. In his disappointment, the latter retained certain family papers which the Baron had intrusted to his keeping. The ring was a gift, and he wore it in remembrance of his benefactor.

Wandering about, Micawber-like, in hopes that something might turn up, he reached Posen, and there either met or heard of the Polish Count, Ladislas Kasincsky, who was seeking a tutor for his only son. His accomplishments, and perhaps, also, a certain aristocratic grace of manner unconsciously caught from the Baron von Herisau, speedily won for him the favor of the Count and Countess Kasincsky, and emboldened him to hope for the hand of the Countess' sister, Helmine — —, to whom he was no doubt sincerely attached. Here Johann Helm, or "Jean," a confidential servant of the Count, who looked upon the new tutor as a rival, yet adroitly flattered his vanity for the purpose of misleading and displacing him, appears upon the stage. "Jean" first detected Otto's passion; "Jean," at an epicurean dinner, wormed out of Otto the secret of the Herisau documents, and perhaps suggested the part which the latter afterwards played.

This "Jean" seemed to me to have been the evil agency in the miserable history which followed. After Helmine's rejection of Otto's suit, and the flight or captivity of Count Kasincsky, leaving a large sum of money in Otto's hands, it would be easy for "Jean," by mingled persuasions and threats, to move the latter to flight, after dividing the money still remaining in his hands. After the theft, and the partition, which took place beyond the Polish frontier, "Jean" in turn, stole his accomplice's share, together with the Von Herisau documents.

Exile and a year's experience of organized mendicancy did the rest.

Otto Lindenschmidt was one of those natures which possess no moral elasticity—which have neither the power nor the comprehension of atonement. The first real, unmitigated guilt—whether great or small—breaks them down hopelessly. He expected no chance of self-redemption, and he found none. His life in America was so utterly dark and hopeless that the brightest moment in it must have been that which showed him the approach of death.

My task was done. I had tracked this weak, vain, erring, hunted soul to its last refuge, and the knowledge bequeathed to me but a single duty. His sins were balanced by his temptations; his vanity and weakness had revenged themselves; and there only remained to tell the simple, faithful sister that her sacrifices were no longer required. I burned the evidences of guilt, despair and suicide, and sent the other papers, with a letter relating the time and circumstances of Otto Lindenschmidt's death, to the civil authorities of Breslau, requesting that they might be placed in the hands of his sister Elise.

This, I supposed, was the end of the history, so far as my connection with it was concerned. But one cannot track a secret with impunity; the fatality connected with the act and the actor clings even to the knowledge of the act. I had opened my door a little, in order to look out upon the life of another, but in doing so a ghost had entered in, and was not to be dislodged until I had done its service.

In the summer of 1867 I was in Germany, and during a brief journey of idlesse and enjoyment came to the lovely little watering-place of Liebenstein, on the southern slope of the Thuringian Forest. I had no expectation or even desire of making new acquaintances among the gay company who took their afternoon coffee under the noble linden trees on the terrace; but, within the first hour of my after-dinner leisure, I was greeted by an old friend, an author, from Coburg, and carried away, in my own despite, to a group of his associates. My friend and his friends had already been at the place a fortnight, and knew the very tint and texture of its gossip. While I sipped my coffee, I listened to them with one ear, and to Wagner's overture to "Lohengrin" with the other; and I should soon have been wholly occupied with the fine orchestra had I not been caught and startled by an unexpected name.

"Have you noticed," some one asked, "how much attention the Baron von Herisau is paying her?"

I whirled round and exclaimed, in a breath, "The Baron von Herisau!"

"Yes," said my friend; "do you know him?"

I was glad that three crashing, tremendous chords came from the orchestra just then, giving me time to collect myself before I replied: "I am not sure whether it is the same person: I knew a Baron von Herisau long ago: how old is the gentleman here?"

"About thirty-five, I should think," my friend answered.

"Ah, then it can't be the same person," said I: "still, if he should happen to pass near us, will you point him out to me?"

It was an hour later, and we were all hotly discussing the question of Lessing's obligations to English literature, when one of the gentlemen at the table said: "There goes the Baron von Herisau: is it perhaps your friend, sir?"

I turned and saw a tall man, with prominent nose, opaque black eyes, and black mustache, walking beside a pretty, insipid girl. Behind the pair went an elderly couple, overdressed and snobbish in appearance. A carriage, with servants in livery, waited in the open space below the terrace, and having received the two couples, whirled swiftly away towards Altenstein.

Had I been more of a philosopher I should have wasted no second thought on the Baron von Herisau. But the Nemesis of the knowledge which I had throttled poor Otto Lindenschmidt's ghost to obtain had come upon me at last, and there was no rest for me until I had discovered who and what was the Baron. The list of guests which the landlord gave me whetted my curiosity to a painful degree; for on it I found the entry: "Aug. 15.—Otto V. Herisau, Rentier, East Prussia."

It was quite dark when the carriage returned. I watched the company into the supper-room, and then, whisking in behind them, secured a place at the nearest table. I had an hour of quiet, stealthy observation before my Coburg friend discovered me, and by that time I was glad of his company and had need of his confidence. But, before making use of him in the second capacity, I desired to make the acquaintance of the adjoining partie carree. He had bowed to them familiarly in passing, and when the old gentleman said, "Will you not join us, Herr — —?" I answered my friend's interrogative glance with a decided affirmative, and we moved to the other table.

My seat was beside the Baron von Herisau, with whom I exchanged the usual commonplaces after an introduction. His manner was cold and taciturn, I thought, and there was something forced in the smile which accompanied his replies to the remarks of the coarse old lady, who continually referred to the "Herr Baron" as authority upon every possible subject. I noticed, however, that he cast a sudden, sharp glance at me, when I was presented to the company as an American.

The man's neighborhood disturbed me. I was obliged to let the conversation run in the channels already selected, and stupid enough I found them. I was considering whether I should not give a signal to my friend and withdraw, when the Baron stretched his hand across the table for a bottle of Affenthaler, and I caught sight of a massive gold ring on his middle finger. Instantly I remembered the ring which "B. V. H." had given to Otto Lindenschmidt, and I said to myself, "That is it!" The inference followed like lightning that it was "Johann Helm" who sat beside me, and not a Baron von Herisau!

That evening my friend and I had a long, absorbing conversation in my room. I told him the whole story, which came back vividly to memory, and learned, in return, that the reputed Baron was supposed to be wealthy, that the old gentleman was a Bremen merchant or banker, known to be rich, that neither was considered by those who had met them to be particularly intelligent or refined, and that the wooing of the daughter had already become so marked as to be a general subject of gossip. My friend was inclined to think my conjecture correct, and willingly co-operated with me in a plan to test the matter. We had no considerable sympathy with the snobbish parents, whose servility to a title was so apparent; but the daughter seemed to be an innocent and amiable creature, however silly, and we determined to spare her the shame of an open scandal.

If our scheme should seem a little melodramatic, it must not be forgotten that my friend was an author. The next morning, as the Baron came up the terrace after his visit to the spring, I stepped forward and greeted him politely, after which I said: "I see by the strangers' list that you are from East Prussia, Baron; have you ever been in Poland?" At that moment, a voice behind him called out rather sharply, "Jean!" The Baron started, turned round and then back to me, and all his art could not prevent the blood from rushing to his face. I made, as if by accident, a gesture with my hand, indicating success, and went a step further.

"Because," said I, "I am thinking of making a visit to Cracow and Warsaw, and should be glad of any information—"

"Certainly!" he interrupted me, "and I should be very glad to give it, if I had ever visited Poland."

"At least," I continued, "you can advise me upon one point; but excuse me, shall we not sit down a moment yonder? As my question relates to money, I should not wish to be overheard."

I pointed out a retired spot, just before reaching which we were joined by my friend, who suddenly stepped out from behind a clump of lilacs. The Baron and he saluted each other.

"Now," said I to the former, "I can ask your advice, Mr. Johann Helm!"

He was not an adept, after all. His astonishment and confusion were brief, to be sure, but they betrayed him so completely that his after-impulse to assume a haughty, offensive air only made us smile.

"If I had a message to you from Otto Lindenschmidt, what then?" I asked.

He turned pale, and presently stammered out, "He—he is dead!"

"Now," said my friend, "it is quite time to drop the mask before us. You see we know you, and we know your history. Not from Otto Lindenschmidt alone; Count Ladislas Kasincsky—"

"What! Has he come back from Siberia?" exclaimed Johann Helm. His face expressed abject terror; I think he would have fallen upon his knees before us if he had not somehow felt, by a rascal's instinct, that we had no personal wrongs to redress in unmasking him.

Our object, however, was to ascertain through him the complete facts of Otto Lindenschmidt's history, and then to banish him from Liebenstein. We allowed him to suppose for awhile that we were acting under the authority of persons concerned, in order to make the best possible use of his demoralized mood, for we knew it would not last long.

My guesses were very nearly correct. Otto Lindenschmidt had been educated by an old Baron, Bernhard von Herisau, on account of his resemblance in person to a dead son, whose name had also been Otto.

He could not have adopted the plebeian youth, at least to the extent of giving him an old and haughty name, but this the latter nevertheless expected, up to the time of the Baron's death. He had inherited a little property from his benefactor, but soon ran through it. "He was a lightheaded fellow," said Johann Helm, "but he knew how to get the confidence of the old Junkers. If he hadn't been so cowardly and fidgety, he might have made himself a career."

The Polish episode differed so little from my interpretation that I need not repeat Helm's version. He denied having stolen Otto's share of the money, but could not help admitting his possession of the Von Herisau papers, among which were the certificates of birth and baptism of the old Baron's son, Otto. It seems that he had been fearful of Lindenschmidt's return from America, for he managed to communicate with his sister in Breslau, and in this way learned the former's death. Not until then had he dared to assume his present disguise.

We let him go, after exacting a solemn pledge that he would betake himself at once to Hamburg, and there ship for Australia. (I judged that America was already amply supplied with individuals of his class.) The sudden departure of the Baron von Herisau was a two days' wonder at Liebenstein; but besides ourselves, only the Bremen banker knew the secret. He also left, two days afterwards, with his wife and daughter—their cases, it was reported, requiring Kissingen.

Otto Lindenschmidt's life, therefore, could not hide itself. Can any life?

# TWIN-LOVE

When John Vincent, after waiting twelve years, married Phebe Etheridge, the whole neighborhood experienced that sense of relief and satisfaction which follows the triumph of the right. Not that the fact of a true love is ever generally recognized and respected when it is first discovered; for there is a perverse quality in American human nature which will not accept the existence of any fine, unselfish passion, until it has been tested and established beyond peradventure. There were two views of the case when John Vincent's love for Phebe, and old Reuben Etheridge's hard prohibition of the match, first became known to the community. The girls and boys, and some of the matrons, ranged themselves at once on the side of the lovers, but a large majority of the older men and a few of the younger supported the tyrannical father.

Reuben Etheridge was rich, and, in addition to what his daughter would naturally inherit from him, she already possessed more than her lover, at the time of their betrothal. This in the eyes of one class was a sufficient reason for the father's hostility. When low natures live (as they almost invariably do) wholly in the present, they neither take tenderness from the past nor warning from the possibilities of the future. It is the exceptional men and women who remember their youth. So, these lovers received a nearly equal amount of sympathy and condemnation; and only slowly, partly through their quiet fidelity and patience, and partly through the improvement in John Vincent's worldly circumstances, was the balance changed. Old Reuben remained an unflinching despot to the last: if any relenting softness touched his heart, he sternly concealed it; and such inference as could be drawn from the fact that he, certainly knowing what would follow his death, bequeathed his daughter her proper share of his goods, was all that could be taken for consent.

They were married: John, a grave man in middle age, weather-beaten and worn by years of hard work and self-denial, yet not beyond the restoration of a milder second youth; and Phebe a sad, weary woman, whose warmth of longing had been exhausted, from whom youth and its uncalculating surrenders of hope and feeling had gone forever. They began their wedded life under the shadow of the death out of which it grew; and when, after a ceremony in which neither bridesmaid nor groomsman stood by their side, they united their divided homes, it seemed to their neighbors that a separated husband and wife had come together again, not that the relation was new to either.

John Vincent loved his wife with the tenderness of an innocent man, but all his tenderness could not avail to lift the weight of settled melancholy which had gathered upon her. Disappointment, waiting, yearning, indulgence in long lament and self-pity, the morbid cultivation of unhappy fancies—all this had wrought its work upon her, and it was too late to effect a cure. In the night she awoke to weep at his side, because of the years when she had awakened to weep alone; by day she kept up her old habit of foreboding, although the evening steadily refuted the morning; and there were times when, without any apparent cause, she would fall into a dark, despairing mood which her husband's greatest care and cunning could only slowly dispel.

Two or three years passed, and new life came to the Vincent farm. One day, between midnight and dawn, the family pair was doubled; the cry of twin sons was heard in the hushed house. The father restrained his happy wonder in his concern for the imperilled life of the mother; he guessed that she had anticipated death, and she now hung by a thread so slight that her simple will might snap it. But her will, fortunately, was as faint as her consciousness; she gradually drifted out of danger, taking her returning strength with a passive acquiescence rather than with joy. She was hardly paler than her wont, but the lurking shadow seemed to have vanished from her eyes, and John Vincent felt that her features had assumed a new expression, the faintly perceptible stamp of some spiritual change.

It was a happy day for him when, propped against his breast and gently held by his warm, strong arm, the twin boys were first brought to be laid upon her lap. Two staring, dark-faced creatures, with restless fists and feet, they were alike in every least feature of their grotesque animality. Phebe placed a hand under the head of each, and looked at them for a long time in silence.

"Why is this?" she said, at last, taking hold of a narrow pink ribbon, which was tied around the wrist of one.

"He's the oldest, sure," the nurse answered. "Only by fifteen minutes or so, but it generally makes a difference when twins come to be named; and you may see with your own eyes that there's no telling of 'em apart otherways."

"Take off the ribbon, then," said Phebe quietly; "*I* know them."

"Why, ma'am, it's always done, where they're so like! And I'll never be able to tell which is which; for they sleep and wake and feed by the same clock. And you might mistake, after all, in giving 'em names—"

"There is no oldest or youngest, John; they are two and yet one: this is mine, and this is yours."

"I see no difference at all, Phebe," said John; "and how can we divide them?"

"We will not divide," she answered; "I only meant it as a sign."

She smiled, for the first time in many days. He was glad of heart, but did not understand her. "What shall we call them?" he asked. "Elias and Reuben, after our fathers?"

"No, John; their names must be David and Jonathan."

And so they were called. And they grew, not less, but more alike, in passing through the stages of babyhood. The ribbon of the older one had been removed, and the nurse would have been distracted, but for Phebe's almost miraculous instinct. The former comforted herself with the hope that teething would bring a variation to the two identical mouths; but no! they teethed as one child. John, after desperate attempts, which always failed in spite of the headaches they gave him, postponed the idea of distinguishing one from the other, until they should be old enough to develop some dissimilarity of speech, or gait, or habit. All trouble might have been avoided, had Phebe consented to the least variation in their dresses; but herein she was mildly immovable.

"Not yet," was her set reply to her husband; and one day, when he manifested a little annoyance at her persistence, she turned to him, holding a child on each knee, and said with a gravity which silenced him thenceforth: "John, can you not see that our burden has passed into them? Is there no meaning in this—that two children who are one in body and face and nature, should be given to us at our time of life, after such long disappointment and trouble? Our lives were held apart; theirs were united before they were born, and I dare not turn them in different directions. Perhaps I do not know all that the Lord intended to say to us, in sending them; but His hand is here!"

"I was only thinking of their good," John meekly answered. "If they are spared to grow up, there must be some way of knowing one from the other."

"THEY will not need it, and I, too, think only of them. They have taken the cross from my heart, and I will lay none on theirs. I am reconciled to my life through them, John; you have been very patient and good with me, and I will yield to you in all things but in this. I do not think I shall live to see them as men grown; yet, while we are together, I feel clearly what it is right to do. Can you not, just once, have a little faith without knowledge, John?"

"I'll try, Phebe," he said. "Any way, I'll grant that the boys belong to you more than to me."

Phebe Vincent's character had verily changed. Her attacks of semi-hysterical despondency never returned; her gloomy prophecies ceased. She was still grave, and the trouble of so many years never wholly vanished from her face; but she performed every duty of her life with at least a quiet willingness, and her home became the abode of peace; for passive content wears longer than demonstrative happiness.

David and Jonathan grew as one boy: the taste and temper of one was repeated in the other, even as the voice and features. Sleeping or waking, grieved or joyous, well or ill, they lived a single life, and it seemed so natural for one to answer to the other's name, that they probably would have themselves confused their own identities, but for their mother's unerring knowledge. Perhaps unconsciously guided by her, perhaps through the voluntary action of their own natures, each quietly took the other's place when called upon, even to the sharing of praise or blame at school, the friendships and quarrels of the playground. They were healthy and happy lads, and John Vincent was accustomed to say to his neighbors, "They're no more trouble than one would be; and yet they're four hands instead of two."

Phebe died when they were fourteen, saying to them, with almost her latest breath, "Be one, always!" Before her husband could decide whether to change her plan of domestic education, they were passing out of boyhood, changing in voice, stature, and character with a continued likeness which bewildered and almost terrified him. He procured garments of different colors, but they were accustomed to wear each article in common, and the result was only a mixture of tints for both. They were sent to different schools, to be returned the next day, equally pale, suffering, and incapable of study. Whatever device was employed, they evaded it by a mutual instinct which rendered all external measures unavailing. To John Vincent's mind their resemblance was an accidental misfortune, which had been confirmed through their mother's fancy. He felt that they were bound by some deep, mysterious tie, which, inasmuch as it might interfere with all practical aspects of life, ought to be gradually weakened. Two bodies, to him, implied two distinct men, and it was wrong to permit a mutual dependence which prevented either from exercising his own separate will and judgment.

But, while he was planning and pondering, the boys became young men, and he was an old man. Old, and prematurely broken; for he had worked much, borne much, and his large frame held only a moderate measure of vital force. A great weariness fell upon him, and his powers began to give way, at first slowly, but then with accelerated failure. He saw the end coming, long before his sons suspected it; his doubt, for their sakes, was the only thing which made it unwelcome. It was "upon his mind" (as his Quaker neighbors would say) to speak to them of the future, and at last the proper moment came.

It was a stormy November evening. Wind and rain whirled and drove among the trees outside, but the sitting-room of the old farm-house was bright and warm. David and Jonathan, at the table, with their arms over each other's backs and their brown locks mixed together, read from the same book: their father sat in the ancient rocking-chair before the fire, with his feet upon a stool. The housekeeper and hired man had gone to bed, and all was still in the house.

John waited until he heard the volume closed, and then spoke.

"Boys," he said, "let me have a bit of talk with you. I don't seem to get over my ailments rightly,—never will, maybe. A man must think of things while there's time, and say them when they HAVE to be said. I don't know as there's any particular hurry in my case; only, we never can tell, from one day to another. When I die, every thing will belong to you two, share and share alike, either to buy another farm with the money out, or divide this: I won't tie you up in any way. But two of you will need two farms for two families; for you won't have to wait twelve years, like your mother and me."

"We don't want another farm, father!" said David and Jonathan together.

"I know you don't think so, now. A wife seemed far enough off from me when I was your age. You've always been satisfied to be with each other, but that can't last. It was partly your mother's notion; I remember her saying that our burden had passed into you. I never quite understood what she meant, but I suppose it must rather be the opposite of what WE had to bear."

The twins listened with breathless attention while their father, suddenly stirred by the past, told them the story of his long betrothal.

"And now," he exclaimed, in conclusion, "it may be putting wild ideas into your two heads, but I must say it! THAT was where I did wrong— wrong to her and to me,—in waiting! I had no right to spoil the best of our lives; I ought to have gone boldly, in broad day, to her father's house, taken her by the hand, and led her forth to be my wife. Boys, if either of you comes to love a woman truly, and she to love you, and there is no reason why God (I don't say man) should put you asunder, do as I ought to have done, not as I did! And, maybe, this advice is the best legacy I can leave you."

"But, father," said David, speaking for both, "we have never thought of marrying."

"Likely enough," their father answered; "we hardly ever think of what surely comes. But to me, looking back, it's plain. And this is the reason why I want you to make me a promise, and as solemn as if I was on my death-bed. Maybe I shall be, soon."

Tears gathered in the eyes of the twins. "What is it, father?" they both said.

"Nothing at all to any other two boys, but I don't know how YOU'll take it. What if I was to ask you to live apart for a while?"

"Oh father!" both cried. They leaned together, cheek pressing cheek, and hand clasping hand, growing white and trembling. John Vincent, gazing into the fire, did not see their faces, or his purpose might have been shaken.

"I don't say NOW," he went on. "After a while, when—well, when I'm dead. And I only mean a beginning, to help you toward what HAS to be. Only a month; I don't want to seem hard to you; but that's little, in all conscience. Give me your word: say, 'For mother's sake!'"

There was a long pause. Then David and Jonathan said, in low, faltering voices, "For mother's sake, I promise."

"Remember that you were only boys to her. She might have made all this seem easier, for women have reasons for things no man can answer. Mind, within a year after I'm gone!"

He rose and tottered out of the room.

The twins looked at each other: David said, "Must we?" and Jonathan, "How can we?" Then they both thought, "It may be a long while yet." Here was a present comfort, and each seemed to hold it firmly in holding the hand of the other, as they fell asleep side by side.

The trial was nearer than they imagined. Their father died before the winter was over; the farm and other property was theirs, and they might have allowed life to solve its mysteries as it rolled onwards, but for their promise to the dead. This must be fulfilled, and then—one thing was certain; they would never again separate.

"The sooner the better," said David. "It shall be the visit to our uncle and cousins in Indiana. You will come with me as far as Harrisburg; it may be easier to part there than here. And our new neighbors, the Bradleys, will want your help for a day or two, after getting home."

"It is less than death," Jonathan answered, "and why should it seem to be more? We must think of father and mother, and all those twelve years; now I know what the burden was."

"And we have never really borne any part of it! Father must have been right in forcing us to promise."

Every day the discussion was resumed, and always with the same termination. Familiarity with the inevitable step gave them increase of courage; yet, when the moment had come and gone, when, speeding on opposite trains, the hills and valleys multiplied between them with terrible velocity, a pang like death cut to the heart of each, and the divided life became a chill, oppressive dream.

During the separation no letters passed between them. When the neighbors asked Jonathan for news of his brother, he always replied, "He is well," and avoided further speech with such evidence of pain that they spared him. An hour before the month drew to an end, he walked forth alone, taking the road to the nearest railway station. A stranger who passed him at the entrance of a thick wood, three miles from home, was thunderstruck on meeting the same person shortly after, entering the wood from the other side; but the farmers in the near fields saw two figures issuing from the shade, hand in hand.

Each knew the other's month, before they slept, and the last thing Jonathan said, with his head on David's shoulder, was, "You must know our neighbors, the Bradleys, and especially Ruth." In the morning, as they dressed, taking each other's garments at random, as of old, Jonathan again said, "I have never seen a girl that I like so well as Ruth Bradley. Do you remember what father said about loving and marrying? It comes into my mind whenever I see Ruth; but she has no sister."

"But we need not both marry," David replied, "that might part us, and this will not. It is for always now."

"For always, David."

Two or three days later Jonathan said, as he started on an errand to the village: "I shall stop at the Bradleys this evening, so you must walk across and meet me there."

When David approached the house, a slender, girlish figure, with her back towards him, was stooping over a bush of great crimson roses, cautiously clipping a blossom here and there. At the click of the gate-latch she started and turned towards him. Her light gingham bonnet, falling back, disclosed a long oval face, fair and delicate, sweet brown eyes, and brown hair laid smoothly over the temples. A soft flush rose suddenly to her cheeks, and he felt that his own were burning.

"Oh Jonathan!" she exclaimed, transferring the roses to her left hand, and extending her right, as she came forward.

He was too accustomed to the name to recognize her mistake at once, and the word "Ruth!" came naturally to his lips.

"I should know your brother David has come," she then said; "even if I had not heard so. You look so bright. How glad I am!"

"Is he not here?" David asked.

"No; but there he is now, surely!" She turned towards the lane, where Jonathan was dismounting. "Why, it is yourself over again, Jonathan!"

As they approached, a glance passed between the twins, and a secret transfer of the riding-whip to David set their identity right with Ruth, whose manner toward the latter innocently became shy with all its friendliness, while her frank, familiar speech was given to Jonathan, as was fitting. But David also took the latter to himself, and when they left, Ruth had apparently forgotten that there was any difference in the length of their acquaintance.

On their way homewards David said: "Father was right. We must marry, like others, and Ruth is the wife for us,—I mean for you, Jonathan. Yes, we must learn to say MINE and YOURS, after all, when we speak of her."

"Even she cannot separate us, it seems," Jonathan answered. "We must give her some sign, and that will also be a sign for others. It will seem strange to divide ourselves; we can never learn it properly; rather let us not think of marriage."

"We cannot help thinking of it; she stands in mother's place now, as we in father's."

Then both became silent and thoughtful. They felt that something threatened to disturb what seemed to be the only possible life for them, yet were unable to distinguish its features, and therefore powerless to resist it. The same instinct which had been born of their wonderful spiritual likeness told them that Ruth Bradley already loved Jonathan: the duty was established, and they must conform their lives to it. There was, however, this slight difference between their natures—that David was generally the first to utter the thought which came to the minds of both. So when he said,

"We shall learn what to do when the need comes," it was a postponement of all foreboding. They drifted contentedly towards the coming change.

The days went by, and their visits to Ruth Bradley were continued. Sometimes Jonathan went alone, but they were usually together, and the tie which united the three became dearer and sweeter as it was more closely drawn. Ruth learned to distinguish between the two when they were before her: at least she said so, and they were willing to believe it. But she was hardly aware how nearly alike was the happy warmth in her bosom produced by either pair of dark gray eyes and the soft half-smile which played around either mouth. To them she seemed to be drawn within the mystic circle which separated them from others—she, alone; and they no longer imagined a life in which she should not share.

Then the inevitable step was taken. Jonathan declared his love, and was answered. Alas! he almost forgot David that late summer evening, as they sat in the moonlight, and over and over again assured each other how dear they had grown. He felt the trouble in David's heart when they met.

"Ruth is ours, and I bring her kiss to you," he said, pressing his lips to David's; but the arms flung around him trembled, and David whispered, "Now the change begins."

"Oh, this cannot be our burden!" Jonathan cried, with all the rapture still warm in his heart.

"If it is, it will be light, or heavy, or none at all, as we shall bear it," David answered, with a smile of infinite tenderness.

For several days he allowed Jonathan to visit the Bradley farm alone, saying that it must be so on Ruth's account. Her love, he declared, must give her the fine instinct which only their mother had ever possessed, and he must allow it time to be confirmed. Jonathan, however, insisted that Ruth already possessed it; that she was beginning to wonder at his absence, and to fear that she would not be entirely welcome to the home which must always be equally his.

David yielded at once.

"You must go alone," said Jonathan, "to satisfy yourself that she knows us at last."

Ruth came forth from the house as he drew near. Her face beamed; she laid her hands upon his shoulders and kissed him. "Now you cannot doubt me, Ruth!" he said, gently.

"Doubt you, Jonathan!" she exclaimed with a fond reproach in her eyes. "But you look troubled; is any thing the matter?"

"I was thinking of my brother," said David, in a low tone.

"Tell me what it is," she said, drawing him into the little arbor of woodbine near the gate. They took seats side by side on the rustic bench. "He thinks I may come between you: is it not that?" she asked. Only one thing was clear to David's mind—that she would surely speak more frankly and freely of him to the supposed Jonathan than to his real self. This once he would permit the illusion.

"Not more than must be," he answered. "He knew all from the very beginning. But we have been like one person in two bodies, and any change seems to divide us."

"I feel as you do," said Ruth. "I would never consent to be your wife, if I could really divide you. I love you both too well for that."

"Do you love me?" he asked, entirely forgetting his representative part.

Again the reproachful look, which faded away as she met his eyes. She fell upon his breast, and gave him kisses which were answered with equal tenderness. Suddenly he covered his face with his hands, and burst into a passion of tears.

"Jonathan! Oh Jonathan!" she cried, weeping with alarm and sympathetic pain.

It was long before he could speak; but at last, turning away his head, he faltered, "I am David!"

There was a long silence.

When he looked up she was sitting with her hands rigidly clasped in her lap: her face was very pale.

"There it is, Ruth," he said; "we are one heart and one soul. Could he love, and not I? You cannot decide between us, for one is the other. If I had known you first, Jonathan would be now in my place. What follows, then?"

"No marriage," she whispered.

"No!" he answered; "we brothers must learn to be two men instead of one. You will partly take my place with Jonathan; I must live with half my life, unless I can find, somewhere in the world, your other half."

"I cannot part you, David!"

"Something stronger than you or me parts us, Ruth. If it were death, we should bow to God's will: well, it can no more be got away from than death or judgment. Say no more: the pattern of all this was drawn long before we were born, and we cannot do any thing but work it out."

He rose and stood before her. "Remember this, Ruth," he said; "it is no blame in us to love each other. Jonathan will see the truth in my face when we meet, and I speak for him also. You will not see me again until your wedding-day, and then no more afterwards—but, yes! ONCE, in some far-off time, when you shall know me to be David, and still give me the kiss you gave to-day."

"Ah, after death!" she thought: "I have parted them forever." She was about to rise, but fell upon the seat again, fainting. At the same moment Jonathan appeared at David's side.

No word was said. They bore her forth and supported her between them until the fresh breeze had restored her to consciousness. Her first glance rested on the brother's hands, clasping; then, looking from one to the other, she saw that the cheeks of both were wet.

"Now, leave me," she said, "but come to-morrow, Jonathan!" Even then she turned from one to the other, with a painful, touching uncertainty, and stretched out both hands to them in farewell.

How that poor twin heart struggled with itself is only known to God. All human voices, and as they believed, also the Divine Voice, commanded the division of their interwoven life. Submission would have seemed easier, could they have taken up equal and similar burdens; but David was unable to deny that his pack was overweighted. For the first time, their thoughts began to diverge.

At last David said: "For mother's sake, Jonathan, as we promised. She always called you HER child. And for Ruth's sake, and father's last advice: they all tell me what I must do."

It was like the struggle between will and desire, in the same nature, and none the less fierce or prolonged because the softer quality foresaw its ultimate surrender. Long after he felt the step to be inevitable, Jonathan sought to postpone it, but he was borne by all combined influences nearer and nearer to the time.

And now the wedding-day came. David was to leave home the same evening, after the family dinner under his father's roof. In the morning he said to Jonathan: "I shall not write until I feel that I have become other than now, but I shall always be here, in you, as you will be in me, everywhere. Whenever you want me, I shall know it; and I think I shall know when to return."

The hearts of all the people went out towards them as they stood together in the little village church. Both were calm, but very pale and abstracted in their expression, yet their marvellous likeness was still unchanged. Ruth's eyes were cast down so they could not be seen; she trembled visibly, and her voice was scarcely audible when she spoke the vow. It was only known in the neighborhood that David was going to make another journey. The truth could hardly have been guessed by persons whose ideas follow the narrow round of their own experiences; had it been, there would probably have been more condemnation than sympathy. But in a vague way the presence of some deeper element was felt—the falling of a shadow, although the outstretched wing was unseen. Far above them, and above the shadow, watched the Infinite Pity, which was not denied to three hearts that day.

It was a long time, more than a year, and Ruth was lulling her first child on her bosom, before a letter came from David. He had wandered westwards, purchased some lands on the outer line of settlement, and appeared to be leading a wild and lonely life. "I know now," he wrote, "just how much there is to bear, and how to bear it. Strange men come between us, but you are not far off when I am alone on these plains. There is a place where I can always meet you, and I know that you have found it,—under the big ash-tree by the barn. I think I am nearly always there about sundown, and on moonshiny nights, because we are then nearest together; and I never sleep without leaving you half my blanket. When I first begin to wake I always feel your breath, so we are never really parted for long. I do not know that I can change much; it is not easy; it is like making up your mind to have different colored eyes and hair, and I can only get sunburnt and wear a full beard. But we are hardly as unhappy as we feared to be; mother came the other night, in a dream, and took us on her knees. Oh, come to me, Jonathan, but for one day! No, you will not find me; I am going across the Plains!"

And Jonathan and Ruth? They loved each other tenderly; no external trouble visited them; their home was peaceful and pure; and yet, every room and stairway and chair was haunted by a sorrowful ghost. As a neighbor said after visiting them, "There seemed to be something lost." Ruth saw how constantly and how unconsciously Jonathan turned to see his own every feeling reflected in the missing eyes; how his hand sought another, even while its fellow pressed hers; how half-spoken words, day and night, died upon his lips, because they could not reach the twin-ear. She knew not how it came, but her own nature took upon itself the same habit. She felt that she received a less measure of love than she gave—not from Jonathan, in whose whole, warm, transparent heart no other woman had ever looked, but something of her own passed beyond him and never returned. To both their life was like one of those conjurer's cups, seemingly filled with red wine, which is held from the lips by the false crystal hollow.

Neither spoke of this: neither dared to speak. The years dragged out their slow length, with rare and brief messages from David. Three children were in the house, and still peace and plenty laid their signs upon its lintels. But at last Ruth, who had been growing thinner and paler ever since the birth of her first boy, became seriously ill. Consumption was hers by inheritance, and it now manifested itself in a form which too surely foretold the result. After the physician had gone, leaving his fatal verdict behind him, she called to Jonathan, who, bewildered by his grief, sank down on his knees at her bedside and sobbed upon her breast.

"Don't grieve," she said; "this is my share of the burden. If I have taken too much from you and David, now comes the atonement. Many things have grown clear to me. David was right when he said that there was no blame. But my time is even less than the doctor thinks: where is David? Can you not bid him come?"

"I can only call him with my heart," he answered. "And will he hear me now, after nearly seven years?"

"Call, then!" she eagerly cried. "Call with all the strength of your love for him and for me, and I believe he will hear you!"

The sun was just setting. Jonathan went to the great ash-tree, behind the barn, fell upon his knees, and covered his face, and the sense of an exceeding bitter cry filled his heart. All the suppressed and baffled longing, the want, the hunger, the unremitting pain of years, came upon him and were crowded into the single prayer, "Come, David, or I die!" Before the twilight faded, while he was still kneeling, an arm came upon his shoulder, and the faint touch of another cheek upon his own. It was hardly for the space of a thought, but he knew the sign.

"David will come!" he said to Ruth.

From that day all was changed. The cloud of coming death which hung over the house was transmuted into fleecy gold. All the lost life came back to Jonathan's face, all the unrestful sweetness of Ruth's brightened into a serene beatitude. Months had passed since David had been heard from; they knew not how to reach him without many delays; yet neither dreamed of doubting his coming.

Two weeks passed, three, and there was neither word nor sign. Jonathan and Ruth thought, "He is near," and one day a singular unrest fell upon the former. Ruth saw it, but said nothing until night came, when she sent Jonathan from her bedside with the words, "Go and meet him?"

An hour afterwards she heard double steps on the stone walk in front of the house. They came slowly to the door; it opened; she heard them along the hall and ascending the stairs; then the chamber-lamp showed her the two faces, bright with a single, unutterable joy.

One brother paused at the foot of the bed; the other drew near and bent over her. She clasped her thin hands around his neck, kissed him fondly, and cried, "Dear, dear David!"

"Dear Ruth," he said, "I came as soon as I could. I was far away, among wild mountains, when I felt that Jonathan was calling me. I knew that I must return, never to leave you more, and there was still a little work to finish. Now we shall all live again!"

"Yes," said Jonathan, coming to her other side, "try to live, Ruth!"

Her voice came clear, strong, and full of authority. "I DO live, as never before. I shall take all my life with me when I go to wait for one soul, as I shall find it there! Our love unites, not divides, from this hour!"

The few weeks still left to her were a season of almost superhuman peace. She faded slowly and painlessly, taking the equal love of the twin-hearts, and giving an equal tenderness and gratitude. Then first she saw the mysterious need which united them, the fulness and joy wherewith each completed himself in the other. All the imperfect past was enlightened, and the end, even that now so near, was very good.

Every afternoon they carried her down to a cushioned chair on the veranda, where she could enjoy the quiet of the sunny landscape, the presence of the brothers seated at her feet, and the sports of her children on the grass. Thus, one day, while David and Jonathan held her hands and waited for her to wake from a happy sleep, she went before them, and, ere they guessed the truth, she was waiting for their one soul in the undiscovered land.

And Jonathan's children, now growing into manhood and girlhood, also call David "father." The marks left by their divided lives have long since vanished from their faces; the middle-aged men, whose hairs are turning gray, still walk hand in hand, still sleep upon the same pillow, still have their common wardrobe, as when they were boys. They talk of "our Ruth" with no sadness, for they believe that death will make them one, when, at the same moment, he summons both. And we who know them, to whom they have confided the touching mystery of their nature, believe so too.

# THE EXPERIENCES OF THE A. C.

"Bridgeport! Change cars for the Naugatuck Railroad!" shouted the conductor of the New York and Boston Express Train, on the evening of May 27th, 1858. Indeed, he does it every night (Sundays excepted), for that matter; but as this story refers especially to Mr. J. Edward Johnson, who was a passenger on that train, on the aforesaid evening, I make special mention of the fact. Mr. Johnson, carpet-bag in hand, jumped upon the platform, entered the office, purchased a ticket for Waterbury, and was soon whirling in the Naugatuck train towards his destination.

On reaching Waterbury, in the soft spring twilight, Mr. Johnson walked up and down in front of the station, curiously scanning the faces of the assembled crowd. Presently he noticed a gentleman who was performing the same operation upon the faces of the alighting passengers. Throwing himself directly in the way of the latter, the two exchanged a steady gaze.

"Is your name Billings?" "Is your name Johnson?" were simultaneous questions, followed by the simultaneous exclamations—"Ned!" "Enos!"

Then there was a crushing grasp of hands, repeated after a pause, in testimony of ancient friendship, and Mr. Billings, returning to practical life, asked—

"Is that all your baggage? Come, I have a buggy here: Eunice has heard the whistle, and she'll be impatient to welcome you."

The impatience of Eunice (Mrs. Billings, of course,) was not of long duration, for in five minutes thereafter she stood at the door of her husband's chocolate-colored villa, receiving his friend.

While these three persons are comfortably seated at the tea-table, enjoying their waffles, cold tongue, and canned peaches, and asking and answering questions helter-skelter in the delightful confusion of reunion after long separation, let us briefly inform the reader who and what they are.

Mr. Enos Billings, then, was part owner of a manufactory of metal buttons, forty years old, of middling height, ordinarily quiet and rather shy, but with a large share of latent warmth and enthusiasm in his nature.

His hair was brown, slightly streaked with gray, his eyes a soft, dark hazel, forehead square, eyebrows straight, nose of no very marked character, and a mouth moderately full, with a tendency to twitch a little at the corners. His voice was undertoned, but mellow and agreeable.

Mrs. Eunice Billings, of nearly equal age, was a good specimen of the wide-awake New-England woman. Her face had a piquant smartness of expression, which might have been refined into a sharp edge, but for her natural hearty good-humor. Her head was smoothly formed, her face a full oval, her hair and eyes blond and blue in a strong light, but brown and steel-gray at other times, and her complexion of that ripe fairness into which a ruddier color will sometimes fade. Her form, neither plump nor square, had yet a firm, elastic compactness, and her slightest movement conveyed a certain impression of decision and self-reliance.

As for J. Edward Johnson, it is enough to say that he was a tall, thin gentleman of forty-five, with an aquiline nose, narrow face, and military whiskers, which swooped upwards and met under his nose in a glossy black mustache. His complexion was dark, from the bronzing of fifteen summers in New Orleans. He was a member of a wholesale hardware firm in that city, and had now revisited his native North for the first time since his departure. A year before, some letters relating to invoices of metal buttons signed, "Foster, Kirkup, & Co., per Enos Billings," had accidentally revealed to him the whereabouts of the old friend of his youth, with whom we now find him domiciled. The first thing he did, after attending to some necessary business matters in New York, was to take the train for Waterbury.

"Enos," said he, as he stretched out his hand for the third cup of tea (which he had taken only for the purpose of prolonging the pleasant table-chat), "I wonder which of us is most changed."

"You, of course," said Mr. Billings, "with your brown face and big mustache. Your own brother wouldn't have known you if he had seen you last, as I did, with smooth cheeks and hair of unmerciful length. Why, not even your voice is the same!"

"That is easily accounted for," replied Mr. Johnson. "But in your case, Enos, I am puzzled to find where the difference lies. Your features seem to be but little changed, now that I can examine them at leisure; yet it is not the same face. But, really, I never looked at you for so long a time, in those days. I beg pardon; you used to be so—so remarkably shy."

Mr. Billings blushed slightly, and seemed at a loss what to answer.

His wife, however, burst into a merry laugh, exclaiming—

"Oh, that was before the days of the A. C!"

He, catching the infection, laughed also; in fact Mr. Johnson laughed, but without knowing why.

"The 'A. C.'!" said Mr. Billings. "Bless me, Eunice! how long it is since we have talked of that summer! I had almost forgotten that there ever was an A. C."

"Enos, COULD you ever forget Abel Mallory and the beer?—or that scene between Hollins and Shelldrake?—or" (here SHE blushed the least bit) "your own fit of candor?" And she laughed again, more heartily than ever.

"What a precious lot of fools, to be sure!" exclaimed her husband.

Mr. Johnson, meanwhile, though enjoying the cheerful humor of his hosts, was not a little puzzled with regard to its cause.

"What is the A. C.?" he ventured to ask.

Mr. and Mrs. Billings looked at each other, and smiled without replying.

"Really, Ned," said the former, finally, "the answer to your question involves the whole story."

"Then why not tell him the whole story, Enos?" remarked his wife.

"You know I've never told it yet, and it's rather a hard thing to do, seeing that I'm one of the heroes of the farce—for it wasn't even genteel comedy, Ned," said Mr. Billings. "However," he continued, "absurd as the story may seem, it's the only key to the change in my life, and I must run the risk of being laughed at."

"I'll help you through, Enos," said his wife, encouragingly; "and besides, my role in the farce was no better than yours. Let us resuscitate, for to-night only, the constitution of the A. C."

"Upon my word, a capital idea! But we shall have to initiate Ned."

Mr. Johnson merrily agreeing, he was blindfolded and conducted into another room. A heavy arm-chair, rolling on casters, struck his legs in the rear, and he sank into it with lamb-like resignation.

"Open your mouth!" was the command, given with mock solemnity.

He obeyed.

"Now shut it!"

And his lips closed upon a cigar, while at the same time the handkerchief was whisked away from his eyes. He found himself in Mr. Billing's library.

"Your nose betrays your taste, Mr. Johnson," said the lady, "and I am not hard-hearted enough to deprive you of the indulgence. Here are matches."

"Well," said he, acting upon the hint, "if the remainder of the ceremonies are equally agreeable, I should like to be a permanent member of your order."

By this time Mr. and Mrs. Billings, having between them lighted the lamp, stirred up the coal in the grate, closed the doors, and taken possession of comfortable chairs, the latter proclaimed—

"The Chapter (isn't that what you call it?) will now be held!"

"Was it in '43 when you left home, Ned?" asked Mr. B.

"Yes."

"Well, the A. C. culminated in '45. You remember something of the society of Norridgeport, the last winter you were there? Abel Mallory, for instance?"

"Let me think a moment," said Mr. Johnson reflectively. "Really, it seems like looking back a hundred years. Mallory—wasn't that the sentimental young man, with wispy hair, a tallowy skin, and big, sweaty hands, who used to be spouting Carlyle on the 'reading evenings' at Shelldrake's? Yes, to be sure; and there was Hollins, with his clerical face and infidel talk,—and Pauline Ringtop, who used to say, 'The Beautiful is the Good.' I can still hear her shrill voice, singing, 'Would that *I* were beautiful, would that *I* were fair!'"

There was a hearty chorus of laughter at poor Miss Ringtop's expense. It harmed no one, however; for the tar-weed was already thick over her Californian grave.

"Oh, I see," said Mr. Billings, "you still remember the absurdities of those days. In fact, I think you partially saw through them then. But I was younger, and far from being so clear-headed, and I looked upon those evenings at Shelldrake's as being equal, at least, to the symposia of Plato. Something in Mallory always repelled me. I detested the sight of his thick nose, with the flaring nostrils, and his coarse, half-formed lips, of the bluish color of raw corned-beef. But I looked upon these feelings as unreasonable prejudices, and strove to conquer them, seeing the admiration which he received from others. He was an oracle on the subject of 'Nature.' Having eaten nothing for two years, except Graham bread, vegetables without salt, and fruits, fresh or dried, he considered himself to have attained an antediluvian purity of health—or that he would attain it, so soon as two pimples on his left temple should have healed. These pimples he looked upon as the last feeble stand made by the pernicious juices left from the meat he had formerly eaten and the coffee he had drunk. His theory was, that through a body so purged and purified none but true and natural impulses could find access to the soul. Such, indeed, was the theory we all held. A Return to Nature was the near Millennium, the dawn of which we already beheld in the sky. To be sure there was a difference in our individual views as to how this should be achieved, but we were all agreed as to what the result should be.

"I can laugh over those days now, Ned; but they were really happy while they lasted. We were the salt of the earth; we were lifted above those grovelling instincts which we saw manifested in the lives of others. Each contributed his share of gas to inflate the painted balloon to which we all clung, in the expectation that it would presently soar with us to the stars. But it only went up over the out-houses, dodged backwards and forwards two or three times, and finally flopped down with us into a swamp."

"And that balloon was the A. C.?" suggested Mr. Johnson.

"As President of this Chapter, I prohibit questions," said Eunice. "And, Enos, don't send up your balloon until the proper time. Don't anticipate the programme, or the performance will be spoiled."

"I had almost forgotten that Ned is so much in the dark," her obedient husband answered. "You can have but a slight notion," he continued, turning to his friend, "of the extent to which this sentimental, or transcendental, element in the little circle at Shelldrake's increased after you left Norridgeport. We read the 'Dial,' and Emerson; we believed in Alcott as the 'purple Plato' of modern times; we took psychological works out of the library, and would listen for hours to Hollins while he read Schelling or Fichte, and then go home with a misty impression of having imbibed infinite wisdom. It was, perhaps, a natural, though very eccentric rebound from the hard, practical, unimaginative New-England mind which surrounded us; yet I look back upon it with a kind of wonder. I was then, as you know, unformed mentally, and might have been so still, but for the experiences of the A. C."

Mr. Johnson shifted his position, a little impatiently. Eunice looked at him with laughing eyes, and shook her finger with a mock threat.

"Shelldrake," continued Mr. Billings, without noticing this by-play, "was a man of more pretence than real cultivation, as I afterwards discovered. He was in good circumstances, and always glad to receive us at his house, as this made him, virtually, the chief of our tribe, and the outlay for refreshments involved only the apples from his own orchard and water from his well. There was an entire absence of conventionality at our meetings, and this, compared with the somewhat stiff society of the village, was really an attraction. There was a mystic bond of union in our ideas: we discussed life, love, religion, and the future state, not only with the utmost candor, but with a warmth of feeling which, in many of us, was genuine. Even I (and you know how painfully shy and bashful I was) felt myself more at home there than in my father's house; and if I didn't talk much, I had a pleasant feeling of being in harmony with those who did.

"Well, 'twas in the early part of '45—I think in April,—when we were all gathered together, discussing, as usual, the possibility of leading a life in accordance with Nature. Abel Mallory was there, and Hollins, and Miss Ringtop, and Faith Levis, with her knitting,—and also Eunice Hazleton, a lady whom you have never seen, but you may take my wife at her representative—"

"Stick to the programme, Enos," interrupted Mrs. Billings.

"Eunice Hazleton, then. I wish I could recollect some of the speeches made on that occasion. Abel had but one pimple on his temple (there was a purple spot where the other had been), and was estimating that in two or three months more he would be a true, unspoiled man. His complexion, nevertheless, was more clammy and whey-like than ever.

"'Yes,' said he, 'I also am an Arcadian! This false dual existence which I have been leading will soon be merged in the unity of Nature. Our lives must conform to her sacred law. Why can't we strip off these hollow Shams,' (he made great use of that word,) 'and be our true selves, pure, perfect, and divine?'

"Miss Ringtop heaved a sigh, and repeated a stanza from her favorite poet:

"'*Ah, when wrecked are my desires*
*On the everlasting Never,*
*And my heart with all its fires*
*Out forever,*
*In the cradle of Creation*
*Finds the soul resuscitation!*

"Shelldrake, however, turning to his wife, said—

"'Elviry, how many up-stairs rooms is there in that house down on the Sound?'

"'Four,—besides three small ones under the roof. Why, what made you think of that, Jesse?' said she.

"'I've got an idea, while Abel's been talking,' he answered. 'We've taken a house for the summer, down the other side of Bridgeport, right on the water, where there's good fishing and a fine view of the Sound. Now, there's room enough for all of us—at least all that can make it suit to go. Abel, you and Enos, and Pauline and Eunice might fix matters so that we could all take the place in partnership, and pass the summer together, living a true and beautiful life in the bosom of Nature. There we shall be perfectly free and untrammelled by the chains which still hang around us in Norridgeport. You know how often we have wanted to be set on some island in the Pacific Ocean, where we could build up a true society, right from the start. Now, here's a chance to try the experiment for a few months, anyhow.'

"Eunice clapped her hands (yes, you did!) and cried out—

"'Splendid! Arcadian! I'll give up my school for the summer.'

"Miss Ringtop gave her opinion in another quotation:

"'*The rainbow hues of the Ideal*

*Condense to gems, and form the Real!'*

"Abel Mallory, of course, did not need to have the proposal repeated. He was ready for any thing which promised indulgence, and the indulgence of his sentimental tastes. I will do the fellow the justice to say that he was not a hypocrite. He firmly believed both in himself and his ideas—especially the former. He pushed both hands through the long wisps of his drab-colored hair, and threw his head back until his wide nostrils resembled a double door to his brain.

"'Oh Nature!' he said, 'you have found your lost children! We shall obey your neglected laws! we shall hearken to your divine whispers I we shall bring you back from your ignominious exile, and place you on your ancestral throne!'

"'Let us do it!' was the general cry.

"A sudden enthusiasm fired us, and we grasped each other's hands in the hearty impulse of the moment. My own private intention to make a summer trip to the White Mountains had been relinquished the moment I heard Eunice give in her adhesion. I may as well confess, at once, that I was desperately in love, and afraid to speak to her.

"By the time Mrs. Sheldrake brought in the apples and water we were discussing the plan as a settled thing. Hollins had an engagement to deliver Temperance lectures in Ohio during the summer, but decided to postpone his departure until August, so that he might, at least, spend two months with us. Faith Levis couldn't go—at which, I think, we were all secretly glad. Some three or four others were in the same case, and the company was finally arranged to consist of the Shelldrakes, Hollins, Mallory, Eunice,

Miss Ringtop, and myself. We did not give much thought, either to the preparations in advance, or to our mode of life when settled there. We were to live near to Nature: that was the main thing.

"'What shall we call the place?' asked Eunice.

"'Arcadia!' said Abel Mallory, rolling up his large green eyes.

"'Then,' said Hollins, 'let us constitute ourselves the Arcadian Club!'"

"Aha!" interrupted Mr. Johnson, "I see! The A. C.!"

"Yes, you can see the A. C. now," said Mrs. Billings; "but to understand it fully, you should have had a share in those Arcadian experiences."

"I am all the more interested in hearing them described. Go on, Enos."

"The proposition was adopted. We called ourselves The Arcadian Club; but in order to avoid gossip, and the usual ridicule, to which we were all more or less sensitive, in case our plan should become generally known, it was agreed that the initials only should be used. Besides, there was an agreeable air of mystery about it: we thought of Delphi, and Eleusis, and Samothrace: we should discover that Truth which the dim eyes of worldly men and women were unable to see, and the day of disclosure would be the day of Triumph. In one sense we were truly Arcadians: no suspicion of impropriety, I verily believe, entered any of our minds. In our aspirations after what we called a truer life there was no material taint. We were fools, if you choose, but as far as possible from being sinners. Besides, the characters of Mr. and Mrs. Shelldrake, who naturally became the heads of our proposed community were sufficient to preserve us from slander or suspicion, if even our designs had been publicly announced.

"I won't bore you with an account of our preparations. In fact, there was very little to be done. Mr. Shelldrake succeeded in hiring the house, with most of its furniture, so that but a few articles had to be supplied. My trunk contained more books than boots, more blank paper than linen.

"'Two shirts will be enough,' said Abel: 'you can wash one of them any day, and dry it in the sun.'

"The supplies consisted mostly of flour, potatoes, and sugar. There was a vegetable-garden in good condition, Mr. Shelldrake said, which would be our principal dependence.

"'Besides, the clams!' I exclaimed unthinkingly.

"'Oh, yes!' said Eunice, 'we can have chowder-parties: that will be delightful!'

"'Clams! chowder! oh, worse than flesh!' groaned Abel. 'Will you reverence Nature by outraging her first laws?'

"I had made a great mistake, and felt very foolish. Eunice and I looked at each other, for the first time."

"Speak for yourself only, Enos," gently interpolated his wife.

"It was a lovely afternoon in the beginning of June when we first approached Arcadia. We had taken two double teams at Bridgeport, and drove slowly forward to our destination, followed by a cart containing our trunks and a few household articles. It was a bright, balmy day: the wheat-fields were rich and green, the clover showed faint streaks of ruby mist along slopes leaning southward, and the meadows were yellow with buttercups. Now and then we caught glimpses of the Sound, and, far beyond it, the dim Long Island shore. Every old white farmhouse, with its gray-walled garden, its clumps of lilacs, viburnums, and early roses, offered us a picture of pastoral simplicity and repose. We passed them, one by one, in the happiest mood, enjoying the earth around us, the sky above, and ourselves most of all.

"The scenery, however, gradually became more rough and broken. Knobs of gray gneiss, crowned by mournful cedars, intrenched upon the arable land, and the dark-blue gleam of water appeared through the trees. Our road, which had been approaching the Sound, now skirted the head of a deep, irregular inlet, beyond which extended a beautiful promontory, thickly studded with cedars, and with scattering groups of elm, oak and maple trees. Towards the end of the promontory stood a house, with white walls shining against the blue line of the Sound.

"'There is Arcadia, at last!' exclaimed Mr. Shelldrake.

"A general outcry of delight greeted the announcement. And, indeed, the loveliness of the picture surpassed our most poetic anticipations. The low sun was throwing exquisite lights across the point, painting the slopes of grass of golden green, and giving a pearly softness to the gray rocks. In the back-ground was drawn the far-off water-line, over which a few specks of sail glimmered against the sky. Miss Ringtop, who, with Eunice, Mallory, and myself, occupied one carriage, expressed her 'gushing' feelings in the usual manner:

> "'Where the turf is softest, greenest,
> Doth an angel thrust me on,—
> Where the landscape lies serenest,
> In the journey of the sun!'

"'Don't, Pauline!' said Eunice; 'I never like to hear poetry flourished in the face of Nature. This landscape surpasses any poem in the world. Let us enjoy the best thing we have, rather than the next best.'

"'Ah, yes!' sighed Miss Ringtop, "tis true!

"'*They sing to the ear; this sings to the eye!*'

"Thenceforward, to the house, all was childish joy and jubilee. All minor personal repugnances were smoothed over in the general exultation. Even Abel Mallory became agreeable; and Hollins, sitting beside Mrs. Shelldrake on the back seat of the foremost carriage, shouted to us, in boyish lightness of heart.

"Passing the head of the inlet, we left the country-road, and entered, through a gate in the tottering stone wall, on our summer domain. A track, open to the field on one side, led us past a clump of deciduous trees, between pastures broken by cedared knolls of rock, down the centre of the peninsula, to the house. It was quite an old frame-building, two stories high, with a gambrel roof and tall chimneys. Two slim Lombardy poplars and a broad-leaved catalpa shaded the southern side, and a kitchen-garden, divided in the centre by a double row of untrimmed currant-bushes, flanked it on the east. For flowers, there were masses of blue flags and coarse tawny-red lilies, besides a huge trumpet-vine which swung its pendent arms from one of the gables. In front of the house a natural lawn of mingled turf and rock sloped steeply down to the water, which was not more than two hundred yards distant. To the west was another and broader inlet of the Sound, out of which our Arcadian promontory rose bluff and bold, crowned with a thick fringe of pines. It was really a lovely spot which Shelldrake had chosen — so secluded, while almost surrounded by the winged and moving life of the Sound, so simple, so pastoral and home-like. No one doubted the success of our experiment, for that evening at least.

"Perkins Brown, Shelldrake's boy-of-all-work, awaited us at the door. He had been sent on two or three days in advance, to take charge of the house, and seemed to have had enough of hermit-life, for he hailed us with a wild whoop, throwing his straw hat half-way up one of the poplars. Perkins was a boy of fifteen, the child of poor parents, who were satisfied to get him off their hands, regardless as to what humanitarian theories might be tested upon him. As the Arcadian Club recognized no such thing as caste, he was always admitted to our meetings, and understood just enough of our conversation to excite a silly ambition in his slow mind. His animal nature was predominant, and this led him to be deceitful. At that time, however, we all looked upon him as a proper young Arcadian, and hoped that he would develop into a second Abel Mallory.

"After our effects had been deposited on the stoop, and the carriages had driven away, we proceeded to apportion the rooms, and take possession. On the first floor there were three rooms, two of which would serve us as dining and drawing rooms, leaving the third for the Shelldrakes. As neither Eunice and Miss Ringtop, nor Hollins and Abel showed any disposition to room together, I quietly gave up to them the four rooms in the second story, and installed myself in one of the attic chambers. Here I could hear the music of the rain close above my head, and through the little gable window, as I lay in bed, watch the colors of the morning gradually steal over the distant shores. The end was, we were all satisfied.

"'Now for our first meal in Arcadia!' was the next cry. Mrs. Shelldrake, like a prudent housekeeper, marched off to the kitchen, where Perkins had already kindled a fire. We looked in at the door, but thought it best to allow her undisputed sway in such a narrow realm. Eunice was unpacking some loaves of bread and paper bags of crackers; and Miss Ringtop, smiling through her ropy curls, as much as to say, 'You see, *I* also can perform the coarser tasks of life!' occupied herself with plates and cups. We men, therefore, walked out to the garden, which we found in a promising condition. The usual vegetables had been planted and were growing finely, for the season was yet scarcely warm enough for the weeds to make much headway. Radishes, young onions, and lettuce formed our contribution to the table. The Shelldrakes, I should explain, had not yet advanced to the antediluvian point, in diet: nor, indeed, had either Eunice or myself. We acknowledged the fascination of tea, we saw a very mitigated evil in milk and butter, and we were conscious of stifled longings after the abomination of meat. Only Mallory, Hollins, and Miss Ringtop had reached that loftiest round on the ladder of progress where the material nature loosens the last fetter of the spiritual. They looked down upon us, and we meekly admitted their right to do so.

"Our board, that evening, was really tempting. The absence of meat was compensated to us by the crisp and racy onions, and I craved only a little salt, which had been interdicted, as a most pernicious substance. I sat at one corner of the table, beside Perkins Brown, who took an opportunity, while the others were engaged in conversation, to jog my elbow gently. As I turned towards him, he said nothing, but dropped his eyes significantly. The little rascal had the lid of a blacking-box, filled with salt, upon his knee, and was privately seasoning his onions and radishes.

I blushed at the thought of my hypocrisy, but the onions were so much better that I couldn't help dipping into the lid with him.

"'Oh,' said Eunice, 'we must send for some oil and vinegar! This lettuce is very nice.'

"'Oil and vinegar?' exclaimed Abel.

"'Why, yes,' said she, innocently: 'they are both vegetable substances.'

"Abel at first looked rather foolish, but quickly recovering himself, said—

"'All vegetable substances are not proper for food: you would not taste the poison-oak, or sit under the upas-tree of Java.'

"'Well, Abel,' Eunice rejoined, 'how are we to distinguish what is best for us? How are we to know WHAT vegetables to choose, or what animal and mineral substances to avoid?'

"'I will tell you,' he answered, with a lofty air. 'See here!' pointing to his temple, where the second pimple—either from the change of air, or because, in the excitement of the last few days, he had forgotten it—was actually healed. 'My blood is at last pure. The struggle between the natural and the unnatural is over, and I am beyond the depraved influences of my former taste. My instincts are now, therefore, entirely pure also. What is good for man to eat, that I shall have a natural desire to eat: what is bad will be naturally repelled. How does the cow distinguish between the wholesome and the poisonous herbs of the meadow? And is man less than a cow, that he cannot cultivate his instincts to an equal point? Let me walk through the woods and I can tell you every berry and root which God designed for food, though I know not its name, and have never seen it before. I shall make use of my time, during our sojourn here, to test, by my purified instinct, every substance, animal, mineral, and vegetable, upon which the human race subsists, and to create a catalogue of the True Food of Man!'

"Abel was eloquent on this theme, and he silenced not only Eunice, but the rest of us. Indeed, as we were all half infected with the same delusions, it was not easy to answer his sophistries.

"After supper was over, the prospect of cleaning the dishes and putting things in order was not so agreeable; but Mrs. Shelldrake and Perkins undertook the work, and we did not think it necessary to interfere with them. Half an hour afterwards, when the full moon had risen, we took our chairs upon the sloop, to enjoy the calm, silver night, the soft sea-air, and our summer's residence in anticipatory talk.

"'My friends,' said Hollins (and HIS hobby, as you may remember, Ned, was the organization of Society, rather than those reforms which apply directly to the Individual),—'my friends, I think we are sufficiently advanced in progressive ideas to establish our little Arcadian community upon what I consider the true basis: not Law, nor Custom, but the uncorrupted impulses of our nature. What Abel said in regard to dietetic reform is true; but that alone will not regenerate the race. We must rise superior to those conventional ideas of Duty whereby Life is warped and crippled. Life must not be a prison, where each one must come and go, work, eat, and sleep, as the jailer commands. Labor must not be a necessity, but a spontaneous joy. 'Tis true, but little labor is required of us here: let us, therefore, have no set tasks, no fixed rules, but each one work, rest, eat, sleep, talk or be silent, as his own nature prompts.'

"Perkins, sitting on the steps, gave a suppressed chuckle, which I think no one heard but myself. I was vexed with his levity, but, nevertheless, gave him a warning nudge with my toe, in payment for the surreptitious salt.

"'That's just the notion I had, when I first talked of our coming here,' said Shelldrake. 'Here we're alone and unhindered; and if the plan shouldn't happen to work well (I don't see why it shouldn't though), no harm will be done. I've had a deal of hard work in my life, and I've been badgered and bullied so much by your strait-laced professors, that I'm glad to get away from the world for a spell, and talk and do rationally, without being laughed at.'

"'Yes,' answered Hollins, 'and if we succeed, as I feel we shall, for I think I know the hearts of all of us here, this may be the commencement of a new Epoch for the world. We may become the turning-point between two dispensations: behind us every thing false and unnatural, before us every thing true, beautiful, and good.'

"'Ah,' sighed Miss Ringtop, 'it reminds me of Gamaliel J. Gawthrop's beautiful lines:

"'Unrobed man is lying hoary

In the distance, gray and dead;

There no wreaths of godless glory

To his mist-like tresses wed,

And the foot-fall of the Ages

Reigns supreme, with noiseless tread.'

"'I am willing to try the experiment,' said I, on being appealed to by Hollins; 'but don't you think we had better observe some kind of order, even in yielding every thing to impulse? Shouldn't there be, at least, a platform, as the politicians call it—an agreement by which we shall all be bound, and which we can afterwards exhibit as the basis of our success?'

"He meditated a few moments, and then answered—

"'I think not. It resembles too much the thing we are trying to overthrow. Can you bind a man's belief by making him sign certain articles of Faith? No: his thought will be free, in spite of it; and I would have Action—Life— as free as Thought. Our platform—to adopt your image—has but one plank: Truth. Let each only be true to himself: BE himself, ACT himself, or herself with the uttermost candor. We can all agree upon that.'

"The agreement was accordingly made. And certainly no happier or more hopeful human beings went to bed in all New England that night.

"I arose with the sun, went into the garden, and commenced weeding, intending to do my quota of work before breakfast, and then devote the day to reading and conversation. I was presently joined by Shelldrake and Mallory, and between us we finished the onions and radishes, stuck the peas, and cleaned the alleys. Perkins, after milking the cow and turning her out to pasture, assisted Mrs. Shelldrake in the kitchen. At breakfast we were joined by Hollins, who made no excuse for his easy morning habits; nor was one expected. I may as well tell you now, though, that his natural instincts never led him to work. After a week, when a second crop of weeds was coming on, Mallory fell off also, and thenceforth Shelldrake and myself had the entire charge of the garden. Perkins did the rougher work, and was always on hand when he was wanted. Very soon, however, I noticed that he was in the habit of disappearing for two or three hours in the afternoon.

"Our meals preserved the same Spartan simplicity. Eunice, however, carried her point in regard to the salad; for Abel, after tasting and finding it very palatable, decided that oil and vinegar might be classed in the catalogue of True Food. Indeed, his long abstinence from piquant flavors gave him such an appetite for it that our supply of lettuce was soon exhausted. An embarrassing accident also favored us with the use of salt. Perkins happening to move his knee at the moment I was dipping an onion into the blacking-box lid, our supply was knocked upon the floor. He picked it up, and we both hoped the accident might pass unnoticed. But Abel, stretching his long neck across the corner of the table, caught a glimpse of what was going on.

"'What's that?' he asked.

"'Oh, it's—it's only,' said I, seeking for a synonyme, 'only chloride of sodium!'

"'Chloride of sodium! what do you do with it?'

"'Eat it with onions,' said I, boldly: 'it's a chemical substance, but I believe it is found in some plants.'

"Eunice, who knew something of chemistry (she taught a class, though you wouldn't think it), grew red with suppressed fun, but the others were as ignorant as Abel Mallory himself.

"'Let me taste it,' said he, stretching out an onion.

"I handed him the box-lid, which still contained a portion of its contents. He dipped the onion, bit off a piece, and chewed it gravely.

"'Why,' said he, turning to me, 'it's very much like salt.'

"Perkins burst into a spluttering yell, which discharged an onion-top he had just put between his teeth across the table; Eunice and I gave way at the same moment; and the others, catching the joke, joined us. But while we were laughing, Abel was finishing his onion, and the result was that Salt was added to the True Food, and thereafter appeared regularly on the table.

"The forenoons we usually spent in reading and writing, each in his or her chamber. (Oh, the journals, Ned!—but you shall not see mine.) After a midday meal,—I cannot call it dinner,—we sat upon the stoop, listening while one of us read aloud, or strolled down the shores on either side, or, when the sun was not too warm, got into a boat, and rowed or floated lazily around the promontory.

"One afternoon, as I was sauntering off, past the garden, towards the eastern inlet, I noticed Perkins slipping along behind the cedar knobs, towards the little woodland at the end of our domain. Curious to find out the cause of his mysterious disappearances, I followed cautiously. From the edge of the wood I saw him enter a little gap between the rocks, which led down to the water. Presently a thread of blue smoke stole up. Quietly creeping along, I got upon the nearer bluff and looked down. There was a sort of hearth built up at the base of the rock, with a brisk little fire burning upon it, but Perkins had disappeared. I stretched myself out upon the moss, in the shade, and waited. In about half an hour up came Perkins, with a large fish in one hand and a lump of clay in the other. I now understood the mystery. He carefully imbedded the fish in a thin layer of clay, placed it on the coals, and then went down to the shore to wash his hands. On his return he found me watching the fire.

"'Ho, ho, Mr. Enos!' said he, 'you've found me out; But you won't say nothin'. Gosh! you like it as well I do. Look 'ee there!'—breaking open the clay, from which arose 'a steam of rich distilled perfumes,'—'and, I say, I've got the box-lid with that 'ere stuff in it,—ho! ho!'—and the scamp roared again.

"Out of a hole in the rock he brought salt and the end of a loaf, and between us we finished the fish. Before long, I got into the habit of disappearing in the afternoon.

"Now and then we took walks, alone or collectively, to the nearest village, or even to Bridgeport, for the papers or a late book. The few purchases we required were made at such times, and sent down in a cart, or, if not too heavy, carried by Perkins in a basket. I noticed that Abel, whenever we had occasion to visit a grocery, would go sniffing around, alternately attracted or repelled by the various articles: now turning away with a shudder from a ham,—now inhaling, with a fearful delight and uncertainty, the odor of smoked herrings. 'I think herrings must feed on sea-weed,' said he, 'there is such a vegetable attraction about them.' After his violent vegetarian harangues, however, he hesitated about adding them to his catalogue.

"But, one day, as we were passing through the village, he was reminded by the sign of 'WARTER CRACKERS' in the window of an obscure grocery that he required a supply of these articles, and we therefore entered. There was a splendid Rhode Island cheese on the counter, from which the shop-mistress was just cutting a slice for a customer. Abel leaned over it, inhaling the rich, pungent fragrance.

"'Enos,' said he to me, between his sniffs, 'this impresses me like flowers—like marigolds. It must be—really—yes, the vegetable element is predominant. My instinct towards it is so strong that I cannot be mistaken. May I taste it, ma'am?'

"The woman sliced off a thin corner, and presented it to him on the knife.

"'Delicious!' he exclaimed; 'I am right,—this is the True Food. Give me two pounds—and the crackers, ma'am.'

"I turned away, quite as much disgusted as amused with this charlatanism. And yet I verily believe the fellow was sincere—self-deluded only. I had by this time lost my faith in him, though not in the great Arcadian principles. On reaching home, after an hour's walk, I found our household in unusual commotion. Abel was writhing in intense pain: he had eaten the whole two pounds of cheese, on his way home! His stomach, so weakened by years of unhealthy abstinence from true nourishment, was now terribly tortured by this sudden stimulus. Mrs. Shelldrake, fortunately, had some mustard among her stores, and could therefore administer a timely emetic. His life was saved, but he was very ill for two or three days. Hollins did not fail to take advantage of this circumstance to overthrow the authority which Abel had gradually acquired on the subject of food. He was so arrogant in his nature that he could not tolerate the same quality in another, even where their views coincided.

"By this time several weeks had passed away. It was the beginning of July, and the long summer heats had come. I was driven out of my attic during the middle hours of the day, and the others found it pleasanter on the doubly shaded stoop than in their chambers. We were thus thrown more together than usual—a circumstance which made our life more monotonous to the others, as I could see; but to myself, who could at last talk to Eunice, and who was happy at the very sight of her, this 'heated term' seemed borrowed from Elysium.

"I read aloud, and the sound of my own voice gave me confidence; many passages suggested discussions, in which I took a part; and you may judge, Ned, how fast I got on, from the fact that I ventured to tell Eunice of my fish-bakes with Perkins, and invite her to join them. After that, she also often disappeared from sight for an hour or two in the afternoon."

— — "Oh, Mr. Johnson," interrupted Mrs. Billings, "it wasn't for the fish!"

"Of course not," said her husband; "it was for my sake."

"No, you need not think it was for you. Enos," she added, perceiving the feminine dilemma into which she had been led, "all this is not necessary to the story."

"Stop!" he answered. "The A. C. has been revived for this night only. Do you remember our platform, or rather no-platform? I must follow my impulses, and say whatever comes uppermost."

"Right, Enos," said Mr. Johnson; "I, as temporary Arcadian, take the same ground. My instinct tells me that you, Mrs. Billings, must permit the confession."

She submitted with a good grace, and her husband continued:

"I said that our lazy life during the hot weather had become a little monotonous. The Arcadian plan had worked tolerably well, on the whole, for there was very little for any one to do—Mrs. Shelldrake and Perkins Brown excepted. Our conversation, however, lacked spirit and variety. We were, perhaps unconsciously, a little tired of hearing and assenting to the same sentiments. But one evening, about this time, Hollins struck upon a variation, the consequences of which he little foresaw. We had been reading one of Bulwer's works (the weather was too hot for Psychology), and came upon this paragraph, or something like it:

"'Ah, Behind the Veil! We see the summer smile of the Earth—enamelled meadow and limpid stream,—but what hides she in her sunless heart? Caverns of serpents, or grottoes of priceless gems? Youth, whose soul sits on thy countenance, thyself wearing no mask, strive not to lift the masks of others! Be content with what thou seest; and wait until Time and Experience shall teach thee to find jealousy behind the sweet smile, and hatred under the honeyed word!'

"This seemed to us a dark and bitter reflection; but one or another of us recalled some illustration of human hypocrisy, and the evidences, by the simple fact of repetition, gradually led to a division of opinion—Hollins, Shelldrake, and Miss Ringtop on the dark side, and the rest of us on the bright. The last, however, contented herself with quoting from her favorite poet, Gamaliel J. Gawthrop:

*"'I look beyond thy brow's concealment!*
*I see thy spirit's dark revealment!*
*Thy inner self betrayed I see:*
*Thy coward, craven, shivering ME!'*

"'We think we know one another,' exclaimed Hollins; 'but do we? We see the faults of others, their weaknesses, their disagreeable qualities, and we keep silent. How much we should gain, were candor as universal as concealment! Then each one, seeing himself as others see him, would truly know himself. How much misunderstanding might be avoided—how much hidden shame be removed—hopeless, because unspoken, love made glad— honest admiration cheer its object—uttered sympathy mitigate misfortune— in short, how much brighter and happier the world would become if each one expressed, everywhere and at all times, his true and entire feeling! Why, even Evil would lose half its power!'

"There seemed to be so much practical wisdom in these views that we were all dazzled and half-convinced at the start. So, when Hollins, turning towards me, as he continued, exclaimed—'Come, why should not this candor be adopted in our Arcadia? Will any one—will you, Enos— commence at once by telling me now—to my face—my principal faults?' I answered after a moment's reflection—'You have a great deal of intellectual arrogance, and you are, physically, very indolent'

"He did not flinch from the self-invited test, though he looked a little surprised.

"'Well put,' said he, 'though I do not say that you are entirely correct. Now, what are my merits?'

"'You are clear-sighted,' I answered, 'an earnest seeker after truth, and courageous in the avowal of your thoughts.'

"This restored the balance, and we soon began to confess our own private faults and weaknesses. Though the confessions did not go very deep,—no one betraying anything we did not all know already,—yet they were sufficient to strength Hollins in his new idea, and it was unanimously resolved that Candor should thenceforth be the main charm of our Arcadian life. It was the very thing *I* wanted, in order to make a certain communication to Eunice; but I should probably never have reached the point, had not the same candor been exercised towards me, from a quarter where I least expected it.

"The next day, Abel, who had resumed his researches after the True Food, came home to supper with a healthier color than I had before seen on his face.

"'Do you know,' said he, looking shyly at Hollins, 'that I begin to think Beer must be a natural beverage? There was an auction in the village to-day, as I passed through, and I stopped at a cake-stand to get a glass of water, as it was very hot. There was no water—only beer: so I thought I would try a glass, simply as an experiment. Really, the flavor was very agreeable. And it occurred to me, on the way home, that all the elements contained in beer are vegetable. Besides, fermentation is a natural process. I think the question has never been properly tested before.'

"'But the alcohol!' exclaimed Hollins.

"'I could not distinguish any, either by taste or smell. I know that chemical analysis is said to show it; but may not the alcohol be created, somehow, during the analysis?'

"'Abel,' said Hollins, in a fresh burst of candor, 'you will never be a Reformer, until you possess some of the commonest elements of knowledge.'

"The rest of us were much diverted: it was a pleasant relief to our monotonous amiability.

"Abel, however, had a stubborn streak in his character. The next day he sent Perkins Brown to Bridgeport for a dozen bottles of 'Beer.' Perkins, either intentionally or by mistake, (I always suspected the former,) brought pint-bottles of Scotch ale, which he placed in the coolest part of the cellar. The evening happened to be exceedingly hot and sultry, and, as we were all fanning ourselves and talking languidly, Abel bethought him of his beer. In his thirst, he drank the contents of the first bottle, almost at a single draught.

"'The effect of beer,' said he, 'depends, I think, on the commixture of the nourishing principle of the grain with the cooling properties of the water. Perhaps, hereafter, a liquid food of the same character may be invented, which shall save us from mastication and all the diseases of the teeth.'

"Hollins and Shelldrake, at his invitation, divided a bottle between them, and he took a second. The potent beverage was not long in acting on a brain so unaccustomed to its influence. He grew unusually talkative and sentimental, in a few minutes.

"'Oh, sing, somebody!' he sighed in a hoarse rapture: 'the night was made for Song.'

"Miss Ringtop, nothing loath, immediately commenced, 'When stars are in the quiet skies;' but scarcely had she finished the first verse before Abel interrupted her.

"'Candor's the order of the day, isn't it?' he asked.

"'Yes!' 'Yes!' two or three answered.

"'Well then,' said he, 'candidly, Pauline, you've got the darn'dest squeaky voice'—

"Miss Ringtop gave a faint little scream of horror.

"'Oh, never mind!' he continued. 'We act according to impulse, don't we? And I've the impulse to swear; and it's right. Let Nature have her way. Listen! Damn, damn, damn, damn! I never knew it was so easy. Why, there's a pleasure in it! Try it, Pauline! try it on me!'

"'Oh-ooh!' was all Miss Ringtop could utter.

"'Abel! Abel!' exclaimed Hollins, 'the beer has got into your head.'

"'No, it isn't Beer,—it's Candor!' said Abel. 'It's your own proposal, Hollins. Suppose it's evil to swear: isn't it better I should express it, and be done with it, than keep it bottled up to ferment in my mind? Oh, you're a precious, consistent old humbug, you are!'

"And therewith he jumped off the stoop, and went dancing awkwardly down towards the water, singing in a most unmelodious voice, ''Tis home where'er the heart is.'

"'Oh, he may fall into the water!' exclaimed Eunice, in alarm.

"'He's not fool enough to do that,' said Shelldrake. 'His head is a little light, that's all. The air will cool him down presently.'

"But she arose and followed him, not satisfied with this assurance. Miss Ringtop sat rigidly still. She would have received with composure the news of his drowning.

"As Eunice's white dress disappeared among the cedars crowning the shore, I sprang up and ran after her. I knew that Abel was not intoxicated, but simply excited, and I had no fear on his account: I obeyed an involuntary impulse. On approaching the water, I heard their voices—hers in friendly persuasion, his in sentimental entreaty,—then the sound of oars in the rowlocks. Looking out from the last clump of cedars, I saw them seated in the boat, Eunice at the stern, while Abel, facing her, just dipped an oar now and then to keep from drifting with the tide. She had found him already in the boat, which was loosely chained to a stone. Stepping on one of the forward thwarts in her eagerness to persuade him to return, he sprang past her, jerked away the chain, and pushed off before she could escape. She would have fallen, but he caught her and placed her in the stern, and then seated himself at the oars. She must have been somewhat alarmed, but there was only indignation in her voice. All this had transpired before my arrival, and the first words I heard bound me to the spot and kept me silent.

"'Abel, what does this mean?' she asked

"'It means Fate—Destiny!' he exclaimed, rather wildly. 'Ah, Eunice, ask the night, and the moon,—ask the impulse which told you to follow me! Let us be candid like the old Arcadians we imitate. Eunice, we know that we love each other: why should we conceal it any longer? The Angel of Love comes down from the stars on his azure wings, and whispers to our hearts. Let us confess to each other! The female heart should not be timid, in this pure and beautiful atmosphere of Love which we breathe. Come, Eunice! we are alone: let your heart speak to me!'

"Ned, if you've ever been in love, (we'll talk of that after a while,) you will easily understand what tortures I endured, in thus hearing him speak. That HE should love Eunice! It was a profanation to her, an outrage to me. Yet the assurance with which he spoke! COULD she love this conceited, ridiculous, repulsive fellow, after all? I almost gasped for breath, as I clinched the prickly boughs of the cedars in my hands, and set my teeth, waiting to hear her answer.

"'I will not hear such language! Take me back to the shore!' she said, in very short, decided tones.

"'Oh, Eunice,' he groaned, (and now, I think he was perfectly sober,) 'don't you love me, indeed? *I* love you,—from my heart I do: yes, I love you. Tell me how you feel towards me.'

"'Abel,' said she, earnestly, 'I feel towards you only as a friend; and if you wish me to retain a friendly interest in you, you must never again talk in this manner. I do not love you, and I never shall. Let me go back to the house.'

"His head dropped upon his breast, but he rowed back to the shore, drew the bow upon the rocks, and assisted her to land. Then, sitting down, he groaned forth—

"'Oh, Eunice, you have broken my heart!' and putting his big hands to his face, began to cry.

"She turned, placed one hand on his shoulder, and said in a calm, but kind tone—

"'I am very sorry, Abel, but I cannot help it.'

"I slipped aside, that she might not see me, and we returned by separate paths.

"I slept very little that night. The conviction which I chased away from my mind as often as it returned, that our Arcadian experiment was taking a ridiculous and at the same time impracticable development, became clearer and stronger. I felt sure that our little community could not hold together much longer without an explosion. I had a presentiment that Eunice shared my impressions. My feelings towards her had reached that crisis where a declaration was imperative: but how to make it? It was a terrible struggle between my shyness and my affection. There was another circumstance in connection with this subject, which troubled me not a little. Miss Ringtop evidently sought my company, and made me, as much as possible, the recipient of her sentimental outpourings. I was not bold enough to repel her—indeed I had none of that tact which is so useful in such emergencies,—and she seemed to misinterpret my submission. Not only was her conversation pointedly directed to me, but she looked at me, when singing, (especially, 'Thou, thou, reign'st in this bosom!') in a way that made me feel very uncomfortable. What if Eunice should suspect an attachment towards her, on my part. What if—oh, horror!—I had unconsciously said or done something to impress Miss Ringtop herself with the same conviction? I shuddered as the thought crossed my mind. One thing was very certain: this suspense was not to be endured much longer.

"We had an unusually silent breakfast the next morning. Abel scarcely spoke, which the others attributed to a natural feeling of shame, after his display of the previous evening. Hollins and Shelldrake discussed Temperance, with a special view to his edification, and Miss Ringtop favored us with several quotations about 'the maddening bowl,'—but he paid no attention to them. Eunice was pale and thoughtful. I had no doubt in my mind, that she was already contemplating a removal from Arcadia. Perkins, whose perceptive faculties were by no means dull, whispered to me, 'Shan't I bring up some porgies for supper?' but I shook my head. I was busy with other thoughts, and did not join him in the wood, that day.

"The forenoon was overcast, with frequent showers. Each one occupied his or her room until dinner-time, when we met again with something of the old geniality. There was an evident effort to restore our former flow of good feeling. Abel's experience with the beer was freely discussed. He insisted strongly that he had not been laboring under its effects, and proposed a mutual test. He, Shelldrake, and Hollins were to drink it in equal measures, and compare observations as to their physical sensations. The others agreed,—quite willingly, I thought,—but I refused. I had determined to make a desperate attempt at candor, and Abel's fate was fresh before my eyes.

"My nervous agitation increased during the day, and after sunset, fearing lest I should betray my excitement in some way, I walked down to the end of the promontory, and took a seat on the rocks. The sky had cleared, and the air was deliciously cool and sweet. The Sound was spread out before me like a sea, for the Long Island shore was veiled in a silvery mist. My mind was soothed and calmed by the influences of the scene, until the moon arose. Moonlight, you know, disturbs—at least, when one is in love. (Ah, Ned, I see you understand it!) I felt blissfully miserable, ready to cry with joy at the knowledge that I loved, and with fear and vexation at my cowardice, at the same time.

"Suddenly I heard a rustling beside me. Every nerve in my body tingled, and I turned my head, with a beating and expectant heart. Pshaw! It was Miss Ringtop, who spread her blue dress on the rock beside me, and shook back her long curls, and sighed, as she gazed at the silver path of the moon on the water.

"'Oh, how delicious!' she cried. 'How it seems to set the spirit free, and we wander off on the wings of Fancy to other spheres!'

"'Yes,' said I, 'It is very beautiful, but sad, when one is alone.'

"I was thinking of Eunice.

"'How inadequate,' she continued, 'is language to express the emotions which such a scene calls up in the bosom! Poetry alone is the voice of the spiritual world, and we, who are not poets, must borrow the language of the gifted sons of Song. Oh, Enos, I WISH you were a poet! But you FEEL poetry, I know you do. I have seen it in your eyes, when I quoted the burning lines of Adeliza Kelley, or the soul-breathings of Gamaliel J. Gawthrop. In HIM, particularly, I find the voice of my own nature. Do you know his 'Night-Whispers?' How it embodies the feelings of such a scene as this!

"*Star-drooping bowers bending down the spaces,*
*And moonlit glories sweep star-footed on;*
*And pale, sweet rivers, in their shining races,*
*Are ever gliding through the moonlit places,*
*With silver ripples on their tranced faces,*
*And forests clasp their dusky hands, with low and sullen moan!*'

"'Ah!' she continued, as I made no reply, 'this is an hour for the soul to unveil its most secret chambers! Do you not think, Enos, that love rises superior to all conventionalities? that those whose souls are in unison should be allowed to reveal themselves to each other, regardless of the world's opinions?'

"'Yes!' said I, earnestly.

"'Enos, do you understand me?' she asked, in a tender voice—almost a whisper.

"'Yes,' said I, with a blushing confidence of my own passion.

"'Then,' she whispered, 'our hearts are wholly in unison. I know you are true, Enos. I know your noble nature, and I will never doubt you. This is indeed happiness!'

"And therewith she laid her head on my shoulder, and sighed—

"'*Life remits his tortures cruel,*
*Love illumes his fairest fuel,*
*When the hearts that once were dual*
*Meet as one, in sweet renewal!*'

"'Miss Ringtop!' I cried, starting away from her, in alarm, 'you don't mean that—that—'

"I could not finish the sentence.

"'Yes, Enos, DEAR Enos! henceforth we belong to each other.'

"The painful embarrassment I felt, as her true meaning shot through my mind, surpassed anything I had imagined, or experienced in anticipation, when planning how I should declare myself to Eunice. Miss Ringtop was at least ten years older than I, far from handsome (but you remember her face,) and so affectedly sentimental, that I, sentimental as I was then, was sick of hearing her talk. Her hallucination was so monstrous, and gave me such a shock of desperate alarm, that I spoke, on the impulse of the moment, with great energy, without regarding how her feelings might be wounded.

"'You mistake!' I exclaimed. 'I didn't mean that,—I didn't understand you. Don't talk to me that way,—don't look at me in that way, Miss Ringtop! We were never meant for each other—I wasn't——You're so much older—I mean different. It can't be—no, it can never be! Let us go back to the house: the night is cold.'

"I rose hastily to my feet. She murmured something,—what, I did not stay to hear,—but, plunging through the cedars, was hurrying with all speed to the house, when, half-way up the lawn, beside one of the rocky knobs, I met Eunice, who was apparently on her way to join us.

"In my excited mood, after the ordeal through which I had passed, everything seemed easy. My usual timidity was blown to the four winds. I went directly to her, took her hand, and said—

"'Eunice, the others are driving me mad with their candor; will you let me be candid, too?'

"'I think you are always candid, Enos,' she answered.

"Even then, if I had hesitated, I should have been lost. But I went on, without pausing—

"'Eunice, I love you—I have loved you since we first met. I came here that I might be near you; but I must leave you forever, and to-night, unless you can trust your life in my keeping. God help me, since we have been together I have lost my faith in almost everything but you. Pardon me, if I am impetuous—different from what I have seemed. I have struggled so hard to speak! I have been a coward, Eunice, because of my love. But now I have spoken, from my heart of hearts. Look at me: I can bear it now. Read the truth in my eyes, before you answer.'

"I felt her hand tremble while I spoke. As she turned towards me her face, which had been averted, the moon shone full upon it, and I saw that tears were upon her cheeks. What was said—whether anything was said—I cannot tell. I felt the blessed fact, and that was enough. That was the dawning of the true Arcadia."

Mrs. Billings, who had been silent during this recital, took her husband's hand and smiled. Mr. Johnson felt a dull pang about the region of his heart. If he had a secret, however, I do not feel justified in betraying it.

"It was late," Mr. Billings continued, "before we returned to the house. I had a special dread of again encountering Miss Ringtop, but she was wandering up and down the bluff, under the pines, singing, 'The dream is past.' There was a sound of loud voices, as we approached the stoop. Hollins, Shelldrake and his wife, and Abel Mallory were sitting together near the door. Perkins Brown, as usual, was crouched on the lowest step, with one leg over the other, and rubbing the top of his boot with a vigor which betrayed to me some secret mirth. He looked up at me from under his straw hat with the grin of a malicious Puck, glanced towards the group, and made a curious gesture with his thumb. There were several empty pint-bottles on the stoop.

"'Now, are you sure you can bear the test?' we heard Hollins ask, as we approached.

"'Bear it? Why to be sure!' replied Shelldrake; 'if I couldn't bear it, or if YOU couldn't, your theory's done for. Try! I can stand it as long as you can.'

"'Well, then,' said Hollins, 'I think you are a very ordinary man. I derive no intellectual benefit from my intercourse with you, but your house is convenient to me. I'm under no obligations for your hospitality, however, because my company is an advantage to you. Indeed if I were treated according to my deserts, you couldn't do enough for me.'

"Mrs. Shelldrake was up in arms.

"'Indeed,' she exclaimed, 'I think you get as good as you deserve, and more too.'

"'Elvira,' said he, with a benevolent condescension, 'I have no doubt you think so, for your mind belongs to the lowest and most material sphere. You have your place in Nature, and you fill it; but it is not for you to judge of intelligences which move only on the upper planes.'

"'Hollins,' said Shelldrake, 'Elviry's a good wife and a sensible woman, and I won't allow you to turn up your nose at her.'

"'I am not surprised,' he answered, 'that you should fail to stand the test. I didn't expect it.'

"'Let me try it on YOU!' cried Shelldrake. 'You, now, have some intellect,—I don't deny that,—but not so much, by a long shot, as you think you have. Besides that, you're awfully selfish in your opinions. You won't admit that anybody can be right who differs from you. You've sponged on me for a long time; but I suppose I've learned something from you, so we'll call it even. I think, however, that what you call acting according to impulse is simply an excuse to cover your own laziness.'

"'Gosh! that's it!' interrupted Perkins, jumping up; then, recollecting himself, he sank down on the steps again, and shook with a suppressed 'Ho! ho! ho!'

"Hollins, however, drew himself up with an exasperated air.

"'Shelldrake,' said he, 'I pity you. I always knew your ignorance, but I thought you honest in your human character. I never suspected you of envy and malice. However, the true Reformer must expect to be misunderstood and misrepresented by meaner minds. That love which I bear to all creatures teaches me to forgive you. Without such love, all plans of progress must fail. Is it not so, Abel?'

"Shelldrake could only ejaculate the words, 'Pity!' 'Forgive?' in his most contemptuous tone; while Mrs. Shelldrake, rocking violently in her chair, gave utterance to that peculiar clucking, 'TS, TS, TS, TS,' whereby certain women express emotions too deep for words.

"Abel, roused by Hollins's question, answered, with a sudden energy—

"'Love! there is no love in the world. Where will you find it? Tell me, and I'll go there. Love! I'd like to see it! If all human hearts were like mine, we might have an Arcadia; but most men have no hearts. The world is a miserable, hollow, deceitful shell of vanity and hypocrisy. No: let us give up. We were born before our time: this age is not worthy of us.'

"Hollins stared at the speaker in utter amazement. Shelldrake gave a long whistle, and finally gasped out—

"'Well, what next?'

"None of us were prepared for such a sudden and complete wreck of our Arcadian scheme. The foundations had been sapped before, it is true; but we had not perceived it; and now, in two short days, the whole edifice tumbled about our ears. Though it was inevitable, we felt a shock of sorrow, and a silence fell upon us. Only that scamp of a Perkins Brown, chuckling and rubbing his boot, really rejoiced. I could have kicked him.

"We all went to bed, feeling that the charm of our Arcadian life was over. I was so full of the new happiness of love that I was scarcely conscious of regret. I seemed to have leaped at once into responsible manhood, and a glad rush of courage filled me at the knowledge that my own heart was a better oracle than those—now so shamefully overthrown—on whom I had so long implicitly relied. In the first revulsion of feeling, I was perhaps unjust to my associates. I see now, more clearly, the causes of those vagaries, which originated in a genuine aspiration, and failed from an ignorance of the true nature of Man, quite as much as from the egotism of the individuals. Other attempts at reorganizing Society were made about the same time by men of culture and experience, but in the A. C. we had neither. Our leaders had caught a few half-truths, which, in their minds, were speedily warped into errors. I can laugh over the absurdities I helped to perpetrate, but I must confess that the experiences of those few weeks went far towards making a man of me."

"Did the A. C. break up at once?" asked Mr. Johnson.

"Not precisely; though Eunice and I left the house within two days, as we had agreed. We were not married immediately, however. Three long years—years of hope and mutual encouragement—passed away before that happy consummation. Before our departure, Hollins had fallen into his old manner, convinced, apparently, that Candor must be postponed to a better age of the world. But the quarrel rankled in Shelldrake's mind, and especially in that of his wife. I could see by her looks and little fidgety ways that his further stay would be very uncomfortable. Abel Mallory, finding himself gaining in weight and improving in color, had no thought of returning. The day previous, as I afterwards learned, he had discovered Perkins Brown's secret kitchen in the woods.

"'Golly!' said that youth, in describing the circumstance to me, 'I had to ketch TWO porgies that day.'

"Miss Ringtop, who must have suspected the new relation between Eunice and myself, was for the most part rigidly silent. If she quoted, it was from the darkest and dreariest utterances of her favorite Gamaliel.

"What happened after our departure I learned from Perkins, on the return of the Shelldrakes to Norridgeport, in September. Mrs. Shelldrake stoutly persisted in refusing to make Hollins's bed, or to wash his shirts. Her brain was dull, to be sure; but she was therefore all the more stubborn in her resentment. He bore this state of things for about a week, when his engagements to lecture in Ohio suddenly called him away. Abel and Miss Ringtop were left to wander about the promontory in company, and to exchange lamentations on the hollowness of human hopes or the pleasures of despair. Whether it was owing to that attraction of sex which would make any man and any woman, thrown together on a desert island, finally become mates, or whether she skilfully ministered to Abel's sentimental vanity, I will not undertake to decide: but the fact is, they were actually betrothed, on leaving Arcadia. I think he would willingly have retreated, after his return to the world; but that was not so easy. Miss Ringtop held him with an inexorable clutch. They were not married, however, until just before his departure for California, whither she afterwards followed him. She died in less than a year, and left him free."

"And what became of the other Arcadians?" asked Mr. Johnson.

"The Shelldrakes are still living in Norridgeport. They have become Spiritualists, I understand, and cultivate Mediums. Hollins, when I last heard of him, was a Deputy-Surveyor in the New York Custom-House. Perkins Brown is our butcher here in Waterbury, and he often asks me—'Do you take chloride of soda on your beefsteaks?' He is as fat as a prize ox, and the father of five children."

"Enos!" exclaimed Mrs. Billings, looking at the clock, "it's nearly midnight! Mr. Johnson must be very tired, after such a long story."

"The Chapter of the A. C. is hereby closed!"

# FRIEND ELI'S DAUGHTER

I

The mild May afternoon was drawing to a close, as Friend Eli Mitchenor reached the top of the long hill, and halted a few minutes, to allow his horse time to recover breath. He also heaved a sigh of satisfaction, as he saw again the green, undulating valley of the Neshaminy, with its dazzling squares of young wheat, its brown patches of corn-land, its snowy masses of blooming orchard, and the huge, fountain like jets of weeping willow, half concealing the gray stone fronts of the farm-houses. He had been absent from home only six days, but the time seemed almost as long to him as a three years' cruise to a New Bedford whaleman. The peaceful seclusion and pastoral beauty of the scene did not consciously appeal to his senses; but he quietly noted how much the wheat had grown during his absence, that the oats were up and looking well, that Friend Comly's meadow had been ploughed, and Friend Martin had built his half of the line-fence along the top of the hill-field. If any smothered delight in the loveliness of the spring-time found a hiding-place anywhere in the well-ordered chambers of his heart, it never relaxed or softened the straight, inflexible lines of his face. As easily could his collarless drab coat and waistcoat have flushed with a sudden gleam of purple or crimson.

Eli Mitchenor was at peace with himself and the world—that is, so much of the world as he acknowledged. Beyond the community of his own sect, and a few personal friends who were privileged to live on its borders, he neither knew nor cared to know much more of the human race than if it belonged to a planet farther from the sun. In the discipline of the Friends he was perfect; he was privileged to sit on the high seats, with the elders of the Society; and the travelling brethren from other States, who visited Bucks County, invariably blessed his house with a family-meeting. His farm was one of the best on the banks of the Neshaminy, and he also enjoyed the annual interest of a few thousand dollars, carefully secured by mortgages on real estate. His wife, Abigail, kept even pace with him in the consideration she enjoyed within the limits of the sect; and his two children, Moses and

Asenath, vindicated the paternal training by the strictest sobriety of dress and conduct. Moses wore the plain coat, even when his ways led him among "the world's people;" and Asenath had never been known to wear, or to express a desire for, a ribbon of a brighter tint than brown or fawn-color. Friend Mitchenor had thus gradually ripened to his sixtieth year in an atmosphere of life utterly placid and serene, and looked forward with confidence to the final change, as a translation into a deeper calm, a serener quiet, a prosperous eternity of mild voices, subdued colors, and suppressed emotions.

He was returning home, in his own old-fashioned "chair," with its heavy square canopy and huge curved springs, from the Yearly Meeting of the Hicksite Friends, in Philadelphia. The large bay farm-horse, slow and grave in his demeanor, wore his plain harness with an air which made him seem, among his fellow-horses, the counterpart of his master among men. He would no more have thought of kicking than the latter would of swearing a huge oath. Even now, when the top of the hill was gained, and he knew that he was within a mile of the stable which had been his home since colthood, he showed no undue haste or impatience, but waited quietly, until Friend Mitchenor, by a well-known jerk of the lines, gave him the signal to go on. Obedient to the motion, he thereupon set forward once more, jogging soberly down the eastern slope of the hill,—across the covered bridge, where, in spite of the tempting level of the hollow-sounding floor, he was as careful to abstain from trotting as if he had read the warning notice,—along the wooded edge of the green meadow, where several cows of his acquaintance were grazing,—and finally, wheeling around at the proper angle, halted squarely in front of the gate which gave entrance to the private lane.

The old stone house in front, the spring-house in a green little hollow just below it, the walled garden, with its clumps of box and lilac, and the vast barn on the left, all joining in expressing a silent welcome to their owner, as he drove up the lane. Moses, a man of twenty-five, left his work in the garden, and walked forward in his shirt-sleeves.

"Well, father, how does thee do?" was his quiet greeting, as they shook hands.

"How's mother, by this time?" asked Eli.

"Oh, thee needn't have been concerned," said the son. "There she is. Go in: I'll tend to the horse."

Abigail and her daughter appeared on the piazza. The mother was a woman of fifty, thin and delicate in frame, but with a smooth, placid beauty of countenance which had survived her youth. She was dressed in a simple dove-colored gown, with book-muslin cap and handkerchief, so scrupulously arranged that one might have associated with her for six months without ever discovering a spot on the former, or an uneven fold in the latter. Asenath, who followed, was almost as plainly attired, her dress being a dark-blue calico, while a white pasteboard sun-bonnet, with broad cape, covered her head.

"Well, Abigail, how art thou?" said Eli, quietly giving his hand to his wife.

"I'm glad to see thee back," was her simple welcome.

No doubt they had kissed each other as lovers, but Asenath had witnessed this manifestation of affection but once in her life—after the burial of a younger sister. The fact impressed her with a peculiar sense of sanctity and solemnity: it was a caress wrung forth by a season of tribulation, and therefore was too earnest to be profaned to the uses of joy. So far, therefore, from expecting a paternal embrace, she would have felt, had it been given, like the doomed daughter of the Gileadite, consecrated to sacrifice.

Both she and her mother were anxious to hear the proceedings of the meeting, and to receive personal news of the many friends whom Eli had seen; but they asked few questions until the supper-table was ready and Moses had come in from the barn. The old man enjoyed talking, but it must be in his own way and at his own good time. They must wait until the communicative spirit should move him. With the first cup of coffee the inspiration came. Hovering at first over indifferent details, he gradually approached those of more importance,—told of the addresses which had been made, the points of discipline discussed, the testimony borne, and the appearance and genealogy of any new Friends who had taken a prominent part therein. Finally, at the close of his relation, he said—

"Abigail, there is one thing I must talk to thee about. Friend Speakman's partner,—perhaps thee's heard of him, Richard Hilton,—has a son who is weakly. He's two or three years younger than Moses. His mother was consumptive, and they're afraid he takes after her. His father wants to send him into the country for the summer—to some place where he'll have good air, and quiet, and moderate exercise, and Friend Speakman spoke of us. I thought I'd mention it to thee, and if thee thinks well of it, we can send word down next week, when Josiah Comly goes"

"What does THEE think?" asked his wife, after a pause

"He's a very quiet, steady young man, Friend Speakman says, and would be very little trouble to thee. I thought perhaps his board would buy the new yoke of oxen we must have in the fall, and the price of the fat ones might go to help set up Moses. But it's for thee to decide."

"I suppose we could take him," said Abigail, seeing that the decision was virtually made already; "there's the corner room, which we don't often use. Only, if he should get worse on our hands—"

"Friend Speakman says there's no danger. He is only weak-breasted, as yet, and clerking isn't good for him. I saw the young man at the store. If his looks don't belie him, he's well-behaved and orderly."

So it was settled that Richard Hilton the younger was to be an inmate of Friend Mitchenor's house during the summer.

## II

At the end of ten days he came.

In the under-sized, earnest, dark-haired and dark-eyed young man of three-and-twenty, Abigail Mitchenor at once felt a motherly interest. Having received him as a temporary member of the family, she considered him entitled to the same watchful care as if he were in reality an invalid son. The ice over an hereditary Quaker nature is but a thin crust, if one knows how to break it; and in Richard Hilton's case, it was already broken before his arrival. His only embarrassment, in fact, arose from the difficulty which he naturally experienced in adapting himself to the speech and address of the Mitchenor family. The greetings of old Eli, grave, yet kindly, of Abigail, quaintly familiar and tender, of Moses, cordial and slightly condescending, and finally of Asenath, simple and natural to a degree which impressed him like a new revelation in woman, at once indicated to him his position among them. His city manners, he felt, instinctively, must be unlearned, or at least laid aside for a time. Yet it was not easy for him to assume, at such short notice, those of his hosts. Happening to address Asenath as "Miss Mitchenor," Eli turned to him with a rebuking face.

"We do not use compliments, Richard," said he; "my daughter's name is Asenath."

"I beg pardon. I will try to accustom myself to your ways, since you have been so kind as to take me for a while," apologized Richard Hilton.

"Thee's under no obligation to us," said Friend Mitchenor, in his strict sense of justice; "thee pays for what thee gets."

The finer feminine instinct of Abigail led her to interpose.

"We'll not expect too much of thee, at first, Richard," she remarked, with a kind expression of face, which had the effect of a smile: "but our ways are plain and easily learned. Thee knows, perhaps, that we're no respecters of persons."

It was some days, however, before the young man could overcome his natural hesitation at the familiarity implied by these new forms of speech. "Friend Mitchenor" and "Moses" were not difficult to learn, but it seemed a want of respect to address as "Abigail" a woman of such sweet and serene dignity as the mother, and he was fain to avoid either extreme by calling her, with her cheerful permission, "Aunt Mitchenor." On the other hand, his own modest and unobtrusive nature soon won the confidence and cordial regard of the family. He occasionally busied himself in the garden, by way of exercise, or accompanied Moses to the corn-field or the woodland on the hill, but was careful never to interfere at inopportune times, and willing to learn silently, by the simple process of looking on.

One afternoon, as he was idly sitting on the stone wall which separated the garden from the lane, Asenath, attired in a new gown of chocolate-colored calico, with a double-handled willow work-basket on her arm, issued from the house. As she approached him, she paused and said—

"The time seems to hang heavy on thy hands, Richard. If thee's strong enough to walk to the village and back, it might do thee more good than sitting still."

Richard Hilton at once jumped down from the wall.

"Certainly I am able to go," said he, "if you will allow it."

"Haven't I asked thee?" was her quiet reply.

"Let me carry your basket," he said, suddenly, after they had walked, side by side, some distance down the lane.

"Indeed, I shall not let thee do that. I'm only going for the mail, and some little things at the store, that make no weight at all. Thee mustn't think I'm like the young women in the city, who, I'm told, if they buy a spool of Cotton, must have it sent home to them. Besides, thee mustn't over-exert thy strength."

Richard Hilton laughed merrily at the gravity with which she uttered the last sentence.

"Why, Miss—Asenath, I mean—what am I good for; if I have not strength enough to carry a basket?"

"Thee's a man, I know, and I think a man would almost as lief be thought wicked as weak. Thee can't help being weakly-inclined, and it's only right that thee should be careful of thyself. There's surely nothing in that that thee need be ashamed of."

While thus speaking, Asenath moderated her walk, in order, unconsciously to her companion, to restrain his steps.

"Oh, there are the dog's-tooth violets in blossom?" she exclaimed, pointing to a shady spot beside the brook; "does thee know them?"

Richard immediately gathered and brought to her a handful of the nodding yellow bells, trembling above their large, cool, spotted leaves.

"How beautiful they are!" said he; "but I should never have taken them for violets."

"They are misnamed," she answered. "The flower is an Erythronium; but I am accustomed to the common name, and like it. Did thee ever study botany?"

"Not at all. I can tell a geranium, when I see it, and I know a heliotrope by the smell. I could never mistake a red cabbage for a rose, and I can recognize a hollyhock or a sunflower at a considerable distance. The wild flowers are all strangers to me; I wish I knew something about them."

"If thee's fond of flowers, it would be very easy to learn. I think a study of this kind would pleasantly occupy thy mind. Why couldn't thee try? I would be very willing to teach thee what little I know. It's not much, indeed, but all thee wants is a start. See, I will show thee how simple the principles are."

Taking one of the flowers from the bunch, Asenath, as they slowly walked forward, proceeded to dissect it, explained the mysteries of stamens and pistils, pollen, petals, and calyx, and, by the time they had reached the village, had succeeded in giving him a general idea of the Linnaean system of classification. His mind took hold of the subject with a prompt and profound interest. It was a new and wonderful world which suddenly opened before him. How surprised he was to learn that there were signs by which a poisonous herb could be detected from a wholesome one, that cedars and pine-trees blossomed, that the gray lichens on the rocks belonged to the vegetable kingdom! His respect for Asenath's knowledge thrust quite out of sight the restraint which her youth and sex had imposed upon him. She was teacher, equal, friend; and the simple candid manner which was the natural expression of her dignity and purity thoroughly harmonized with this relation.

Although, in reality, two or three years younger than he, Asenath had a gravity of demeanor, a calm self-possession, a deliberate balance of mind, and a repose of the emotional nature, which he had never before observed, except in much older women. She had had, as he could well imagine, no romping girlhood, no season of careless, light-hearted dalliance with opening life, no violent alternation even of the usual griefs and joys of youth. The social calm in which she had expanded had developed her nature as gently and securely as a sea-flower is unfolded below the reach of tides and storms.

She would have been very much surprised if any one had called her handsome: yet her face had a mild, unobtrusive beauty which seemed to grow and deepen from day to day. Of a longer oval than the Greek standard, it was yet as harmonious in outline; the nose was fine and straight, the dark-blue eyes steady and untroubled, and the lips calmly, but not too firmly closed. Her brown hair, parted over a high white forehead, was smoothly laid across the temples, drawn behind the ears, and twisted into a simple knot. The white cape and sun-bonnet gave her face a nun-like character, which set her apart, in the thoughts of "the world's people" whom she met, as one sanctified for some holy work. She might have gone around the world, repelling every rude word, every bold glance, by the protecting atmosphere of purity and truth which inclosed her.

The days went by, each bringing some new blossom to adorn and illustrate the joint studies of the young man and maiden. For Richard Hilton had soon mastered the elements of botany, as taught by Priscilla Wakefield,—the only source of Asenath's knowledge,—and entered, with her, upon the text-book of Gray, a copy of which he procured from Philadelphia. Yet, though he had overtaken her in his knowledge of the technicalities of the science, her practical acquaintance with plants and their habits left her still his superior. Day by day, exploring the meadows, the woods, and the clearings, he brought home his discoveries to enjoy her aid in classifying and assigning them to their true places. Asenath had generally an hour or two of leisure from domestic duties in the afternoons, or after the early supper of summer was over; and sometimes, on "Seventh-days," she would be his guide to some locality where the rarer plants were known to exist. The parents saw this community of interest and exploration without a thought of misgiving. They trusted their daughter as themselves; or, if any possible fear had flitted across their hearts, it was allayed by the absorbing delight with which Richard Hilton pursued his study. An earnest discussion as to whether a certain leaf was ovate or lanceolate, whether a certain plant belonged to the species scandens or canadensis, was, in their eyes, convincing proof that the young brains were touched, and therefore NOT the young hearts.

But love, symbolized by a rose-bud, is emphatically a botanical emotion. A sweet, tender perception of beauty, such as this study requires, or develops, is at once the most subtle and certain chain of communication between impressible natures. Richard Hilton, feeling that his years were numbered, had given up, in despair, his boyish dreams, even before he understood them: his fate seemed to preclude the possibility of love. But, as he gained a little strength from the genial season, the pure country air, and the release from gloomy thoughts which his rambles afforded, the end was farther removed, and a future—though brief, perhaps, still a FUTURE—began to glimmer before him. If this could be his life,—an endless summer, with a search for new plants every morning, and their classification every evening, with Asenath's help on the shady portico of Friend Mitchenor's house,—he could forget his doom, and enjoy the blessing of life unthinkingly.

The azaleas succeeded to the anemones, the orchis and trillium followed, then the yellow gerardias and the feathery purple pogonias, and finally the growing gleam of the golden-rods along the wood-side and the red umbels of the tall eupatoriums in the meadow announced the close of summer. One evening, as Richard, in displaying his collection, brought to view the blood-red leaf of a gum-tree, Asenath exclaimed—

"Ah, there is the sign! It is early, this year."

"What sign?" he asked.

"That the summer is over. We shall soon have frosty nights, and then nothing will be left for us except the asters and gentians and golden-rods."

Was the time indeed so near? A few more weeks, and this Arcadian life would close. He must go back to the city, to its rectilinear streets, its close brick walls, its artificial, constrained existence. How could he give up the peace, the contentment, the hope he had enjoyed through the summer? The question suddenly took a more definite form in his mind: How could he give up Asenath? Yes—the quiet, unsuspecting girl, sitting beside him, with her lap full of the September blooms he had gathered, was thenceforth a part of his inmost life. Pure and beautiful as she was, almost sacred in his regard, his heart dared to say—"I need her and claim her!"

"Thee looks pale to-night, Richard," said Abigail, as they took their seats at the supper-table. "I hope thee has not taken cold."

# III

"Will thee go along, Richard? I know where the rudbeckias grow," said Asenath, on the following "Seventh-day" afternoon.

They crossed the meadows, and followed the course of the stream, under its canopy of magnificent ash and plane trees, into a brake between the hills. It was an almost impenetrable thicket, spangled with tall autumnal flowers. The eupatoriums, with their purple crowns, stood like young trees, with an undergrowth of aster and blue spikes of lobelia, tangled in a golden mesh of dodder. A strong, mature odor, mixed alike of leaves and flowers, and very different from the faint, elusive sweetness of spring, filled the air. The creek, with a few faded leaves dropped upon its bosom, and films of gossamer streaming from its bushy fringe, gurgled over the pebbles in its bed. Here and there, on its banks, shone the deep yellow stars of the flower they sought.

Richard Hilton walked as in a dream, mechanically plucking a stem of rudbeckia, only to toss it, presently, into the water.

"Why, Richard! what's thee doing?" cried Asenath; "thee has thrown away the very best specimen."

"Let it go," he answered, sadly. "I am afraid everything else is thrown away."

"What does thee mean?" she asked, with a look of surprised and anxious inquiry.

"Don't ask me, Asenath. Or—yes, I WILL tell you. I must say it to you now, or never afterwards. Do you know what a happy life I've been leading since I came here?—that I've learned what life is, as if I'd never known it before? I want to live, Asenath,—and do you know why?"

"I hope thee will live, Richard," she said, gently and tenderly, her deep-blue eyes dim with the mist of unshed tears.

"But, Asenath, how am I to live without you? But you can't understand that, because you do not know what you are to me. No, you never guessed that all this while I've been loving you more and more, until now I have no other idea of death than not to see you, not to love you, not to share your life!"

"Oh, Richard!"

"I knew you would be shocked, Asenath. I meant to have kept this to myself. You never dreamed of it, and I had no right to disturb the peace of your heart. The truth is told now,—and I cannot take it back, if I wished. But if you cannot love, you can forgive me for loving you—forgive me now and every day of my life."

He uttered these words with a passionate tenderness, standing on the edge of the stream, and gazing into its waters. His slight frame trembled with the violence of his emotion. Asenath, who had become very pale as he commenced to speak, gradually flushed over neck and brow as she listened. Her head drooped, the gathered flowers fell from her hands, and she hid her face. For a few minutes no sound was heard but the liquid gurgling of the water, and the whistle of a bird in the thicket beside them. Richard Hilton at last turned, and, in a voice of hesitating entreaty, pronounced her name—

"Asenath!"

She took away her hands, and slowly lifted her face. She was pale, but her eyes met his with a frank, appealing, tender expression, which caused his heart to stand still a moment. He read no reproach, no faintest thought of blame; but—was it pity?—was it pardon?—or——

"We stand before God, Richard," said she, in a low, sweet, solemn tone. "He knows that I do not need to forgive thee. If thee requires it, I also require His forgiveness for myself."

Though a deeper blush now came to cheek and brow, she met his gaze with the bravery of a pure and innocent heart. Richard, stunned with the sudden and unexpected bliss, strove to take the full consciousness of it into a being which seemed too narrow to contain it. His first impulse was to rush forward, clasp her passionately in his arms, and hold her in the embrace which encircled, for him, the boundless promise of life; but she stood there, defenceless, save in her holy truth and trust, and his heart bowed down and gave her reverence.

"Asenath," said he, at last, "I never dared to hope for this. God bless you for those words! Can you trust me?—can you indeed love me?"

"I can trust thee,—I DO love thee!"

They clasped each other's hands in one long, clinging pressure. No kiss was given, but side by side they walked slowly up the dewy meadows, in happy and hallowed silence. Asenath's face became troubled as the old farmhouse appeared through the trees.

"Father and mother must know of this, Richard," said she. "I am afraid it may be a cross to them."

The same fear had already visited his own mind, but he answered, cheerfully—

"I hope not. I think I have taken a new lease of life, and shall soon be strong enough to satisfy them. Besides, my father is in prosperous business."

"It is not that," she answered; "but thee is not one of us."

It was growing dusk when they reached the house. In the dim candle-light Asenath's paleness was not remarked; and Richard's silence was attributed to fatigue.

The next morning the whole family attended meeting at the neighboring Quaker meeting-house, in the preparation for which, and the various special occupations of their "First-day" mornings, the unsuspecting parents overlooked that inevitable change in the faces of the lovers which they must otherwise have observed. After dinner, as Eli was taking a quiet walk in the garden, Richard Hilton approached him.

"Friend Mitchenor," said he, "I should like to have some talk with thee."

"What is it, Richard?" asked the old man, breaking off some pods from a seedling radish, and rubbing them in the palm of his hand.

"I hope, Friend Mitchenor," said the young man, scarcely knowing how to approach so important a crisis in his life, "I hope thee has been satisfied with my conduct since I came to live with thee, and has no fault to find with me as a man."

"Well," exclaimed Eli, turning around and looking up, sharply, "does thee want a testimony from me? I've nothing, that I know of, to say against thee."

"If I were sincerely attached to thy daughter, Friend Mitchenor, and she returned the attachment, could thee trust her happiness in my hands?"

"What!" cried Eli, straightening himself and glaring upon the speaker, with a face too amazed to express any other feeling.

"Can you confide Asenath's happiness to my care? I love her with my whole heart and soul, and the fortune of my life depends on your answer."

The straight lines in the old man's face seemed to grow deeper and more rigid, and his eyes shone with the chill glitter of steel. Richard, not daring to say a word more, awaited his reply in intense agitation.

"So!" he exclaimed at last, "this is the way thee's repaid me! I didn't expect THIS from thee! Has thee spoken to her?"

"I have."

"Thee has, has thee? And I suppose thee's persuaded her to think as thee does. Thee'd better never have come here. When I want to lose my daughter, and can't find anybody else for her, I'll let thee know."

"What have you against me, Friend Mitchenor?" Richard sadly asked, forgetting, in his excitement, the Quaker speech he had learned.

"Thee needn't use compliments now! Asenath shall be a Friend while *I* live; thy fine clothes and merry-makings and vanities are not for her. Thee belongs to the world, and thee may choose one of the world's women."

"Never!" protested Richard; but Friend Mitchenor was already ascending the garden-steps on his way to the house.

The young man, utterly overwhelmed, wandered to the nearest grove and threw himself on the ground. Thus, in a miserable chaos of emotion, unable to grasp any fixed thought, the hours passed away. Towards evening, he heard a footstep approaching, and sprang up. It was Moses.

The latter was engaged, with the consent of his parents and expected to "pass meeting" in a few weeks. He knew what had happened, and felt a sincere sympathy for Richard, for whom he had a cordial regard. His face was very grave, but kind.

"Thee'd better come in, Richard," said he; "the evenings are damp, and I v'e brought thy overcoat. I know everything, and I feel that it must be a great cross for thee. But thee won't be alone in bearing it."

"Do you think there is no hope of your father relenting?" he asked, in a tone of despondency which anticipated the answer.

"Father's very hard to move," said Moses; "and when mother and Asenath can't prevail on him, nobody else need try. I'm afraid thee must make up thy mind to the trial. I'm sorry to say it, Richard, but I think thee'd better go back to town."

"I'll go to-morrow,—go and die!" he muttered hoarsely, as he followed Moses to the house.

Abigail, as she saw his haggard face, wept quietly. She pressed his hand tenderly, but said nothing. Eli was stern and cold as an Iceland rock. Asenath did not make her appearance. At supper, the old man and his son exchanged a few words about the farm-work to be done on the morrow, but nothing else was said. Richard soon left the room and went up to his chamber to spend his last, his only unhappy night at the farm. A yearning, pitying look from Abigail accompanied him.

"Try and not think hard of us!" was her farewell the next morning, as he stepped into the old chair, in which Moses was to convey him to the village where he should meet the Doylestown stage. So, without a word of comfort from Asenath's lips, without even a last look at her beloved face, he was taken away.

# IV

True and firm and self-reliant as was the nature of Asenath Mitchenor, the thought of resistance to her father's will never crossed her mind. It was fixed that she must renounce all intercourse with Richard Hilton; it was even sternly forbidden her to see him again during the few hours he remained in the house; but the sacred love, thus rudely dragged to the light and outraged, was still her own. She would take it back into the keeping of her heart, and if a day should ever come when he would be free to return and demand it of her, he would find it there, unwithered, with all the unbreathed perfume hoarded in its folded leaves. If that day came not, she would at the last give it back to God, saying, "Father, here is Thy most precious gift, bestow it as Thou wilt."

As her life had never before been agitated by any strong emotion, so it was not outwardly agitated now. The placid waters of her soul did not heave and toss before those winds of passion and sorrow: they lay in dull, leaden calm, under a cold and sunless sky. What struggles with herself she underwent no one ever knew. After Richard Hilton's departure, she never mentioned his name, or referred, in any way, to the summer's companionship with him. She performed her household duties, if not cheerfully, at least as punctually and carefully as before; and her father congratulated himself that the unfortunate attachment had struck no deeper root. Abigail's finer sight, however, was not deceived by this external resignation. She noted the faint shadows under the eyes, the increased whiteness of the temples, the unconscious traces of pain which sometimes played about the dimpled corners of the mouth, and watched her daughter with a silent, tender solicitude.

The wedding of Moses was a severe test of Asenath's strength, but she stood the trial nobly, performing all the duties required by her position with such sweet composure that many of the older female Friends remarked to Abigail, "How womanly Asenath has grown!" Eli Mitchenor noted, with peculiar satisfaction, that the eyes of the young Friends—some of them of great promise in the sect, and well endowed with worldly goods—followed her admiringly.

"It will not be long," he thought, "before she is consoled."

Fortune seemed to favor his plans, and justify his harsh treatment of Richard Hilton. There were unfavorable accounts of the young man's conduct. His father had died during the winter, and he was represented as having become very reckless and dissipated. These reports at last assumed such a definite form that Friend Mitchenor brought them to the notice of his family.

"I met Josiah Comly in the road," said he, one day at dinner. "He's just come from Philadelphia, and brings bad news of Richard Hilton. He's taken to drink, and is spending in wickedness the money his father left him. His friends have a great concern about him, but it seems he's not to be reclaimed."

Abigail looked imploringly at her husband, but he either disregarded or failed to understand her look. Asenath, who had grown very pale, steadily met her father's gaze, and said, in a tone which he had never yet heard from her lips—

"Father, will thee please never mention Richard Hilton's name when I am by?"

The words were those of entreaty, but the voice was that of authority. The old man was silenced by a new and unexpected power in his daughter's heart: he suddenly felt that she was not a girl, as heretofore, but a woman, whom he might persuade, but could no longer compel.

"It shall be as thee wishes, Asenath," he said; "we had best forget him."

Of their friends, however, she could not expect this reserve, and she was doomed to hear stories of Richard which clouded and embittered her thoughts of him. And a still severer trial was in store. She accompanied her father, in obedience to his wish, and against her own desire, to the Yearly Meeting in Philadelphia. It has passed into a proverb that the Friends, on these occasions, always bring rain with them; and the period of her visit was no exception to the rule. The showery days of "Yearly Meeting Week" glided by, until the last, and she looked forward with relief to the morrow's return to Bucks County, glad to have escaped a meeting with Richard Hilton, which might have confirmed her fears and could but have given her pain in any case.

As she and her father joined each other, outside the meeting-house, at the close of the afternoon meeting, a light rain was falling. She took his arm, under the capacious umbrella, and they were soon alone in the wet streets, on their way to the house of the Friends who entertained them. At a crossing, where the water pouring down the gutter towards the Delaware, caused them to halt a man, plashing through the flood, staggered towards them. Without an umbrella, with dripping, disordered clothes, yet with a hot, flushed face, around which the long black hair hung wildly, he approached, singing to himself with maudlin voice a song that would have been sweet and tender in a lover's mouth. Friend Mitchenor drew to one side, lest his spotless drab should be brushed by the unclean reveller; but the latter, looking up, stopped suddenly face to face with them.

"Asenath!" he cried, in a voice whose anguish pierced through the confusion of his senses, and struck down into the sober quick of his soul.

"Richard!" she breathed, rather than spoke, in a low, terrified voice.

It was indeed Richard Hilton who stood before her, or rather—as she afterwards thought, in recalling the interview—the body of Richard Hilton possessed by an evil spirit. His cheeks burned with a more than hectic red, his eyes were wild and bloodshot, and though the recognition had suddenly sobered him, an impatient, reckless devil seemed to lurk under the set mask of his features.

"Here I am, Asenath," he said at length, hoarsely. "I said it was death, didn't I? Well, it's worse than death, I suppose; but what matter? You can't be more lost to me now than you were already. This is THY doing, Friend Eli," he continued, turning to the old man, with a sneering emphasis on the "THY." "I hope thee's satisfied with thy work!"

Here he burst into a bitter, mocking laugh, which it chilled Asenath's blood to hear.

The old man turned pale. "Come away, child!" said he, tugging at her arm. But she stood firm, strengthened for the moment by a solemn feeling of duty which trampled down her pain.

"Richard," she said, with the music of an immeasurable sorrow in her voice, "oh, Richard, what has thee done? Where the Lord commands resignation, thee has been rebellious; where he chasteneth to purify, thee turns blindly to sin. I had not expected this of thee, Richard; I thought thy regard for me was of the kind which would have helped and uplifted thee,— not through me, as an unworthy object, but through the hopes and the pure desires of thy own heart. I expected that thee would so act as to justify what I felt towards thee, not to make my affection a reproach,—oh, Richard, not to cast over my heart the shadow of thy sin!"

The wretched young man supported himself against the post of an awning, buried his face in his hands, and wept passionately. Once or twice he essayed to speak, but his voice was choked by sobs, and, after a look from the streaming eyes which Asenath could scarcely bear to meet, he again covered his face. A stranger, coming down the street, paused out of curiosity. "Come, come!" cried Eli, once more, eager to escape from the scene. His daughter stood still, and the man slowly passed on.

Asenath could not thus leave her lost lover, in his despairing grief. She again turned to him, her own tears flowing fast and free.

"I do not judge thee, Richard, but the words that passed between us give me a right to speak to thee. It was hard to lose sight of thee then, but it is still harder for me to see thee now. If the sorrow and pity I feel could save thee, I would be willing never to know any other feelings. I would still do anything for thee except that which thee cannot ask, as thee now is, and I could not give. Thee has made the gulf between us so wide that it cannot be crossed. But I can now weep for thee and pray for thee as a fellow-creature whose soul is still precious in the sight of the Lord. Fare thee well!"

He seized the hand she extended, bowed down, and showered mingled tears and kisses upon it. Then, with a wild sob in his throat, he started up and rushed down the street, through the fast-falling rain. The father and daughter walked home in silence. Eli had heard every word that was spoken, and felt that a spirit whose utterances he dared not question had visited Asenath's tongue.

She, as year after year went by, regained the peace and patience which give a sober cheerfulness to life. The pangs of her heart grew dull and transient; but there were two pictures in her memory which never blurred in outline or faded in color: one, the brake of autumn flowers under the bright autumnal sky, with bird and stream making accordant music to the new voice of love; the other a rainy street, with a lost, reckless man leaning against an awning-post, and staring in her face with eyes whose unutterable woe, when she dared to recall it, darkened the beauty of the earth, and almost shook her trust in the providence of God.

# V

Year after year passed by, but not without bringing change to the Mitchenor family. Moses had moved to Chester County soon after his marriage, and had a good farm of his own. At the end of ten years Abigail died; and the old man, who had not only lost his savings by an unlucky investment, but was obliged to mortgage his farm, finally determined to sell it and join his son. He was getting too old to manage it properly, impatient under the unaccustomed pressure of debt, and depressed by the loss of the wife to whom, without any outward show of tenderness, he was, in truth, tenderly attached. He missed her more keenly in the places where she had lived and moved than in a neighborhood without the memory of her presence. The pang with which he parted from his home was weakened by the greater pang which had preceded it.

It was a harder trial to Asenath. She shrank from the encounter with new faces, and the necessity of creating new associations. There was a quiet satisfaction in the ordered, monotonous round of her life, which might be the same elsewhere, but here alone was the nook which held all the morning sunshine she had ever known. Here still lingered the halo of the sweet departed summer,—here still grew the familiar wild-flowers which THE FIRST Richard Hilton had gathered. This was the Paradise in which the Adam of her heart had dwelt, before his fall. Her resignation and submission entitled her to keep those pure and perfect memories, though she was scarcely conscious of their true charm. She did not dare to express to herself, in words, that one everlasting joy of woman's heart, through all trials and sorrows—"I have loved, I have been beloved."

On the last "First-day" before their departure, she walked down the meadows to the lonely brake between the hills. It was the early spring, and the black buds of the ash had just begun to swell. The maples were dusted with crimson bloom, and the downy catkins of the swamp-willow dropped upon the stream and floated past her, as once the autumn leaves. In the edges of the thickets peeped forth the blue, scentless violet, the fairy cups of the anemone, and the pink-veined bells of the miskodeed. The tall blooms through which the lovers walked still slept in the chilly earth; but the sky above her was mild and blue, and the remembrance of the day came back to her with a delicate, pungent sweetness, like the perfume of the trailing arbutus in the air around her. In a sheltered, sunny nook, she found a single erythronium, lured forth in advance of its proper season, and gathered it as a relic of the spot, which she might keep without blame. As she stooped to pluck it, her own face looked up at her out of a little pool filled by the spring rains. Seen against the reflected sky, it shone with a soft radiance, and the earnest eyes met hers, as if it were her young self, evoked from the past, to bid her farewell. "Farewell!" she whispered, taking leave at once, as she believed, of youth and the memory of love.

During those years she had more than once been sought in marriage, but had steadily, though kindly, refused. Once, when the suitor was a man whose character and position made the union very desirable in Eli Mitchenor's eyes, he ventured to use his paternal influence. Asenath's gentle resistance was overborne by his arbitrary force of will, and her protestations were of no avail.

"Father," she finally said, in the tone which he had once heard and still remembered, "thee can take away, but thee cannot give."

He never mentioned the subject again.

Richard Hilton passed out of her knowledge shortly after her meeting with him in Philadelphia. She heard, indeed, that his headlong career of dissipation was not arrested,—that his friends had given him up as hopelessly ruined,—and, finally, that he had left the city. After that, all reports ceased. He was either dead, or reclaimed and leading a better life, somewhere far away. Dead, she believed—almost hoped; for in that case might he not now be enjoying the ineffable rest and peace which she trusted might be her portion? It was better to think of him as a purified spirit, waiting to meet her in a holier communion, than to know that he was still bearing the burden of a soiled and blighted life. In any case, her own future was plain and clear. It was simply a prolongation of the present—an alternation of seed-time and harvest, filled with humble duties and cares, until the Master should bid her lay down her load and follow Him.

Friend Mitchenor bought a small cottage adjacent to his son's farm, in a community which consisted mostly of Friends, and not far from the large old meeting-house in which the Quarterly Meetings were held. He at once took his place on the upper seat, among the elders, most of whom he knew already, from having met them, year after year, in Philadelphia. The charge of a few acres of ground gave him sufficient occupation; the money left to him after the sale of his farm was enough to support him comfortably; and a late Indian summer of contentment seemed now to have come to the old man. He was done with the earnest business of life. Moses was gradually taking his place, as father and Friend; and Asenath would be reasonably provided for at his death. As his bodily energies decayed, his imperious temper softened, his mind became more accessible to liberal influences, and he even cultivated a cordial friendship with a neighboring farmer who was one of "the world's people." Thus, at seventy-five he was really younger, because tenderer of heart and more considerate, than he had been at sixty.

Asenath was now a woman of thirty-five, and suitors had ceased to approach her. Much of her beauty still remained, but her face had become thin and wasted, and the inevitable lines were beginning to form around her eyes. Her dress was plainer than ever, and she wore the scoop-bonnet of drab silk, in which no woman can seem beautiful, unless she be very old. She was calm and grave in her demeanor, save that her perfect goodness and benevolence shone through and warmed her presence; but, when earnestly interested, she had been known to speak her mind so clearly and forcibly that it was generally surmised among the Friends that she possessed "a gift," which might, in time, raise her to honor among them. To the children of Moses she was a good genius, and a word from "Aunt 'Senath" oftentimes prevailed when the authority of the parents was disregarded. In them she found a new source of happiness; and when her old home on the Neshaminy had been removed a little farther into the past, so that she no longer looked, with every morning's sun, for some familiar feature of its scenery, her submission brightened into a cheerful content with life.

It was summer, and Quarterly-Meeting Day had arrived. There had been rumors of the expected presence of "Friends from a distance," and not only those of the district, but most of the neighbors who were not connected with the sect, attended. By the by-road, through the woods, it was not more than half a mile from Friend Mitchenor's cottage to the meeting-house, and Asenath, leaving her father to be taken by Moses in his carriage, set out on foot. It was a sparkling, breezy day, and the forest was full of life. Squirrels chased each other along the branches of the oaks, and the air was filled with fragrant odors of hickory-leaves, sweet fern, and spice-wood. Picking up a flower here and there, Asenath walked onward, rejoicing alike in shade and sunshine, grateful for all the consoling beauty which the earth offers to a lonely heart. That serene content which she had learned to call happiness had filled her being until the dark canopy was lifted and the waters took back their transparency under a cloudless sky.

Passing around to the "women's side" of the meeting-house, she mingled with her friends, who were exchanging information concerning the expected visitors. Micajah Morrill had not arrived, they said, but Ruth Baxter had spent the last night at Friend Way's, and would certainly be there. Besides, there were Friend Chandler, from Nine Partners, and Friend

Carter, from Maryland: they had been seen on the ground. Friend Carter was said to have a wonderful gift,—Mercy Jackson had heard him once, in Baltimore. The Friends there had been a little exercised about him, because they thought he was too much inclined to "the newness," but it was known that the Spirit had often manifestly led him. Friend Chandler had visited Yearly Meeting once, they believed. He was an old man, and had been a personal friend of Elias Hicks.

At the appointed hour they entered the house. After the subdued rustling which ensued upon taking their seats, there was an interval of silence, shorter than usual, because it was evident that many persons would feel the promptings of the Spirit. Friend Chandler spoke first, and was followed by Ruth Baxter, a frail little woman, with a voice of exceeding power. The not unmelodious chant in which she delivered her admonitions rang out, at times, like the peal of a trumpet. Fixing her eyes on vacancy, with her hands on the wooden rail before her, and her body slightly swaying to and fro, her voice soared far aloft at the commencement of every sentence, gradually dropping, through a melodious scale of tone, to the close. She resembled an inspired prophetess, an aged Deborah, crying aloud in the valleys of Israel.

The last speaker was Friend Carter, a small man, not more than forty years of age. His face was thin and intense in its expression, his hair gray at the temples, and his dark eye almost too restless for a child of "the stillness and the quietness." His voice, though not loud, was clear and penetrating, with an earnest, sympathetic quality, which arrested, not the ear alone, but the serious attention of the auditor. His delivery was but slightly marked by the peculiar rhythm of the Quaker preachers; and this fact, perhaps, increased the effect of his words, through the contrast with those who preceded him.

His discourse was an eloquent vindication of the law of kindness, as the highest and purest manifestation of true Christian doctrine.

The paternal relation of God to man was the basis of that religion which appealed directly to the heart: so the fraternity of each man with his fellow was its practical application. God pardons the repentant sinner: we can also pardon, where we are offended; we can pity, where we cannot pardon. Both the good and the bad principles generate their like in others. Force begets force; anger excites a corresponding anger; but kindness awakens the slumbering emotions even of an evil heart. Love may not always be answered by an equal love, but it has never yet created hatred. The testimony which Friends bear against war, he said, is but a general assertion, which has no value except in so far as they manifest the principle of peace in their daily lives—in the exercise of pity, of charity, of forbearance, and Christian love.

The words of the speaker sank deeply into the hearts of his hearers. There was an intense hush, as if in truth the Spirit had moved him to speak, and every sentence was armed with a sacred authority. Asenath Mitchenor looked at him, over the low partition which divided her and her sisters from the men's side, absorbed in his rapt earnestness and truth. She forgot that other hearers were present: he spake to her alone. A strange spell seemed to seize upon her faculties and chain them at his feet: had he beckoned to her, she would have arisen and walked to his side.

Friend Carter warmed and deepened as he went on. "I feel moved to-day," he said,—"moved, I know not why, but I hope for some wise purpose,—to relate to you an instance of Divine and human kindness which has come directly to my own knowledge. A young man of delicate constitution, whose lungs were thought to be seriously affected, was sent to the house of a Friend in the country, in order to try the effect of air and exercise."

Asenath almost ceased to breathe, in the intensity with which she gazed and listened. Clasping her hands tightly in her lap to prevent them from trembling, and steadying herself against the back of the seat, she heard the story of her love for Richard Hilton told by the lips of a stranger!—not merely of his dismissal from the house, but of that meeting in the street, at which only she and her father were present! Nay, more, she heard her own words repeated, she heard Richard's passionate outburst of remorse described in language that brought his living face before her! She gasped for breath—his face WAS before her! The features, sharpened by despairing grief, which her memory recalled, had almost anticipated the harder lines which fifteen years had made, and which now, with a terrible shock and choking leap of the heart, she recognized. Her senses faded, and she would have fallen from her seat but for the support of the partition against which she leaned. Fortunately, the women near her were too much occupied with the narrative to notice her condition. Many of them wept silently, with their handkerchiefs pressed over their mouths.

The first shock of death-like faintness passed away, and she clung to the speaker's voice, as if its sound alone could give her strength to sit still and listen further.

"Deserted by his friends, unable to stay his feet on the evil path," he continued, "the young man left his home and went to a city in another State. But here it was easier to find associates in evil than tender hearts that might help him back to good. He was tired of life, and the hope of a speedier death hardened him in his courses. But, my friends, Death never comes to those who wickedly seek him. The Lord withholds destruction from the hands that are madly outstretched to grasp it, and forces His pity and forgiveness on the unwilling soul. Finding that it was the principle of LIFE which grew stronger within him, the young man at last meditated an awful crime. The thought of self-destruction haunted him day and night. He lingered around the wharves, gazing into the deep waters, and was restrained from the deed only by the memory of the last loving voice he had heard. One gloomy evening, when even this memory had faded, and he awaited the approaching darkness to make his design secure, a hand was laid on his arm. A man in the simple garb of the Friends stood beside him, and a face which reflected the kindness of the Divine Father looked upon him. 'My child,' said he, 'I am drawn to thee by the great trouble of thy mind. Shall I tell thee what it is thee meditates?' The young man shook his head. 'I will be silent, then, but I will save thee. I know the human heart, and its trials and weaknesses, and it may be put into my mouth to give thee strength.' He took the young man's hand, as if he had been a little child, and led him to his home. He heard the sad story, from beginning to end; and the young man wept upon his breast, to hear no word of reproach, but only the largest and tenderest pity bestowed upon him. They knelt down, side by side, at midnight; and the Friend's right hand was upon his head while they prayed.

"The young man was rescued from his evil ways, to acknowledge still further the boundless mercy of Providence. The dissipation wherein he had recklessly sought death was, for him, a marvellous restoration to life. His lungs had become sound and free from the tendency to disease. The measure of his forgiveness was almost more than he could bear. He bore his cross thenceforward with a joyful resignation, and was mercifully drawn nearer and nearer to the Truth, until, in the fulness of his convictions, he entered into the brotherhood of the Friends.

"I have been powerfully moved to tell you this story." Friend Carter concluded, "from a feeling that it may be needed, here, at this time, to influence some heart trembling in the balance. Who is there among you, my friends, that may not snatch a brand from the burning! Oh, believe that pity and charity are the most effectual weapons given into the hands of us imperfect mortals, and leave the awful attribute of wrath in the hands of the Lord!"

He sat down, and dead silence ensued. Tears of emotion stood in the eyes of the hearers, men as well as women, and tears of gratitude and thanksgiving gushed warmly from those of Asenath. An ineffable peace and joy descended upon her heart.

When the meeting broke up, Friend Mitchenor, who had not recognized Richard Hilton, but had heard the story with feelings which he endeavored in vain to control, approached the preacher.

"The Lord spoke to me this day through thy lips," said he; "will thee come to one side, and hear me a minute?"

"Eli Mitchenor!" exclaimed Friend Carter; "Eli! I knew not thee was here! Doesn't thee know me?"

The old man stared in astonishment. "It seems like a face I ought to know," he said, "but I can't place thee." They withdrew to the shade of one of the poplars. Friend Carter turned again, much moved, and, grasping the old man's hands in his own, exclaimed—

"Friend Mitchenor, I was called upon to-day to speak of myself. I am—or, rather, I WAS—the Richard Hilton whom thee knew."

Friend Mitchenor's face flushed with mingled emotions of shame and joy, and his grasp on the preacher's hands tightened.

"But thee calls thyself Carter?" he finally said.

"Soon after I was saved," was the reply, "an aunt on the mother's side died, and left her property to me, on condition that I should take her name. I was tired of my own then, and to give it up seemed only like losing my former self; but I should like to have it back again now."

"Wonderful are the ways of the Lord, and past finding out!" said the old man. "Come home with me, Richard,—come for my sake, for there is a concern on my mind until all is clear between us. Or, stay,—will thee walk home with Asenath, while I go with Moses?"

"Asenath?"

"Yes. There she goes, through the gate. Thee can easily overtake her. I 'm coming, Moses!"—and he hurried away to his son's carriage, which was approaching.

Asenath felt that it would be impossible for her to meet Richard Hilton there. She knew not why his name had been changed; he had not betrayed his identity with the young man of his story; he evidently did not wish it to be known, and an unexpected meeting with her might surprise him into an involuntary revelation of the fact. It was enough for her that a saviour had arisen, and her lost Adam was redeemed,—that a holier light than the autumn sun's now rested, and would forever rest, on the one landscape of her youth. Her eyes shone with the pure brightness of girlhood, a soft warmth colored her cheek and smoothed away the coming lines of her brow, and her step was light and elastic as in the old time.

Eager to escape from the crowd, she crossed the highway, dusty with its string of returning carriages, and entered the secluded lane. The breeze had died away, the air was full of insect-sounds, and the warm light of the sinking sun fell upon the woods and meadows. Nature seemed penetrated with a sympathy with her own inner peace.

But the crown of the benignant day was yet to come. A quick footstep followed her, and ere long a voice, near at hand, called her by name.

She stopped, turned, and for a moment they stood silent, face to face.

"I knew thee, Richard!" at last she said, in a trembling voice; "may the Lord bless thee!"

Tears were in the eyes of both.

"He has blessed me," Richard answered, in a reverent tone; "and this is His last and sweetest mercy. Asenath, let me hear that thee forgives me."

"I have forgiven thee long ago, Richard—forgiven, but not forgotten."

The hush of sunset was on the forest, as they walked onward, side by side, exchanging their mutual histories. Not a leaf stirred in the crowns of the tall trees, and the dusk, creeping along between their stems, brought with it a richer woodland odor. Their voices were low and subdued, as if an angel of God were hovering in the shadows, and listening, or God Himself looked down upon them from the violet sky.

At last Richard stopped.

"Asenath," said he, "does thee remember that spot on the banks of the creek, where the rudbeckias grew?"

"I remember it," she answered, a girlish blush rising to her face.

"If I were to say to thee now what I said to thee there, what would be thy answer?"

Her words came brokenly.

"I would say to thee, Richard,—'I can trust thee,—I DO love thee!'"

"Look at me, Asenath."

Her eyes, beaming with a clearer light than even then when she first confessed, were lifted to his. She placed her hands gently upon his shoulders, and bent her head upon his breast. He tenderly lifted it again, and, for the first time, her virgin lips knew the kiss of man.

# MISS BARTRAM'S TROUBLE

## I

It was a day of unusual excitement at the Rambo farm-house. On the farm, it is true, all things were in their accustomed order, and all growths did their accustomed credit to the season. The fences were in good repair; the cattle were healthy and gave promise of the normal increase, and the young corn was neither strangled with weeds nor assassinated by cutworms. Old John Rambo was gradually allowing his son, Henry, to manage in his stead, and the latter shrewdly permitted his father to believe that he exercised the ancient authority. Leonard Clare, the strong young fellow who had been taken from that shiftless adventurer, his father, when a mere child, and brought up almost as one of the family, and who had worked as a joiner's apprentice during the previous six months, had come back for the harvest work; so the Rambos were forehanded, and probably as well satisfied as it is possible for Pennsylvania farmers to be.

In the house, also, Mrs. Priscilla Rambo was not severely haunted by the spectre of any neglected duty. The simple regular routine of the household could not be changed under her charge; each thing had its appropriate order of performance, must be done, and WAS done. If the season were backward, at the time appointed for whitewashing or soap-making, so much the worse for the season; if the unhatched goslings were slain by thunder, she laid the blame on the thunder. And if—but no, it is quite impossible to suppose that, outside of those two inevitable, fearful house-cleaning weeks in each year, there could have been any disorder in the cold prim, varnish-odored best rooms, sacred to company.

It was Miss Betty Rambo, whose pulse beat some ten strokes faster than its wont, as she sat down with the rest to their early country dinner. Whether her brother Henry's participated in the accelerated movement could not be guessed from his demeanor. She glanced at him now and then, with bright eyes and flushed cheeks, eager to speak yet shrinking from the half magisterial air which was beginning to supplant his old familiar banter. Henry was changing with his new responsibility, as she admitted to herself with a sort of dismay; he had the airs of an independent farmer, and she remained only a farmer's daughter,—without any acknowledged rights, until she should acquire them all, at a single blow, by marriage.

Nevertheless, he must have felt what was in her mind; for, as he cut out the quarter of a dried apple pie, he said carelessly:

"I must go down to the Lion, this afternoon. There's a fresh drove of Maryland cattle just come."

"Oh Harry!" cried Betty, in real distress.

"I know," he answered; "but as Miss Bartram is going to stay two weeks, she'll keep. She's not like a drove, that's here one day, and away the next. Besides, it is precious little good I shall have of her society, until you two have used up all your secrets and small talk. I know how it is with girls. Leonard will drive over to meet the train."

"Won't I do on a pinch?" Leonard asked.

"Oh, to be sure," said Betty, a little embarrassed, "only Alice—Miss Bartram—might expect Harry, because her brother came for me when I went up."

"If that's all, make yourself easy, Bet," Henry answered, as he rose from the table. "There's a mighty difference between here and there. Unless you mean to turn us into a town family while she stays—high quality, eh?"

"Go along to your cattle! there's not much quality, high or low, where you are."

Betty was indignant; but the annoyance exhausted itself healthfully while she was clearing away the dishes and restoring the room to its order, so that when Leonard drove up to the gate with the lumbering, old-fashioned carriage two hours afterwards, she came forth calm, cheerful, fresh as a pink in her pink muslin, and entirely the good, sensible country-girl she was.

Two or three years before, she and Miss Alice Bartram, daughter of the distinguished lawyer in the city, had been room-mates at the Nereid Seminary for Young Ladies. Each liked the other for the contrast to her own self; both were honest, good and lovable, but Betty had the stronger nerves and a practical sense which seemed to be admirable courage in the eyes of Miss Alice, whose instincts were more delicate, whose tastes were fine and high, and who could not conceive of life without certain luxurious accessories. A very cordial friendship sprang up between them,—not the effusive girl-love, with its iterative kisses, tears, and flow of loosened hair, but springing from the respect inspired by sound and positive qualities.

The winter before, Betty had been invited to visit her friend in the city, and had passed a very excited and delightful week in the stately Bartram mansion. If she were at first a little fluttered by the manners of the new world, she was intelligent enough to carry her own nature frankly through it, instead of endeavoring to assume its character. Thus her little awkwardnesses became originalities, and she was almost popular in the lofty circle when she withdrew from it. It was therefore, perhaps, slightly inconsistent in Betty, that she was not quite sure how Miss Bartram would accept the reverse side of this social experience. She imagined it easier to look down and make allowances, as a host, than as a guest; she could not understand that the charm of the change might be fully equal.

It was lovely weather, as they drove up the sweet, ever-changing curves of the Brandywine valley. The woods fairly laughed in the clear sunlight, and the soft, incessant, shifting breezes. Leonard, in his best clothes, and with a smoother gloss on his brown hair, sang to himself as he urged the strong-boned horses into a trot along the levels; and Betty finally felt so quietly happy that she forgot to be nervous. When they reached the station they walked up and down the long platform together, until the train from the city thundered up, and painfully restrained its speed. Then Betty, catching sight of a fawn-colored travelling dress issuing from the ladies' car, caught hold of Leonard's arm, and cried: "There she is!"

Miss Bartram heard the words, and looked down with a bright, glad expression on her face. It was not her beauty that made Leonard's heart suddenly stop beating; for she was not considered a beauty, in society. It was something rarer than perfect beauty, yet even more difficult to describe,—a serene, unconscious grace, a pure, lofty maturity of womanhood, such as our souls bow down to in the Santa Barbara of Palma Vecchio. Her features were not "faultlessly regular," but they were informed with the finer harmonies of her character. She was a woman, at whose feet a noble man might kneel, lay his forehead on her knee, confess his sins, and be pardoned.

She stepped down to the platform, and Betty's arms were about her. After a double embrace she gently disengaged herself, turned to Leonard, gave him her hand, and said, with a smile which was delightfully frank and cordial: "I will not wait for Betty's introduction, Mr. Rambo. She has talked to me so much of her brother Harry, that I quite know you already."

Leonard could neither withdraw his eyes nor his hand. It was like a double burst of warmth and sunshine, in which his breast seemed to expand, his stature to grow, and his whole nature to throb with some new and wonderful force. A faint color came into Miss Bartram's cheeks, as they stood thus, for a moment, face to face. She seemed to be waiting for him to speak, but of this he never thought; had any words come to his mind, his tongue could not have uttered them.

"It is not Harry," Betty explained, striving to hide her embarrassment. "This is Leonard Clare, who lives with us."

"Then I do not know you so well as I thought," Miss Bartram said to him; "it is the beginning of a new acquaintance, after all."

"There isn't no harm done," Leonard answered, and instantly feeling the awkwardness of the words, blushed so painfully that Miss Bartram felt the inadequacy of her social tact to relieve so manifest a case of distress. But she did, instinctively, what was really best: she gave Leonard the check for her trunk, divided her satchels with Betty, and walked to the carriage.

He did not sing, as he drove homewards down the valley. Seated on the trunk, in front, he quietly governed the horses, while the two girls, on the seat behind him, talked constantly and gaily. Only the rich, steady tones of Miss Bartram's voice WOULD make their way into his ears, and every light, careless sentence printed itself upon his memory. They came to him as if from some inaccessible planet. Poor fellow! he was not the first to feel "the desire of the moth for the star."

When they reached the Rambo farm-house, it was necessary that he should give his hand to help her down from the clumsy carriage. He held it but a moment; yet in that moment a gentle pulse throbbed upon his hard palm, and he mechanically set his teeth, to keep down the impulse which made him wild to hold it there forever. "Thank you, Mr. Clare!" said Miss Bartram, and passed into the house. When he followed presently, shouldering her trunk into the upper best-room, and kneeling upon the floor to unbuckle the straps, she found herself wondering: "Is this a knightly service, or the menial duty of a porter? Can a man be both sensitive and ignorant, chivalrous and vulgar?"

The question was not so easily decided, though no one guessed how much Miss Bartram pondered it, during the succeeding days. She insisted, from the first, that her coming should make no change in the habits of the household; she rose in the cool, dewy summer dawns, dined at noon in the old brown room beside the kitchen, and only differed from the Rambos in sitting at her moonlit window, and breathing the subtle odors of a myriad leaves, long after Betty was sleeping the sleep of health.

It was strange how frequently the strong, not very graceful figure of Leonard Clare marched through these reveries. She occasionally spoke to him at the common table, or as she passed the borders of the hay-field, where he and Henry were at work: but his words to her were always few and constrained. What was there in his eyes that haunted her? Not merely a most reverent admiration of her pure womanly refinement, although she read that also; not a fear of disparagement, such as his awkward speech implied, but something which seemed to seek agonizingly for another language than that of the lips,—something which appealed to her from equal ground, and asked for an answer.

One evening she met him in the lane, as she returned from the meadow. She carried a bunch of flowers, with delicate blue and lilac bells, and asked him the name.

"Them's Brandywine cowslips," he answered; "I never heard no other name."

"May I correct you?" she said, gently, and with a smile which she meant to be playful. "I suppose the main thing is to speak one's thought, but there are neat and orderly ways, and there are careless ways." Thereupon she pointed out the inaccuracies of his answer, he standing beside her, silent and attentive. When she ceased, he did not immediately reply.

"You will take it in good part, will you not?" she continued. "I hope I have not offended you."

"No!" he exclaimed, firmly, lifting his head, and looking at her. The inscrutable expression in his dark gray eyes was stronger than before, and all his features were more clearly drawn. He reminded her of a picture of Adam which she had once seen: there was the same rather low forehead, straight, even brows, full yet strong mouth, and that broader form of chin which repeats and balances the character of the forehead. He was not positively handsome, but from head to foot he expressed a fresh, sound quality of manhood.

Another question flashed across Miss Bartram's mind: Is life long enough to transform this clay into marble? Here is a man in form, and with all the dignity of the perfect masculine nature: shall the broad, free intelligence, the grace and sweetness, the taste and refinement, which the best culture gives, never be his also? If not, woman must be content with faulty representations of her ideal.

So musing, she walked on to the farm-house. Leonard had picked up one of the blossoms she had let fall, and appeared to be curiously examining it. If he had apologized for his want of grammar, or promised to reform it, her interest in him might have diminished; but his silence, his simple, natural obedience to some powerful inner force, whatever it was, helped to strengthen that phantom of him in her mind, which was now beginning to be a serious trouble.

Once again, the day before she left the Rambo farmhouse to return to the city, she came upon him, alone. She had wandered off to the Brandywine, to gather ferns at a rocky point where some choice varieties were to be found. There were a few charming clumps, half-way up a slaty cliff, which it did not seem possible to scale, and she was standing at the base, looking up in vain longing, when a voice, almost at her ear, said:

"Which ones do you want?"

Afterwards, she wondered that she did not start at the voice. Leonard had come up the road from one of the lower fields: he wore neither coat nor waistcoat, and his shirt, open at the throat, showed the firm, beautiful white of the flesh below the strong tan of his neck. Miss Bartram noticed the sinewy strength and elasticity of his form, yet when she looked again at the ferns, she shook her head, and answered:

"None, since I cannot have them."

Without saying a word, he took off his shoes, and commenced climbing the nearly perpendicular face of the cliff. He had done it before, many a time; but Miss Bartram, although she was familiar with such exploits from the pages of many novels, had never seen the reality, and it quite took away her breath.

When he descended with the ferns in his hand, she said: "It was a great risk; I wish I had not wanted them."

"It was no risk for me," he answered.

"What can I send you in return?" she asked, as they walked forwards. "I am going home to-morrow."

"Betty told me," Leonard said; "please, wait one minute."

He stepped down to the bank of the stream, washed his hands carefully in the clear water, and came back to her, holding them, dripping, at his sides.

"I am very ignorant," he then continued,—"ignorant and rough. You are good, to want to send me something, but I want nothing. Miss Bartram, you are very good."

He paused; but with all her tact and social experience, she did not know what to say.

"Would you do one little thing for me—not for the ferns, that was nothing—no more than you do, without thinking, for all your friends?"

"Oh, surely!" she said.

"Might I—might I—now,—there'll be no chance tomorrow,—shake hands with you?"

The words seemed to be forced from him by the strength of a fierce will. Both stopped, involuntarily.

"It's quite dry, you see," said he, offering his hand. Her own sank upon it, palm to palm, and the fingers softly closed over each, as if with the passion and sweetness of a kiss. Miss Bartram's heart came to her eyes, and read, at last, the question in Leonard's. It was: "I as man, and you, as woman, are equals; will you give me time to reach you?" What her eyes replied she knew not. A mighty influence drew her on, and a mighty doubt and dread restrained her. One said: "Here is your lover, your husband, your cherished partner, left by fate below your station, yet whom you may lift to your side! Shall man, alone, crown the humble maiden,—stoop to love, and, loving, ennoble? Be you the queen, and love him by the royal right of womanhood!" But the other sternly whispered: "How shall your fine and delicate fibres be knit into this coarse texture? Ignorance, which years cannot wash away,—low instincts, what do YOU know?—all the servile side of life, which is turned from you,—what madness to choose this, because some current of earthly magnetism sets along your nerves? He loves you: what of that? You are a higher being to him, and he stupidly adores you. Think,— yes, DARE to think of all the prosaic realities of life, shared with him!"

Miss Bartram felt herself growing dizzy. Behind the impulse which bade her cast herself upon his breast swept such a hot wave of shame and pain that her face burned, and she dropped her eyelids to shut out the sight of his face. But, for one endless second, the sweeter voice spoke through their clasped hands. Perhaps he kissed hers; she did not know; she only heard herself murmur:

"Good-bye! Pray go on; I will rest here."

She sat down upon a bank by the roadside, turned away her head, and closed her eyes. It was long before the tumult in her nature subsided. If she reflected, with a sense of relief, "nothing was said," the thought immediately followed, "but all is known." It was impossible,—yes, clearly impossible; and then came such a wild longing, such an assertion of the right and truth and justice of love, as made her seem a miserable coward, the veriest slave of conventionalities.

Out of this struggle dawned self-knowledge, and the strength which is born of it. When she returned to the house, she was pale and weary, but capable of responding to Betty Rambo's constant cheerfulness. The next day she left for the city, without having seen Leonard Clare again.

# II

Henry Rambo married, and brought a new mistress to the farm-house. Betty married, and migrated to a new home in another part of the State. Leonard Clare went back to his trade, and returned no more in harvest-time. So the pleasant farm by the Brandywine, having served its purpose as a background, will be seen no more in this history.

Miss Bartram's inmost life, as a woman, was no longer the same. The point of view from which she had beheld the world was shifted, and she was obliged to remodel all her feelings and ideas to conform to it. But the process was gradual, and no one stood near enough to her to remark it. She was occasionally suspected of that "eccentricity" which, in a woman of five-and-twenty, is looked upon as the first symptom of a tendency to old-maidenhood, but which is really the sign of an earnest heart struggling with the questions of life. In the society of cities, most men give only the shallow, flashy surface of their natures to the young women they meet, and Miss Bartram, after that revelation of the dumb strength of an ignorant man, sometimes grew very impatient of the platitudes and affectations which came to her clad in elegant words, and accompanied by irreproachable manners.

She had various suitors; for that sense of grace and repose and sweet feminine power, which hung around her like an atmosphere, attracted good and true men towards her. To some, indeed, she gave that noble, untroubled friendship which is always possible between the best of the two sexes, and when she was compelled to deny the more intimate appeal, it was done with such frank sorrow, such delicate tenderness, that she never lost the friend in losing the lover. But, as one year after another went by, and the younger members of her family fell off into their separate domestic orbits, she began to shrink a little at the perspective of a lonely life, growing lonelier as it receded from the Present.

By this time, Leonard Clare had become almost a dream to her. She had neither seen him nor heard of him since he let go her hand on that memorable evening beside the stream. He was a strange, bewildering chance, a cypher concealing a secret which she could not intelligently read. Why should she keep the memory of that power which was, perhaps, some unconscious quality of his nature (no, it was not so! something deeper than reason cried:), or long since forgotten, if felt, by him?

The man whom she most esteemed came back to her. She knew the ripeness and harmony of his intellect, the nobility of his character, and the generosity of a feeling which would be satisfied with only a partial return. She felt sure, also, that she should never possess a sentiment nearer to love than that which pleaded his cause in her heart. But her hand lay quiet in his, her pulses were calm when he spoke, and his face, manly and true as it was, never invaded her dreams. All questioning was vain; her heart gave no solution of the riddle. Perhaps her own want was common to all lives: then she was cherishing a selfish ideal, and rejecting the positive good offered to her hands.

After long hesitation she yielded. The predictions of society came to naught; instead of becoming an "eccentric" spinster, Miss Bartram was announced to be the affianced bride of Mr. Lawrie. A few weeks and months rolled around, and when the wedding-day came, she almost hailed it as the port of refuge, where she should find a placid and peaceful life.

They were married by an aged clergyman, a relative of the bridegroom. The cross-street where his chapel stood, fronting a Methodist church—both of the simplest form of that architecture fondly supposed to be Gothic,—was quite blocked up by the carriages of the party. The pews were crowded with elegant guests, the altar was decorated with flowers, and the ceremony lacked nothing of its usual solemn beauty. The bride was pale, but strikingly calm and self-possessed, and when she moved towards the door as Mrs. Lawrie, on her husband's arm, many matrons, recalling their own experience, marvelled at her unflurried dignity.

Just as they passed out the door, and the bridal carriage was summoned, a singular thing happened. Another bridal carriage drew up from the opposite side, and a newly wedded pair came forth from the portal of the Methodist church. Both parties stopped, face to face, divided only by the narrow street. Mrs. Lawrie first noticed the flushed cheeks of the other bride, her white dress, rather showy than elegant, and the heavy gold ornaments she wore. Then she turned to the bridegroom. He was tall and well-formed, dressed like a gentleman, but like one who is not yet unconscious of his dress, and had the air of a man accustomed to exercise some authority.

She saw his face, and instantly all other faces disappeared. From the opposite brink of a tremendous gulf she looked into his eyes, and their blended ray of love and despair pierced her to the heart.

There was a roaring in her ears, followed a long sighing sound, like that of the wind on some homeless waste; she leaned more heavily on her husband's arm, leaned against his shoulder, slid slowly down into his supporting clasp, and knew no more.

"She's paying for her mock composure, after all," said the matrons.

"It must have been a great effort."

# III

Ten years afterwards, Mrs. Lawrie went on board a steamer at Southampton, bound for New York. She was travelling alone, having been called suddenly from Europe by the approaching death of her aged father. For two or three days after sailing, the thick, rainy spring weather kept all below, except a few hardy gentlemen who crowded together on the lee of the smoke-stack, and kept up a stubborn cheerfulness on a very small capital of comfort. There were few cabin-passengers on board, but the usual crowd of emigrants in the steerage.

Mrs. Lawrie's face had grown calmer and colder during these years. There was yet no gray in her hair, no wrinkles about her clear eyes; each feature appeared to be the same, but the pale, monotonous color which had replaced the warm bloom of her youth, gave them a different character. The gracious dignity of her manner, the mellow tones of her voice, still expressed her unchanging goodness, yet those who met her were sure to feel, in some inexplicable way, that to be good is not always to be happy. Perhaps, indeed, her manner was older than her face and form: she still attracted the interest of men, but with a certain doubt and reserve.

Certain it is that when she made her appearance on deck, glad of the blue sky and sunshine, and threw back her hood to feel the freshness of the sea air, all eyes followed her movements, except those of a forlorn individual, who, muffled in his cloak and apparently sea-sick, lay upon one of the benches. The captain presently joined her, and the gentlemen saw that she was bright and perfectly self-possessed in conversation: some of them immediately resolved to achieve an acquaintance. The dull, passive existence of the beginning of every voyage, seemed to be now at an end. It was time for the little society of the vessel to awake, stir itself, and organize a life of its own, for the few remaining days.

That night, as Mrs. Lawrie was sleeping in her berth, she suddenly awoke with a singular feeling of dread and suspense. She listened silently, but for some time distinguished none other than the small sounds of night on shipboard—the indistinct orders, the dragging of ropes, the creaking of timbers, the dull, regular jar of the engine, and the shuffling noise of feet overhead. But, ere long, she seemed to catch faint, distant sounds, that seemed like cries; then came hurry and confusion on deck; then voices in the cabin, one of which said: "they never can get it under, at this rate!"

She rose, dressed herself hastily, and made her way through pale and excited stewards, and the bewildered passengers who were beginning to rush from their staterooms, to the deck. In the wild tumult which prevailed, she might have been thrown down and trampled under foot, had not a strong arm seized her around the waist, and borne her towards the stern, where there were but few persons.

"Wait here!" said a voice, and her protector plunged into the crowd.

She saw, instantly, the terrible fate which had fallen upon the vessel. The bow was shrouded in whirls of smoke, through which dull red flashes began to show themselves; and all the length and breadth of the deck was filled with a screaming, struggling, fighting mass of desperate human beings. She saw the captain, officers, and a few of the crew working in vain against the disorder: she saw the boats filled before they were lowered, and heard the shrieks as they were capsized; she saw spars and planks and benches cast overboard, and maddened men plunging after them; and then, like the sudden opening of the mouth of Hell, the relentless, triumphant fire burst through the forward deck and shot up to the foreyard.

She was leaning against the mizen shrouds, between the coils of rope. Nobody appeared to notice her, although the quarter-deck was fast filling with persons driven back by the fire, yet still shrinking from the terror and uncertainty of the sea. She thought: "It is but death—why should I fear? The waves are at hand, to save me from all suffering." And the collective horror of hundreds of beings did not so overwhelm her as she had both fancied and feared; the tragedy of each individual life was lost in the confusion, and was she not a sharer in their doom?

Suddenly, a man stood before her with a cork life-preserver in his hands, and buckled it around her securely, under the arms. He was panting and almost exhausted, yet he strove to make his voice firm, and even cheerful, as he said:

"We fought the cowardly devils as long as there was any hope. Two boats are off, and two capsized; in ten minutes more every soul must take to the water. Trust to me, and I will save you or die with you!"

"What else can I do?" she answered.

With a few powerful strokes of an axe, he broke off the top of the pilot-house, bound two or three planks to it with ropes, and dragged the mass to the bulwarks.

"The minute this goes," he then said to her, "you go after it, and I follow. Keep still when you rise to the surface."

She left the shrouds, took hold of the planks at his side, and they heaved the rude raft into the sea. In an instant she was seized and whirled over the side; she instinctively held her breath, felt a shock, felt herself swallowed up in an awful, fathomless coldness, and then found herself floating below the huge towering hull which slowly drifted away.

In another moment there was one at her side. "Lay your hand on my shoulder," he said; and when she did so, swam for the raft, which they soon reached. While she supported herself by one of the planks he so arranged and bound together the pieces of timber that in a short time they could climb upon them and rest, not much washed by the waves. The ship drifted further and further, casting a faint, though awful, glare over the sea, until the light was suddenly extinguished, as the hull sank.

The dawn was in the sky by this time, and as it broadened they could see faint specks here and there, where others, like themselves, clung to drifting spars. Mrs. Lawrie shuddered with cold and the reaction from an excitement which had been far more powerful than she knew at the time.

Her preserver then took off his coat, wrapped it around her, and produced a pocket-flask, saying; "this will support us the longest; it is all I could find, or bring with me."

She sat, leaning against his shoulder, though partly turned away from him: all she could say was: "you are very good."

After awhile he spoke, and his voice seemed changed to her ears. "You must be thinking of Mr. Lawrie. It will, indeed, be terrible for him to hear of the disaster, before knowing that you are saved."

"God has spared him that distress," she answered. "Mr. Lawrie died, a year ago."

She felt a start in the strong frame upon which she leaned. After a few minutes of silence, he slowly shifted his position towards her, yet still without facing her, and said, almost in a whisper:

"You have said that I am very good. Will you put your hand in mine?"

She stretched hers eagerly and gratefully towards him. What had happened? Through all the numbness of her blood, there sprang a strange new warmth from his strong palm, and a pulse, which she had almost forgotten as a dream of the past, began to beat through her frame. She turned around all a-tremble, and saw his face in the glow of the coming day.

"Leonard Clare!" she cried.

"Then you have not forgotten me?"

"Could one forget, when the other remembers?"

The words came involuntarily from her lips. She felt what they implied, the moment afterwards, and said no more. But he kept her hand in his.

"Mrs. Lawrie," he began, after another silence, "we are hanging by a hair on the edge of life, but I shall gladly let that hair break, since I may tell you now, purely and in the hearing of God, how I have tried to rise to you out of the low place in which you found me. At first you seemed too far; but you yourself led me the first step of the way, and I have steadily kept my eyes on you, and followed it. When I had learned my trade, I came to the city. No labor was too hard for me, no study too difficult. I was becoming a new man, I saw all that was still lacking, and how to reach it, and I watched you, unknown, at a distance. Then I heard of your engagement: you were lost, and something of which I had begun to dream, became insanity. I determined to trample it out of my life. The daughter of the master-builder, whose first assistant I was, had always favored me in her society; and I soon persuaded her to love me. I fancied, too, that I loved her as most married men seemed to love their wives; the union would advance me to a partnership in her father's business, and my fortune would then be secured. You know what happened; but you do not know how the sight of your face planted the old madness again in my life, and made me a miserable husband, a miserable man of wealth, almost a scoffer at the knowledge I had acquired for your sake.

"When my wife died, taking an only child with her, there was nothing left to me except the mechanical ambition to make myself, without you, what I imagined I might have become, through you. I have studied and travelled, lived alone and in society, until your world seemed to be almost mine: but you were not there!"

The sun had risen, while they sat, rocking on their frail support. Her hand still lay in his, and her head rested on his shoulder. Every word he spoke sank into her heart with a solemn sweetness, in which her whole nature was silent and satisfied. Why should she speak? He knew all.

Yes, it seemed that he knew. His arm stole around her, and her head was drawn from his shoulder to the warm breadth of his breast.

Something hard pressed her cheek, and she lifted her hand to move it aside. He drew forth a flat medallion case; and to the unconscious question in her face, such a sad, tender smile came to his lips, that she could not repress a sudden pain. Was it the miniature of his dead wife?

He opened the case, and showed her, under the glass, a faded, pressed flower.

"What is it?" she asked.

"The Brandywine cowslip you dropped, when you spoke to me in the lane. Then it was that you showed me the first step of the way."

She laid her head again upon his bosom. Hour after hour they sat, and the light swells of the sea heaved them aimlessly to and fro, and the sun burned them, and the spray drenched their limbs. At last Leonard Clare roused himself and looked around: he felt numb and faint, and he saw, also, that her strength was rapidly failing.

"We cannot live much longer, I fear," he said, clasping her closely in his arms. "Kiss me once, darling, and then we will die."

She clung to him and kissed him.

"There is life, not death, in your lips!" he cried. "Oh, God, if we should live!"

He rose painfully to his feet, stood, tottering? on the raft, and looked across the waves. Presently he began to tremble, then to sob like a child, and at last spoke, through his tears:

"A sail! a sail!—and heading towards us!"

# MRS. STRONGITHARM'S REPORT

Mr. Editor,—If you ever read the "Burroak Banner" (which you will find among your exchanges, as the editor publishes your prospectus for six weeks every year, and sends no bill to you) my name will not be that of a stranger. Let me throw aside all affectation of humility, and say that I hope it is already and not unfavorably familiar to you. I am informed by those who claim to know that the manuscripts of obscure writers are passed over by you editors without examination—in short, that I must first have a name, if I hope to make one. The fact that an article of three hundred and seventy-five pages, which I sent, successively, to the "North American Review," the "Catholic World," and the "Radical," was in each case returned to me with MY knot on the tape by which it was tied, convinces me that such is indeed the case. A few years ago I should not have meekly submitted to treatment like this; but late experiences have taught me the vanity of many womanly dreams.

You are acquainted with the part I took (I am SURE you must have seen it in the "Burroak Banner" eight years ago) in creating that public sentiment in our favor which invested us with all the civil and political rights of men. How the editors of the "Revolution," to which I subscribe, and the conventions in favor of the equal rights of women, recently held in Boston and other cities, have failed to notice our noble struggle, is a circumstance for which I will not try to account. I will only say—and it is a hint which SOME PERSONS will understand—that there are other forms of jealousy than those which spring from love.

It is, indeed, incredible that so little is known, outside the State of Atlantic, of the experiment—I mean the achievement—of the last eight years. While the war lasted, we did not complain that our work was ignored; but now that our sisters in other States are acting as if in complete unconsciousness of what WE have done—now that we need their aid and they need ours (but in different ways), it is time that somebody should speak. Were Selina Whiston living, I should leave the task to her pen; she never recovered from the shock and mortification of her experiences in the State Legislature, in '64—but I will not anticipate the history. Of all the band of female iconoclasts, as the Hon. Mr. Screed called us in jest—it was no jest afterwards, HIS image being the first to go down—of all, I say, "some are married, and some are dead," and there is really no one left so familiar with the circumstances as I am, and equally competent to give a report of them.

Mr. Spelter (the editor of the "Burroak Banner") suggests that I must be brief, if I wish my words to reach the ears of the millions for whom they are designed; and I shall do my best to be so. If I were not obliged to begin at the very beginning, and if the interests of Atlantic had not been swallowed up, like those of other little States, in the whirlpool of national politics, I should have much less to say. But if Mr. George Fenian Brain and Mrs. Candy Station do not choose to inform the public of either the course or the results of our struggle, am I to blame? If I could have attended the convention in Boston, and had been allowed to speak—and I am sure the distinguished Chairwoman would have given me a chance—it would have been the best way, no doubt, to set our case before the world.

I must first tell you how it was that we succeeded in forcing the men to accept our claims, so much in advance of other States. We were indebted for it chiefly to the skill and adroitness of Selina Whiston. The matter had been agitated, it is true, for some years before, and as early as 1856, a bill, drawn up by Mrs. Whiston herself, had been introduced into the Legislature, where it received three votes. Moreover, we had held meetings in almost every election precinct in the State, and our Annual Fair (to raise funds) at Gaston, while the Legislature was in session, was always very brilliant and successful. So the people were not entirely unprepared.

Although our State had gone for Fremont in 1856, by a small majority, the Democrats afterwards elected their Governor; and both parties, therefore, had hopes of success in 1860. The canvass began early, and was very animated. Mrs. Whiston had already inaugurated the custom of attending political meetings, and occasionally putting a question to the stump orator—no matter of which party; of sometimes, indeed, taking the stump herself, after the others had exhausted their wind. She was very witty, as you know, and her stories were so good and so capitally told, that neither Democrat nor Republican thought of leaving the ground while she was upon the stand.

Now, it happened that our Congressional District was one of the closest. It happened, also, that our candidate (I am a Republican, and so is Mr. Strongitharm) was rather favorably inclined to the woman's cause. It happened, thirdly—and this is the seemingly insignificant pivot upon which we whirled into triumph—that he, Mr. Wrangle, and the opposing candidate, Mr. Tumbrill, had arranged to hold a joint meeting at Burroak. This meeting took place on a magnificent day, just after the oats-harvest;

and everybody, for twenty miles around, was there. Mrs. Whiston, together with Sarah Pincher, Olympia Knapp, and several other prominent advocates of our cause, met at my house in the morning; and we all agreed that it was time to strike a blow. The rest of us magnanimously decided to take no part in the concerted plan, though very eager to do so. Selina Whiston declared that she must have the field to herself; and when she said that, we knew she meant it.

It was generally known that she was on the ground. In fact, she spent most of the time while Messrs. Wrangle and Tumbrill were speaking, in walking about through the crowds—so after an hour apiece for the gentlemen, and then fifteen minutes apiece for a rejoinder, and the Star Spangled Banner from the band, for both sides, we were not a bit surprised to hear a few cries of "Whiston!" from the audience. Immediately we saw the compact gray bonnet and brown serge dress (she knew what would go through a crowd without tearing!) splitting the wedge of people on the steps leading to the platform. I noticed that the two Congressional candidates looked at each other and smiled, in spite of the venomous charges they had just been making.

Well—I won't attempt to report her speech, though it was her most splendid effort (as people WILL say, when it was no effort to her at all). But the substance of it was this: after setting forth woman's wrongs and man's tyranny, and taxation without representation, and an equal chance, and fair-play, and a struggle for life (which you know all about from the other conventions), she turned squarely around to the two candidates and said:

"Now to the practical application. You, Mr. Wrangle, and you, Mr. Tumbrill, want to be elected to Congress. The district is a close one: you have both counted the votes in advance (oh, I know your secrets!) and there isn't a difference of a hundred in your estimates. A very little will turn the scale either way. Perhaps a woman's influence—perhaps my voice—might do it. But I will give you an equal chance. So much power is left to woman, despite what you withhold, that we, the women of Putnam, Shinnebaug, and Rancocus counties, are able to decide which of you shall be elected. Either of you would give a great deal to have a majority of the intelligent women of the District on your side: it would already be equivalent to success. Now, to show that we understand the political business from which you have excluded us—to prove that we are capable of imitating the noble example of MEN—we offer to sell our influence, as they their votes, to the highest bidder!"

There was great shouting and cheering among the people at this, but the two candidates, somehow or other, didn't seem much amused.

"I stand here," she continued, "in the interest of my struggling sisters, and with authority to act for them. Which of you will bid the most—not in offices or material advantages, as is the way of your parties, but in the way of help to the Woman's Cause? Which of you will here publicly pledge himself to say a word for us, from now until election-day, whenever he appears upon the stump?"

There was repeated cheering, and cries of "Got 'em there!" (Men are so vulgar).

"I pause for a reply. Shall they not answer me?" she continued, turning to the audience.

Then there were tremendous cries of "Yes! yes! Wrangle! Tumbrill!"

Mr. Wrangle looked at Mr. Tumbrill, and made a motion with his head, signifying that he should speak. Then Mr. Tumbrill looked at Mr. Wrangle, and made a motion that HE should speak. The people saw all this, and laughed and shouted as if they would never finish.

Mr. Wrangle, on second thoughts (this is my private surmise), saw that boldness would just then be popular; so he stepped forward.

"Do I understand," he said, "that my fair and eloquent friend demands perfect political and civil equality for her sex?"

"I do!" exclaimed Selina Whiston, in her firmest manner.

"Let me be more explicit," he continued. "You mean precisely the same rights, the same duties, the same obligations, the same responsibilities?"

She repeated the phrases over after him, affirmatively, with an emphasis which I never heard surpassed.

"Pardon me once more," said Mr. Wrangle; "the right to vote, to hold office, to practise law, theology, medicine, to take part in all municipal affairs, to sit on juries, to be called upon to aid in the execution of the law, to aid in suppressing disturbances, enforcing public order, and performing military duty?"

Here there were loud cheers from the audience; and a good many voices cried out: "Got her there!" (Men are so very vulgar.)

Mrs. Whiston looked troubled for a moment, but she saw that a moment's hesitation would be fatal to our scheme, so she brought out her words as if each one were a maul-blow on the butt-end of a wedge:

"All—that—we—demand!"

"Then," said Mr. Wrangle, "I bid my support in exchange for the women's! Just what the speaker demands, without exception or modification—equal privileges, rights, duties and obligations, without regard to the question of sex! Is that broad enough?"

I was all in a tremble when it came to that. Somehow Mr. Wrangle's acceptance of the bid did not inspire me, although it promised so much. I had anticipated opposition, dissatisfaction, tumult. So had Mrs. Whiston, and I could see, and the crowd could see, that she was not greatly elated.

Mr. Wrangle made a very significant bow to Mr. Tumbrill, and then sat down. There were cries of "Tumbrill!" and that gentleman—none of us, of course, believing him sincere, for we knew his private views—came forward and made exactly the same pledge. I will do both parties the justice to say that they faithfully kept their word; nay, it was generally thought the repetition of their brief pleas for woman, at some fifty meetings before election came, had gradually conducted them to the belief that they were expressing their own personal sentiments. The mechanical echo in public thus developed into an opinion in private. My own political experience has since demonstrated to me that this is a phenomenon very common among men.

The impulse generated at that meeting gradually spread all over the State. We—the leaders of the Women's Movement—did not rest until we had exacted the same pledge from all the candidates of both parties; and the nearer it drew towards election-day, the more prominence was given, in the public meetings, to the illustration and discussion of the subject. Our State went for Lincoln by a majority of 2763 (as you will find by consulting the "Tribune Almanac"), and Mr. Wrangle was elected to Congress, having received a hundred and forty-two more votes than his opponent. Mr. Tumbrill has always attributed his defeat to his want of courage in not taking up at once the glove which Selina Whiston threw down.

I think I have said enough to make it clear how the State of Atlantic came to be the first to grant equal civil and political rights to women. When the Legislature of 1860-'61 met at Gaston, we estimated that we might count upon fifty-three out of the seventy-one Republican Senators and Assemblymen, and on thirty-four out of the sixty-five Democrats. This would give a majority of twenty-eight in the House, and ten in the Senate. Should the bill pass, there was still a possibility that it might be vetoed by the Governor, of whom we did not feel sure. We therefore arranged that our Annual Fair should be held a fortnight later than usual, and that the proceeds (a circumstance known only to the managers) should be devoted to a series of choice suppers, at which we entertained, not only the Governor and our friends in both Houses, but also, like true Christians, our legislatorial enemies. Olympia Knapp, who, you know, is so very beautiful, presided at these entertainments. She put forth all her splendid powers, and with more effect than any of us suspected. On the day before the bill reached its third reading, the Governor made her an offer of marriage. She came to the managers in great agitation, and laid the matter before them, stating that she was overwhelmed with surprise (though Sarah Pincher always maintained that she wasn't in the least), and asking their advice. We discussed the question for four hours, and finally decided that the interests of the cause would oblige her to accept the Governor's hand. "Oh, I am so glad!" cried Olympia, "for I accepted him at once." It was a brave, a noble deed!

Now, I would ask those who assert that women are incapable of conducting the business of politics, to say whether any set of men, of either party, could have played their cards more skilfully? Even after the campaign was over we might have failed, had it not been for the suppers. We owed this idea, like the first, to the immortal Selina Whiston. A lucky accident—as momentous in its way as the fall of an apple to Newton, or the flying of a kite to Dr. Franklin—gave her the secret principle by which the politics of men are directed. Her house in Whittletown was the half of a double frame building, and the rear-end of the other part was the private office of—but no, I will not mention the name—a lawyer and a politician. He was known as a "wirepuller," and the other wire-pullers of his party used to meet in his office and discuss matters. Mrs. Whiston always asserted that there was a mouse-hole through the partition; but she had energy enough to have made a hole herself, for the sake of the cause.

She never would tell us all she overheard. "It is enough," she would say, "that I know how the thing is done."

I remember that we were all considerably startled when she first gave us an outline of her plan. On my saying that I trusted the dissemination of our principles would soon bring us a great adhesion, she burst out with:

"Principles! Why if we trust to principles, we shall never succeed! We must rely upon INFLUENCES, as the men do; we must fight them with their own weapons, and even then we are at a disadvantage, because we cannot very well make use of whiskey and cigars."

We yielded, because we had grown accustomed to be guided by her; and, moreover, we had seen, time and again, how she could succeed—as, for instance, in the Nelson divorce case (but I don't suppose you ever heard of that), when the matter seemed nigh hopeless to all of us. The history of 1860 and the following winter proves that in her the world has lost a stateswoman. Mr. Wrangle and Governor Battle have both said to me that they never knew a measure to be so splendidly engineered both before the public and in the State Legislature.

After the bill had been passed, and signed by the Governor, and so had become a law, and the grand Women's Jubilee had been held at Gaston, the excitement subsided. It would be nearly a year to the next State election, and none of the women seemed to care for the local and municipal elections in the spring. Besides, there was a good deal of anxiety among them in regard to the bill, which was drawn up in almost the exact terms used by Mr. Wrangle at the political meeting. In fact, we always have suspected that he wrote it. The word "male" was simply omitted from all laws. "Nothing is changed," said Mrs. Whiston, quoting Charles X., "there are only 201,758 more citizens in Atlantic!"

This was in January, 1861, you must remember; and the shadow of the coming war began to fall over us. Had the passage of our bill been postponed a fortnight it would have been postponed indefinitely, for other and (for the men) more powerful excitements followed one upon the other. Even our jubilee was thinly attended, and all but two of the members on whom we relied for speeches failed us. Governor Battle, who was to have presided, was at Washington, and Olympia, already his wife, accompanied him. (I may add that she has never since taken any active part with us. They have been in Europe for the last three years.)

Most of the women—here in Burroak, at least—expressed a feeling of disappointment that there was no palpable change in their lot, no sense of extended liberty, such as they imagined would come to transform them into brighter and better creatures. They supposed that they would at once gain in importance in the eyes of the men; but the men were now so preoccupied by the events at the South that they seemed to have forgotten our political value. Speaking for myself, as a good Union woman, I felt that I must lay aside, for a time, the interests of my sex. Once, it is true, I proposed to accompany Mr. Strongitharm to a party caucus at the Wrangle House; but he so suddenly discovered that he had business in another part of the town, that I withdrew my proposition.

As the summer passed over, and the first and second call for volunteers had been met, and more than met, by the patriotic men of the State (how we blessed them!) we began to take courage, and to feel, that if our new civil position brought us no very tangible enjoyment, at least it imposed upon us no very irksome duties.

The first practical effect of the new law came to light at the August term of our County Court. The names of seven women appeared on the list of jurors, but only three of them answered to their names. One, the wife of a poor farmer, was excused by the Judge, as there was no one to look after six small children in her absence; another was a tailoress, with a quantity of work on hand, some of which she proposed bringing with her into Court, in order to save time; but as this could not be allowed, she made so much trouble that she was also finally let off. Only one, therefore, remained to serve; fortunately for the credit of our sex, she was both able and willing to do so; and we afterward made a subscription, and presented her with a silver fish-knife, on account of her having tired out eleven jurymen, and brought in a verdict of $5,000 damages against a young man whom she convicted of seduction. She told me that no one would ever know what she endured during those three days; but the morals of our county have been better ever since.

Mr. Spelter told me that his State exchanges showed that there had been difficulties of the same kind in all the other counties. In Mendip (the county-town of which is Whittletown, Mrs. Whiston's home) the immediate result had been the decision, on the part of the Commissioners, to build an addition at the rear of the Court-House, with large, commodious and well-furnished jury-rooms, so arranged that a comfortable privacy was secured to the jury-women. I did my best to have the same improvement adopted here, but, alas! I have not the ability of Selina Whiston in such matters, and there is nothing to this day but the one vile, miserable room, properly furnished in no particular except spittoons.

The nominating Conventions were held in August, also, and we were therefore called upon to move at once, in order to secure our fair share. Much valuable time had been lost in discussing a question of policy, namely, whether we should attach ourselves to the two parties already in existence, according to our individual inclinations, or whether we should form a third party for ourselves. We finally accepted the former proposition, and I think wisely; for the most of us were so ignorant of political tricks and devices, that we still needed to learn from the men, and we could not afford to draw upon us the hostility of both parties, in the very infancy of our movement.

Never in my life did I have such a task, as in drumming up a few women to attend the primary township meeting for the election of delegates. It was impossible to make them comprehend its importance. Even after I had done my best to explain the technicalities of male politics, and fancied that I had made some impression, the answer would be: "Well, I'd go, I'm sure, just to oblige you, but then there's the tomatoes to be canned"—or, "I'm so behindhand with my darning and patching"—or, "John'll be sure to go, and there's no need of two from the same house"—and so on, until I was mightily discouraged. There were just nine of us, all told, to about a hundred men. I won't deny that our situation that night, at the Wrangle House, was awkward and not entirely agreeable. To be sure the landlord gave us the parlor, and most of the men came in, now and then, to speak to us; but they managed the principal matters all by themselves, in the bar-room, which was such a mess of smoke and stale liquor smells, that it turned my stomach when I ventured in for two minutes.

I don't think we should have accomplished much, but for a 'cute idea of Mrs. Wilbur, the tinman's wife. She went to the leaders, and threatened them that the women's vote should be cast in a body for the Democratic candidates, unless we were considered in making up the ticket. THAT helped: the delegates were properly instructed, and the County Convention afterward nominated two men and one woman as candidates for the Assembly. That woman was—as I need hardly say, for the world knows it—myself. I had not solicited the honor, and therefore could not refuse, especially as my daughter Melissa was then old enough to keep house in my absence. No woman had applied for the nomination for Sheriff, but there were seventeen schoolmistresses anxious for the office of County Treasurer. The only other nomination given to the women, however, was that of Director (or rather, Directress) of the Poor, which was conferred on Mrs. Bassett, wife of a clergyman.

Mr. Strongitharm insisted that I should, in some wise, prepare myself for my new duties, by reading various political works, and I conscientiously tried to do so—but, dear me! it was much more of a task than I supposed. We had all read the debate on our bill, of course; but I always skipped the dry, stupid stuff about the tariff, and finance, and stay laws and exemption laws, and railroad company squabbles; and for the life of me I can't see, to this day, what connection there is between these things and Women's Rights. But, as I said, I did my best, with the help of Webster's Dictionary; although the further I went the less I liked it.

As election-day drew nearer, our prospects looked brighter. The Republican ticket, under the editorial head of the "Burroak Banner," with my name and Mrs. Bassett's among the men's, was such an evidence, that many women, notably opposed to the cause, said: "We didn't want the right, but since we have it, we shall make use of it." This was exactly what Mrs. Whiston had foretold. We estimated that—taking the County tickets all over the State—we had about one-twentieth of the Republican, and one-fiftieth of the Democratic, nominations. This was far from being our due, but still it was a good beginning.

My husband insisted that I should go very early to the polls. I could scarcely restrain a tear of emotion as I gave my first ballot into the hands of the judges. There were not a dozen persons present, and the act did not produce the sensation which I expected. One man cried out: "Three cheers for our Assemblywoman!" and they gave them; and I thereupon returned home in the best spirits. I devoted the rest of the day to relieving poorer women, who could not have spared the time to vote, if I had not, meanwhile, looked after their children. The last was Nancy Black, the shoemaker's wife in our street, who kept me waiting upon her till it was quite dark. When she finally came, the skirt of her dress was ripped nearly off, her hair was down and her comb broken; but she was triumphant, for Sam Black was with her, and SOBER. "The first time since we were married, Mrs. Strongitharm!" she cried. Then she whispered to me, as I was leaving: "And I've killed HIS vote, anyhow!"

When the count was made, our party was far ahead. Up to this time, I think, the men of both parties had believed that only a few women, here and there, would avail themselves of their new right—but they were roundly mistaken. Although only ten per cent. of the female voters went to the polls, yet three-fourths of them voted the Republican ticket, which increased the majority of that party, in the State, about eleven thousand.

It was amazing what an effect followed this result. The whole country would have rung with it, had we not been in the midst of war. Mr. Wrangle declared that he had always been an earnest advocate of the women's cause. Governor Battle, in his next message, congratulated the State on the signal success of the experiment, and the Democratic masses, smarting under their defeat, cursed their leaders for not having been sharp enough to conciliate the new element. The leaders themselves said nothing, and in a few weeks the rank and file recovered their cheerfulness. Even Mrs. Whiston, with all her experience, was a little puzzled by this change of mood. Alas! she was far from guessing the correct explanation.

It was a great comfort to me that Mrs. Whiston was also elected to the Legislature. My husband had just then established his manufactory of patent self-scouring knife-blades (now so celebrated), and could not leave; so I was obliged to go up to Gaston all alone, when the session commenced. There were but four of us Assemblywomen, and although the men treated us with great courtesy, I was that nervous that I seemed to detect either commiseration or satire everywhere. Before I had even taken my seat, I was addressed by fifteen or twenty different gentlemen, either great capitalists, or great engineers, or distinguished lawyers, all interested in various schemes for developing the resources of our State by new railroads, canals or ferries. I then began to comprehend the grandeur of the Legislator's office. My voice could assist in making possible these magnificent improvements, and I promised it to all. Mr. Filch, President of the Shinnebaug and Great Western Consolidated Line, was so delighted with my appreciation of his plan for reducing the freight on grain from Nebraska, that he must have written extravagant accounts of me to his wife; for she sent me, at Christmas, one of the loveliest shawls I ever beheld.

I had frequently made short addresses at our public meetings, and was considered to have my share of self-possession; but I never could accustom myself to the keen, disturbing, irritating atmosphere of the Legislature. Everybody seemed wide-awake and aggressive, instead of pleasantly receptive; there were so many "points of order," and what not; such complete disregard, among the members, of each other's feelings; and, finally—a thing I could never understand, indeed—such inconsistency and lack of principle in the intercourse of the two parties. How could I feel assured of their sincerity, when I saw the very men chatting and laughing together, in the lobbies, ten minutes after they had been facing each other like angry lions in the debate?

Mrs. Whiston, also, had her trials of the same character. Nothing ever annoyed her so much as a little blunder she made, the week after the opening of the session. I have not yet mentioned that there was already a universal dissatisfaction among the women, on account of their being liable to military service. The war seemed to have hardly begun, as yet, and conscription was already talked about; the women, therefore, clamored for an exemption on account of sex. Although we all felt that this was a retrograde movement, the pressure was so great that we yielded. Mrs. Whiston, reluctant at first, no sooner made up her mind that the thing must be done, than she furthered it with all her might. After several attempts to introduce a bill, which were always cut off by some "point of order," she unhappily lost her usual patience.

I don't know that I can exactly explain how it happened, for what the men call "parliamentary tactics" always made me fidgetty. But the "previous question" turned up (as it always seemed to me to do, at the wrong time), and cut her off before she had spoken ten words.

"Mr. Speaker!" she protested; "there is no question, previous to this, which needs the consideration of the house! This is first in importance, and demands your immediate—"

"Order! order!" came from all parts of the house.

"I am in order—the right is always in order!" she exclaimed, getting more and more excited. "We women are not going to be contented with the mere show of our rights on this floor; we demand the substance—"

And so she was going on, when there arose the most fearful tumult. The upshot of it was, that the speaker ordered the sergeant-at-arms to remove Mrs. Whiston; one of the members, more considerate, walked across the floor to her, and tried to explain in what manner she was violating the rules; and in another minute she sat down, so white, rigid and silent that it made me shake in my shoes to look at her.

"I have made a great blunder," she said to me, that evening; "and it may set us back a little; but I shall recover my ground." Which she did, I assure you. She cultivated the acquaintance of the leaders of both parties, studied their tactics, and quietly waited for a good opportunity to bring in her bill. At first, we thought it would pass; but one of the male members presently came out with a speech, which dashed our hopes to nothing. He simply took the ground that there must be absolute equality in citizenship; that every privilege was balanced by a duty, every trust accompanied with its responsibility. He had no objection to women possessing equal rights with men—but to give them all civil rights and exempt them from the most important obligation of service, would be, he said, to create a privileged class—a female aristocracy. It was contrary to the spirit of our institutions. The women had complained of taxation without representation; did they now claim the latter without the former?

The people never look more than half-way into a subject, and so this speech was immensely popular. I will not give Mrs. Whiston's admirable reply; for Mr. Spelter informs me that you will not accept an article, if it should make more than seventy or eighty printed pages. It is enough that our bill was "killed," as the men say (a brutal word); and the women of the State laid the blame of the failure upon us. You may imagine that we suffered under this injustice; but worse was to come.

As I said before, a great many things came up in the Legislature which I did not understand—and, to be candid, did not care to understand. But I was obliged to vote, nevertheless, and in this extremity I depended pretty much on Mrs. Whiston's counsel. We could not well go to the private nightly confabs of the members—indeed, they did not invite us; and when it came to the issue of State bonds, bank charters, and such like, I felt as if I were blundering along in the dark.

One day, I received, to my immense astonishment, a hundred and more letters, all from the northern part of our county. I opened them, one after the other, and—well, it is beyond my power to tell you what varieties of indignation and abuse fell upon me. It seems that I had voted against the bill to charter the Mendip Extension Railroad Co. I had been obliged to vote for or against so many things, that it was impossible to recollect them all. However, I procured the printed journal, and, sure enough! there, among the nays, was "Strongitharm." It was not a week after that—and I was still suffering in mind and body—when the newspapers in the interest of the

Rancocus and Great Western Consolidated accused me (not by name, but the same thing—you know how they do it) of being guilty of taking bribes. Mr. Filch, of the Shinnebaug Consolidated had explained to me so beautifully the superior advantages of his line, that the Directors of the other company took their revenge in this vile, abominable way.

That was only the beginning of my trouble. What with these slanders and longing for the quiet of our dear old home at Burroak, I was almost sick; yet the Legislature sat on, and sat on, until I was nearly desperate. Then one morning came a despatch from my husband: "Melissa is drafted—come home!" How I made the journey I can't tell; I was in an agony of apprehension, and when Mr. Strongitharm and Melissa both met me at the Burroak Station, well and smiling, I fell into a hysterical fit of laughing and crying, for the first time in my life.

Billy Brandon, who was engaged to Melissa, came forward and took her place like a man; he fought none the worse, let me tell you, because he represented a woman, and (I may as well say it now) he came home a Captain, without a left arm—but Melissa seems to have three arms for his sake.

You have no idea what a confusion and lamentation there was all over the State. A good many women were drafted, and those who could neither get substitutes for love nor money, were marched to Gaston, where the recruiting Colonel was considerate enough to give them a separate camp. In a week, however, the word came from Washington that the Army Regulations of the United States did not admit of their being received; and they came home blessing Mr. Stanton. This was the end of drafting women in our State.

Nevertheless, the excitement created by the draft did not subside at once. It was seized upon by the Democratic leaders, as part of a plan already concocted, which they then proceeded to set in operation. It succeeded only too well, and I don't know when we shall ever see the end of it.

We had more friends among the Republicans at the start, because all the original Abolitionists in the State came into that party in 1860. Our success had been so rapid and unforeseen that the Democrats continued their opposition even after female suffrage was an accomplished fact; but the leaders were shrewd enough to see that another such election as the last would ruin their party in the State. So their trains were quietly laid, and the match was not applied until all Atlantic was ringing with the protestations of the unwilling conscripts and the laments of their families. Then came, like three claps of thunder in one, sympathy for the women, acquiescence in their rights, and invitations to them, everywhere, to take part in the

Democratic caucuses and conventions. Most of the prominent women of the State were deluded for a time by this manifestation, and acted with the party for the sake of the sex.

I had no idea, however, what the practical result of this movement would be, until, a few weeks before election, I was calling upon Mrs. Buckwalter, and happened to express my belief that we Republicans were going to carry the State again, by a large majority.

"I am very glad of it," said she, with an expression of great relief, "because then my vote will not be needed."

"Why!" I exclaimed; "you won't decline to vote, surely?"

"Worse than that," she answered, "I am afraid I shall have to vote with the other side."

Now as I knew her to be a good Republican, I could scarcely believe my ears. She blushed, I must admit, when she saw my astonished face.

"I'm so used to Bridget, you know," she continued, "and good girls are so very hard to find, nowadays. She has as good as said that she won't stay a day later than election, if I don't vote for HER candidate; and what am I to do?"

"Do without!" I said shortly, getting up in my indignation.

"Yes, that's very well for you, with your wonderful PHYSIQUE," said Mrs. Buckwalter, quietly, "but think of me with my neuralgia, and the pain in my back! It would be a dreadful blow, if I should lose Bridget."

Well—what with torch-light processions, and meetings on both sides, Burroak was in such a state of excitement when election came, that most of the ladies of my acquaintance were almost afraid to go to the polls. I tried to get them out during the first hours after sunrise, when I went myself, but in vain. Even that early, I heard things that made me shudder. Those who came later, went home resolved to give up their rights rather than undergo a second experience of rowdyism. But it was a jubilee for the servant girls. Mrs. Buckwalter didn't gain much by her apostasy, for Bridget came home singing "The Wearing of the Green," and let fall a whole tray full of the best china before she could be got to bed.

Burroak, which, the year before, had a Republican majority of three hundred, now went for the Democrats by more than five hundred. The same party carried the State, electing their Governor by near twenty thousand. The Republicans would now have gladly repealed the bill giving us equal rights, but they were in a minority, and the Democrats refused to co-operate. Mrs. Whiston, who still remained loyal to our side, collected information from all parts of the State, from which it appeared that four-fifths of all the female citizens had voted the Democratic ticket. In New Lisbon, our great manufacturing city, with its population of nearly one hundred thousand, the party gained three thousand votes, while the accessions to the Republican ranks were only about four hundred.

Mrs. Whiston barely escaped being defeated; her majority was reduced from seven hundred to forty-three. Eleven Democratic Assemblywomen and four Senatoresses were chosen, however, so that she had the consolation of knowing that her sex had gained, although her party had lost. She was still in good spirits: "It will all right itself in time," she said.

You will readily guess, after what I have related, that I was not only not re-elected to the Legislature, but that I was not even a candidate. I could have born the outrageous attacks of the opposite party; but the treatment I had received from my own "constituents" (I shall always hate the word) gave me a new revelation of the actual character of political life. I have not mentioned half the worries and annoyances to which I was subjected—the endless, endless letters and applications for office, or for my influence in some way—the abuse and threats when I could not possibly do what was desired—the exhibitions of selfishness and disregard of all great and noble principles—and finally, the shameless advances which were made by what men call "the lobby," to secure my vote for this, that, and the other thing.

Why, it fairly made my hair stand on end to hear the stories which the pleasant men, whom I thought so grandly interested in schemes for "the material development of the country," told about each other. Mrs. Filch's shawl began to burn my shoulders before I had worn it a half a dozen times. (I have since given it to Melissa, as a wedding-present).

Before the next session was half over, I was doubly glad of being safe at home. Mrs. Whiston supposed that the increased female representation would give her more support, and indeed it seemed so, at first. But after her speech on the Bounty bill, only two of the fifteen Democratic women would even speak to her, and all hope of concord of action in the interests of women was at an end. We read the debates, and my blood fairly boiled when I found what taunts and sneers, and epithets she was forced to endure. I wondered how she could sit still under them.

To make her position worse, the adjoining seat was occupied by an Irishwoman, who had been elected by the votes of the laborers on the new Albemarle Extension, in the neighborhood of which she kept a grocery store. Nelly Kirkpatrick was a great, red-haired giant of a woman, very illiterate, but with some native wit, and good-hearted enough, I am told, when she was in her right mind. She always followed the lead of Mr. Gorham (whose name, you see, came before hers in the call), and a look from him was generally sufficient to quiet her when she was inclined to be noisy.

When the resolutions declaring the war a failure were introduced, the party excitement ran higher than ever. The "lunch-room" (as they called it—I never went there but once, the title having deceived me) in the basement-story of the State House was crowded during the discussion, and every time Nelly Kirkpatrick came up, her face was a shade deeper red. Mr. Gorham's nods and winks were of no avail—speak she would, and speak she did, not so very incoherently, after all, but very abusively. To be sure, you would never have guessed it, if you had read the quiet and dignified report in the papers on her side, the next day.

THEN Mrs. Whiston's patience broke down. "Mr. Speaker," she exclaimed, starting to her feet, "I protest against this House being compelled to listen to such a tirade as has just been delivered. Are we to be disgraced before the world—"

"Oh, hoo! Disgraced, is it?" yelled Nelly Kirkpatrick, violently interrupting her, "and me as dacent a woman as ever she was, or ever will be! Disgraced, hey? Oh, I'll larn her what it is to blaggard her betters!"

And before anybody could imagine what was coming, she pounced upon Mrs. Whiston, with one jerk ripped off her skirt (it was silk, not serge, this time), seized her by the hair, and gave her head such a twist backwards, that the chignon not only came off in her hands, but as her victim opened her mouth too widely in the struggle, the springs of her false teeth were sprung the wrong way, and the entire set flew out and rattled upon the floor.

Of course there were cries of "Order! Order!" and the nearest members—Mr. Gorham among the first—rushed in; but the mischief was done. Mrs. Whiston had always urged upon our minds the necessity of not only being dressed according to the popular fashion, but also as elegantly and becomingly as possible. "If we adopt the Bloomers," she said, "we shall never get our rights, while the world stands. Where it is necessary to influence men, we must be wholly and truly WOMEN, not semi-sexed nondescripts; we must employ every charm Nature gives us and Fashion adds, not hide them under a forked extinguisher!" I give her very words to show you her way of looking at things. Well, now imagine this elegant woman, looking not a day over forty, though she was—but no, I have no right to tell it,—imagine her, I say, with only her scanty natural hair hanging over her ears, her mouth dreadfully fallen in, her skirt torn off, all in open day, before the eyes of a hundred and fifty members (and I am told they laughed immensely, in spite of the scandal that it was), and, if you are human beings, you will feel that she must have been wounded to the very heart.

There was a motion made to expel Nelly Kirkpatrick, and perhaps it might have succeeded—but the railroad hands, all over the State, made a heroine of her, and her party was afraid of losing five or six thousand votes; so only a mild censure was pronounced. But there was no end to the caricatures, and songs, and all sorts of ribaldry, about the occurrence; and even our party said that, although Mrs. Whiston was really and truly a martyr, yet the circumstance was an immense damage to THEM. When she heard THAT, I believe it killed her. She resigned her seat, went home, never appeared again in public, and died within a year. "My dear friend," she wrote to me, not a month before her death, "I have been trying all my life to get a thorough knowledge of the masculine nature, but my woman's plummet will not reach to the bottom of that chaotic pit of selfishness and principle, expedience and firmness for the right, brutality and tenderness, gullibility and devilish shrewdness, which I have tried to sound. Only one thing is clear—we women cannot do without what we have sometimes, alas! sneered at as THE CHIVELRY OF THE SEX. The question of our rights is as clear to me as ever; but we must find a plan to get them without being forced to share, or even to SEE, all that men do in their political lives. We have only beheld some Principle riding aloft, not the mud through which her chariot wheels are dragged. The ways must be swept before we can walk in them—but how and by whom shall this be done?"

For my part, *I* can't say, and I wish somebody would tell me.

Well—after seeing our State, which we used to be proud of, delivered over for two years to the control of a party whose policy was so repugnant to all our feelings of loyalty, we endeavored to procure, at least a qualification of intelligence for voters. Of course, we didn't get it: the exclusion from suffrage of all who were unable to read and write might have turned the scales again, and given us the State. After our boys came back from the war, we might have succeeded—but their votes were over-balanced by those of the servant-girls, every one of whom turned out, making a whole holiday of the election.

I thought, last fall, that my Maria, who is German, would have voted with us. I stayed at home and did the work myself, on purpose that she might hear the oration of Carl Schurz; but old Hammer, who keeps the lager-beer saloon in the upper end of Burroak, gave a supper and a dance to all the German girls and their beaux, after the meeting, and so managed to secure nine out of ten of their votes for Seymour. Maria proposed going away a week before election, up into Decatur County, where, she said, some relations, just arrived from Bavaria, had settled. I was obliged to let her go, or lose her altogether, but I was comforted by the thought that if her vote were lost for Grant, at least it could not be given to Seymour. After the election was over, and Decatur County, which we had always managed to carry hitherto, went against us, the whole matter was explained. About five hundred girls, we were informed, had been COLONIZED in private families, as extra help, for a fortnight, and of course Maria was one of them. (I have looked at the addresses of her letters, ever since, and not one has she sent to Decatur). A committee has been appointed, and a report made on the election frauds in our State, and we shall see, I suppose, whether any help comes of it.

Now, you mustn't think, from all this, that I am an apostate from the principle of Women's Rights. No, indeed! All the trouble we have had, as I think will be evident to the millions who read my words, comes from THE MEN. They have not only made politics their monopoly, but they have fashioned it into a tremendous, elaborate system, in which there is precious little of either principle or honesty. We can and we MUST "run the machine" (to use another of their vulgar expressions) with them, until we get a chance to knock off the useless wheels and thingumbobs, and scour the whole concern, inside and out. Perhaps the men themselves would like to do this, if they only knew how: men have so little talent for cleaning-up. But when it comes to making a litter, they're at home, let me tell you!

Meanwhile, in our State, things are about as bad as they can be. The women are drawn for juries, the same as ever, but (except in Whittletown, where they have a separate room,) no respectable woman goes, and the fines come heavy on some of us. The demoralization among our help is so bad, that we are going to try Co-operative Housekeeping. If that don't succeed, I shall get brother Samuel, who lives in California, to send me two Chinamen, one for cook and chamber-boy, and one as nurse for Melissa. I console myself with thinking that the end of it all must be good, since the principle is right: but, dear me! I had no idea that I should be called upon to go through such tribulation.

Now the reason I write—and I suppose I must hurry to the end, or you will be out of all patience—is to beg, and insist, and implore my sisters in other States to lose no more time, but at once to coax, or melt, or threaten the men into accepting their claims. We are now so isolated in our rights that we are obliged to bear more than our proper share of the burden. When the States around us shall be so far advanced, there will be a chance for new stateswomen to spring up, and fill Mrs. Whiston's place, and we shall then, I firmly believe, devise a plan to cleanse the great Augean stable of politics by turning into it the river of female honesty and intelligence and morality. But they must do this, somehow or other, without letting the river be tainted by the heaps of pestilent offal it must sweep away. As Lord Bacon says (in that play falsely attributed to Shakespeare)—"Ay, there's the rub!"

If you were to ask me, NOW, what effect the right of suffrage, office, and all the duties of men has had upon the morals of the women of our State, I should be puzzled what to say. It is something like this—if you put a chemical purifying agent into a bucket of muddy water, the water gets clearer, to be sure, but the chemical substance takes up some of the impurity. Perhaps that's rather too strong a comparison; but if you say that men are worse than women, as most people do, then of course we improve them by closer political intercourse, and lose a little ourselves in the process. I leave you to decide the relative loss and gain. To tell you the truth, this is a feature of the question which I would rather not discuss; and I see, by the reports of the recent Conventions, that all the champions of our sex feel the same way.

Well, since I must come to an end somewhere, let it be here. To quote Lord Bacon again, take my "round, unvarnished tale," and perhaps the world will yet acknowledge that some good has been done by

Yours truly,

JANE STRONGITHARM.

## FOOTNOTE:

(1) [ Little Boris.]

Milton Keynes UK
Ingram Content Group UK Ltd.
UKHW040712200324
439767UK00006B/238